PLUM JELLY

Jean Bell

authorHOUSE®

AuthorHouse™
1663 Liberty Drive
Bloomington, IN 47403
www.authorhouse.com
Phone: 1 (800) 839-8640

Published by AuthorHouse   02/15/2019

ISBN: 978-1-5462-7996-9 (sc)
ISBN: 978-1-5462-7994-5 (hc)
ISBN: 978-1-5462-7995-2 (e)

Library of Congress Control Number: 2019901702

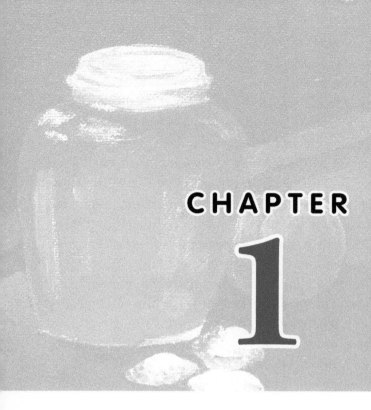

CHAPTER 1

Low taxes were the big advantage in living farther out from the more populated area of Cooperton. Houses had bigger lots. They were older, too.

"More character," Kelwyn, her husband, had explained.

She felt weak. *How could I have been so careless* she thought? *Just graduated, pregnant, back in Cooperton, isolated in the middle of Wisconsin, not in graduate school.* She cuddled her cat, Mewmew, in her arms. *At least there's still you, Mewmew,*

So, this is character, thought Cara Bow Keck. That was her name now. The kitchen, with its cracked glass doors on the tall cabinets had character, Cara Bow had to admit. The handles on the doors were small butterfly shaped knobs, that were hard to turn, because they had been painted over so many times. The frame around the glass was now a color called antique red, the latest color in *home decorating magazines,* explained the realtor.

"What was the year on the magazine, Fred?" she murmured, half to herself. She felt so weak.

The realtor's name was Fred Albert, the sole proprietor of Albert's Cozy Home Realty. There was only one realty place in Cooperton. Not much chance for buying and selling because people tended to stay put and outsiders seldom wanted to buy into the town. It was a small town numbering about 25,000 people. It was trying to be a city. There was even a mall with sort of half-sized department stores offering second tier merchandise. And of course, all the fast food places lining the outskirts as one drove into the town. Taverns popped up here and there, too. There was one featuring Girls, Girls, Girls in pink flashing neon lights.

"I'm not sure about living so far from the town center, Fred," murmured Cara Bow. The winters in central Wisconsin can be pretty brutal. I know. This is where I grew up."

"I really like this place, Caribou. It will give our child a lot of space to run around in and explore nature," said Kelwyn.

"Well, I'm not that much into nature, Kelwyn," she protested, this time finding her voice.

"I've already put down a deposit, Caribou. Mr. Albert went to a lot of trouble finding this place."

"How long has it been on the market, Fred?" asked Cara Bow.

"Not that long, Mrs. Keck. Two or three years, I believe."

Oh, God, thought Cara Bow. *I'm just too tired to argue anymore.* They had not been married long and the prospect of moving from her parents place was compelling. Kelwyn snored.

"We hear him all over the place, Cara Bow. Your father needs his rest," said her mother, Judy.

"Let's fill out the papers, Mr. Albert," said Kelwyn, cutting off Cara Bow from further protest.

Fred Albert smiled with the prospect of selling the white elephant. "You won't be sorry, Mr. and Mrs Keck. This is a great piece of property."

Cara Bow would hear a lot about the Alberts grip on Cooperton in the days and weeks and years to come. She had never paid much attention to the name while growing up. The Alberts were Catholic and the Edens, her parents were proper Presbyterians.

The move happened shortly after the money was paid. A pregnant Cara Bow surveyed the house with mounting despair. "Oh, God, Kelwyn" she cried. "This kitchen definitely needs a complete makeover. There's no dishwasher and the refrigerator must be at least twenty years old. It's not self-defrosting. The water pan under the unit has to be emptied daily."

"You're raising your voice, again, Honey. The neighbors will hear you."

"What neighbors, Kelwyn. Where are the neighbors?"

Kelwyn didn't answer. He put on his jacket and left, saying he had some business in town.

Oh, this house. I hate it. All of it, just look at this place, she thought after Kelwyn had left. *Who lived here before?* She stood in the kitchen in her fluffy slippers, Mewmew at her feet, purring against their soft sides.

"Well, Mewmew, let's explore," she said resolutely.

There were three doors from the kitchen one leading to the dining room, another to the basement and another door next to the basement door that she never used. It led to the attic. She opened it and saw cracked wooden stairs, a single bare bulb at the shadowy top and curtains of cobwebs covering everything, like a shroud. She closed it quickly but not before she felt a cold draft whooshing down as though the attic had been in a vacuum.

In the next weeks, her list grew of the things that had to be replaced of removed. One of her biggest complaints was the furnace. She had to go some evenings to the basement to pry out the glowing clinker from the coal furnace with large metal tongs and place it into the nearby large tin bucket. If it wasn't removed the house would fill with smoggy, smelly gas overnight. That was one chore she could usually count on Kelwyn doing unless he was out with his new buddies in one of the local taverns. Kelwyn liked the bar where there was a dart board on the wall and pickled pig's feet in large glass jars on the bar counter.

Cara Bow usually left the clinker task to Kelwyn unless he was very late. He seemed to enjoy the task, piling the hot clinkers into the metal bin—several bins—because he never removed them to the outdoor ash pile. "We'll have them taken out when they put in the new gas furnace,

Caribou. I talked to the heating company this morning and they've promised to start next week with the installation." Caribou was what he called her as a term of endearment. He'd started calling her that name when he found out that the nickname had been attached to her in first grade

The new teacher had mispronounced her name during roll call. Caribou instead of Cara Bow. "Present," she'd responded. The name caught on. It was a keeper. Cara Bow didn't mind, having no idea at the time what a caribou was. Later, when she saw a picture of a caribou in her geography book, she was so impressed with the great animal and its huge horned rack, that she considered the name an honor, and even repeated it to herself when checking in a mirror for lipstick smudges. That was when she had started wearing lipstick—in the sixth grade. She drew it on her bow lips before class in the girl's bathroom. The teacher never said anything to her about taking it off. She was, after all, the daughter of Judge Eden. Cara Bow's lips were considered her most beautiful asset. Her mother had wanted to name her Clara Bow—after her favorite the silent screen actor—because of her perfect bow lips but finally reached a compromise with the judge and dropped the 'l'.

"Say goodbye to the clinkers," Kelwyn said one morning explaining that the new boiler would be small and compact, no more big aluminum heating vents crisscrossing the bare wooden studs in the basement. "I'll be able to put a pool table down there, you wait and see."

"That'll be nice Kelwyn. A new furnace. But do we really need a pool table?"

"I've always wanted my own pool table, Caribou. It won't be in your way at all. And we'll get a washer and dryer, too. There's room for it in this big kitchen. We won't have to cart the laundry to your parents anymore."

"We, Kelwyn? I'm the one who does all the carting and its getting a bit much with my expanding waistline. And I'm tired of washing out your socks every night in the kitchen sink."

The kitchen sink was ancient, but at least there was hot and cold running water. The drain pipes under the sink were exposed. Cara Bow had managed to conceal them with a curtain of flowered bark cloth, un- hemmed, and chopped off at the proper length. She knew only a little about sewing. Once she had tried to make an apron from a kit, pricking her finger so many times, that she eventually threw the whole thing away unfinished. *Housekeeping is not my thing*, she thought.

The dining room had built in cabinets all along one side, made of wood—"real oak," Fred Albert had gushed in his sales pitch. The cabinets were vertically striated with years of grime. It had an odor of rot. A side door led directly from this room outside to a small cement porch which had no railing. One had to be careful when going out or it would be easy to fall off the edge onto the long gravel driveway which ran alongside the house.

The dining room floor was covered with black and white diamond patterned asphalt tile, the white tiles really a dirty grey shade which Cara Bow made an occasional stab at when wiping down with a floor mop. The stains refused to be lifted off, even with the help of ammonia. The smell of the ammonia made her eyes water.

She decided this would be a good room for the out-of-tune baby grand piano which her mother had let her have when she married Kelwyn. A telephone was in this room, too, screwed to the wall, a non-working rural telephone that had required one to ask an operator for the desired party number. *It's like stepping back a hundred years*, thought Cara Bow. *Thank god for my i-phone.*

The living room was baronial, the biggest room in the house. There was a huge, natural stone fireplace which smoked up the whole house every time it was lit. The chimney draw was unfixable. Brass sconces flanked the fireplace which had once held candles but now held tiny light bulbs that no longer worked as the wiring had been eaten by mice. But the windows were nice. Mullioned. Only a few of the panes were cracked.

"We'll put in gas logs when we get the new boiler," Kelwyn had promised.

"Kelwyn, there are no town gas lines to this place."

"I know, I know. Don't look so worried, Caribou. They're bringing a bottle gas tank at the same time as the new boiler. They'll put the tank right in back of the house. You'll have to be careful with your cigarettes. One little careless match near the tank and the whole house will be blown to kingdom come."

I would like that, thought Cara Bow. *As if I would ever walk in that so-called back yard. And I'm not smoking now because of the baby.* The backyard was scruffy. Rocks and quack grass poked through the sandy soil. A muddy stream ran along the west side of the house, which was a breeding ground for hordes of mosquitos when they emerged from their tiny eggs in June and August. The Kecks had moved in in July, just in time for the second swarm. There appeared to be no natural mosquito predators in the area.

Well, there were the swallows. Vicious birds. They nested under the eaves at the front of the house. When Cara Bow did venture out to pick up the plums that had fallen from the two trees on the property, the swallows, whose two nests were nestled under the eaves, would swoop down, almost hitting her head in their effort to protect their babies who seemed to be perpetually hatching. Cara Bow was not that fond of babies.

There were the wasp nests, too. More environmental misery, especially if she was wearing scent when running for her car to head out for some errand. She complained about the wasps to Kelwyn. Once in that September, while she was eating a golden delicious apple and walking to the mailbox at the end of the drive, a wasp flew into her mouth stinging her tongue.

"My tongue hurts, Kelwyn," she said thickly. Can't you get rid of the wasps?"

"I'll talk to Mr. Olsen," he promised. "He can probably take care of it."

The nearest neighbor was Mr. Olsen. His family—there was a wife and three sons—ran a potato farm. His ground was rocky, too, and in spring he hired local kids to pick rocks. There was no end to the rocks. They kept erupting from underneath the soil, as if there was a mine of evil gnomes below the surface who took delight in enlarging their space by tormenting Mr. Olson with the grey round stones. Cara Bow had met him once when he stopped by the house to give her a plastic container with cookies inside as a welcoming gift.

"My wife baked them," he said.

She thought he had a troubled face, deeply lined. The farmer tied his long straggly hair back in a ponytail. He wore a flat grey hat with a duck brim. The cap had a gold eagle pin fastened to the front.

Trying to make conversation, Cara Bow commented on the pin.

"That's an interesting pin, Mr. Olsen," she said.

He said it was a souvenir from his time in Iraq. "Now, I have to be on my way, Mrs. Keck. Tell your husband I stopped by. Those aren't wasps. Those are sweat bees. They'll only bother you in the fall." I'd probably just leave them be for now. By October they'll be no trouble."

He came with his tiller one day and offered to plow up a plot of ground on their property so the Kecks could have a garden in the spring. Cara Bow saw no point in having a garden, but Kelwyn said, "Go ahead, it'll be good for Caribou to have something to do."

"I have plenty to do, Kelwyn. There's the two-thousand-piece picture puzzle of the Empire State Building on the dining room table, and all those plums that keep falling from the plum trees. I'm always gathering them up and making the plum jelly that you like so much on your morning toast." He made the jelly sandwich in three layers. Three pieces of white bread toast with the jelly oozing from the sides

"Making that jelly is a huge job." The plums had to be boiled with pounds of sugar in a large kettle on the old electric stove, then pectin was added when the thermometer indicated it was time, then the mess had to be ladled into a giant cheese cloth bag to drain the red juice that was then poured into little jelly glasses and topped with melted paraffin, so it would keep. "You have no idea. I don't need a garden to weed." She hated the thought of a garden with the hovering swallows, wasps and mosquitos geared for the attack.

She didn't mind the jelly task that much, as she had majored in chemistry in college, and she thought of the jelly making as a transformation, a combination of elements, a mixture, turning one thing into another. Farmer Olson did plow the area, but nothing was ever planted and in time it was covered with milkweeds, nettles, and quack grass.

The whole front yard was quack grass that Kelwyn paid Mr. Olsen to mow every two weeks on his riding mower. There was a large field of tall grasses to the east of the house. That fall the county workers set fire to the grass—a-controlled burn it was called. The smoke made her eyes water. She had to keep the windows closed but that was little help. Mice and rabbits and other small creatures could be seen scurrying from the blaze. Not all of them escaped, of course. Cara Bow made sure to keep Mewmew, her beloved cat inside. Her parents had given her the ragdoll kitten for her sixteenth birthday.

Mewmew was quite a large cat by this time. There was no longer a cat box. Now she did her business out of doors. Sometimes she brought Cara Bow a gift of a wriggly mouse or a small dead wren. Murdered, thought Cara Bow. She wished the bird was a swallow, but they were just too quick for Mewmew.

Why am I in the hinterlands, she wondered. The center of Cooperton was at least three miles away. No nearby train to Green Bay, no easy walk to the mall, no Starbucks, but there was a gym. She decided to enroll for a class in stretching. It was some break in the tedium, but she felt like an exile, not knowing anyone. She had been away for four years and had had no intention to return.

Evenings, she sat on the black Naugahyde two-piece couch, her rationed cigarette butts filling the marble ashtray on the one end table, silently fuming with the smoke curls as she watched Kelwyn in his easy chair reading the paper that he brought from the office, rarely stirring. He's like a dung beetle, Cara Bow thought. *How did I ever think he was the love of my life?* He rarely looked up or said anything to her. "How was your day?" was never asked. "What's for dinner?" he voiced on occasion. *He doesn't love his Caribou anymore*, she thought. *Well, I don't love him either. I wish he would disappear.* Had she really thought that? She wondered why her thoughts were so often of murder. *I want to murder him. Yes, I do want to murder him.*

CHAPTER

2

Her mother had warned her about marrying Kelwyn Keck. *"He'll never get anywhere in this world, Cara Bow." That may well be,* Cara bow thought. She and Kelwyn had met during Cara Bow's senior year at the University of Wisconsin in Madison. Kelwyn was a Chicago man, a plus in Cara Bow's mind. The boys in Cooperton had never interested her. She envisioned living in Chicago with Kelwyn. They met at a Greek restaurant, where the lamb kebabs were the best. She went there for the first time with her sorority sister, Alecia. Alicia was from Chicago too, the well-to-do north side part of town. Alecia spotted Kelwyn nearby and called out, waving him over to their table. It apparently was all arranged.

"You've got to meet this guy, Caribou. He told me he wants to meet you, too. He said you were the prettiest girl on campus."

"Really, Alecia? I've met a lot of guys since I've been here. None of them stuck around for long. My fault, maybe. I spend a lot of time in the lab. My Quantum Spectroscopy Lab TA thought I should go on for my masters. Maybe even a doctorate. My professor, Dr. Timmer thinks so too."

"You don't want to use those big words around Kelwyn, Caribou. There he comes now. The red-head. Hey, Kelwyn, great to see you,"

"Alecia how are you doing?" said Kelwyn, giving her a peck on the cheek. "Who's your friend?"

"Meet Cara Bow, we're in the same house," she said by way of introduction.

"Well, hello Cara Bow, that's a familiar name. It sounds like someone I know.

Alecia laughed, "You're thinking of a caribou. You're always talking about hunting and fishing, Kelwyn. This is Caribou, that's what she goes by."

"Caribou, of course, lovely handle. Alecia's told me all about you," he said flashing Cara Bow his best smile. *Oh, perfect teeth*, she thought. *What a handsome man. Charming, really.* His reddish hair was thinning a bit, emphasizing his striking widow's peak, and his voice was deep, resonating confidence. Her heart turned over, skipping several beats.

Cara Bow had had a few sexual encounters during the past four years. Her virginity was long gone, but the experiences were almost obligatory given the sorority she was part of. The girls kept calendars with red dots on them for each conquest. For Cara Bow, there was little romance, and there were never more than a few dates because she was intent on her studies. She had applied to graduate school at the same university and had decided to go on for her master's degree in non-organic chemistry and maybe even go on a doctorate. But now, Kelwyn. She was truly smitten for the first time. *He's the real thing*, she thought. She remembered Alecia warning her about using big words. "I've heard about you too, Kelwyn," she said almost shyly and then listened mostly as he and Alecia talked about fun times in Chicago.

Kelwyn asked her to the senior dance that spring. Cara Bow thought him a bit clumsy on the dance floor but overlooked it. They sat out all of the fast dances and had little conversation because of the ear-splitting music thumped out by the DJ.

———— ✦✦✦✦✦✦ ————

Right after graduation she brought Kelwyn to Cooperton to meet her parents—the Edens. "Mom, Dad, this is Kelwyn Keck."

"Hi, Judy, Norman," he said sticking out his hand to the judge. Judge Eden did not offer his hand. Judy asked him if he would like some iced tea.

"Never touch it, Judy," he replied. "A cold beer would be great. Nice place you have here, Norman, with the lake and all. Bet the hunting and fishing is good.

The judge looked taken aback. "How's my little girl?" he asked after a few moments of awkward silence. "I'm sorry your mother and I couldn't make the graduation exercise. We don't go for those big doings. Never did."

"That's all right, Daddy, it was so long. I almost skipped it myself, but Alecia said we had to represent our sorority."

She and Kelwyn had driven up from Madison to Cooperton on Kelwyn's Kawasaki. The ride was uncomfortable for Cara Bow. Her rear end was not used to the bouncing up and down on the hard leather seat, and it had rained during part of the one-hundred-and-fifty-mile trip. Kelwyn kept on going, refusing to stop under an overpass, even during the strongest down pours.

She was not a pretty picture when they finally reached the Eden home. Her mother drew her an Epsom salt bath to soothe her aching bum. She kept Kelwyn sitting at the kitchen table where he could drip-dry. Judy didn't want mud on her white shag carpet in the living room.

The bath was soothing. Cara Bow trailed her fingers along the water's surface, making a wavy pattern. Her cigarette was on a low stool next to the tub. She reached for it and took a long drag, the paper wet between her fingers. The little nicotine high gave her a sense of happiness. *Fake happy, that's what I am*, she thought. *I'm living a fake life. Not my own life. What a mess I've* gotten *myself into.*

The water was beginning to cool, so she reached forward and added a bit more from the hot water tap. The gush from the faucet felt too hot on her toes, but the water was soon pleasant again. She added some fragrant bubble bath from the rack attached to the tile near the tub side. Swish, swish, bubbles right up to her neck. Then she turned on the jets. Roiling, roiling, like her thoughts. Some of the bubbles got into her nose, causing her to sneeze several times.

Kelwyn had wasted no time bedding her down, and she had been compliant, but it was a rough encounter. That's what rape might feel like, she imagined afterwards. Then, *no, it'll be better the next time.* It wasn't.

Alecia crowed to her sorority sisters about Cara Bow's conquest. "Caribou's snagged Kelwyn Keck. They're going to be married! She's so lucky."

She didn't feel lucky, only helpless. Kelwyn wanted to know everything about her at first, where she lived, what she liked, who were her parents? His piercing blue eyes were hypnotic, and she willingly volunteered the tiniest detail. She had never been so completely involved with a man. She even neglected her studies, getting a 'B' on a test which she would have aced with little effort before Kelwyn.

Drying off before the full-length bathroom door mirror, she took an honest account of her body. Long legs, she was five feet eight inches tall, a slender neck, straight nose, not too prominent, a taut tummy, but no longer flat, and small breasts. Her long legs and slender ankles were balanced by her long arms. *I could have been a prima ballerina,* she thought as she leaned forward and tried a dainty pose, then laughed aloud at the idea. *The dance studio in Cooperton mostly teaches tap. That might have been fun, but Dad said dance is for sissys. Ha, most of the residents are on the chunky side. They liked polka bands and square dances.* She gave her nipples a little pinch. Kelwyn thought she should have her breasts enhanced with silicone, but she refused to consider this. Her face was the desired heart shape. Her mouth was still the tiny, puckered bow shape which had engendered her name. Her eyes were wide, hazel, flecked with gold, though one eye, her left, had a greenish tinge. Her skin was too white, like a milky china doll.

She had a sun allergy, discovered at an early age, so her sunbathing was really shade bathing, with big brimmed hats and a white head to toe beach towel covering her whole body like an Egyptian mummy. Dark

12

brown hair cut short, added to her statuesque appearance. *I could be in a museum*, she thought, *frozen in time, or in a puppet show, someone else pulling my life strings. Fake happy.*

She joined Kelwyn and her mother in the kitchen. Her cat, Mewmew, who had been with her parents while she was at school, purred against her leg. Judy didn't look happy. Kelwyn's charm had no effect on her.

"I've been working in my uncle's accounting firm during summer breaks," he said to Judy and the judge. "He's been wanting to branch out into Wisconsin and I've been telling him about Cooperton and how close it is to Green Bay. He wants me to open an office in this area. What with the good hunting and fishing, I think I might be happy in this place. Of course, there's Caribou, I mean Cara Bow," he chuckled. "She's the girl of my dreams. We're going to be married as soon as possible."

He didn't stay long after this announcement. He gave Cara Bow a quick kiss and hug before leaving. Silence reigned as the door banged shut after him and they heard the Kawasaki roar off.

The judge finally broke the silence. "I know you've been seeing this fellow, Cara Bow, and I've been checking on him. He does work at his uncle's firm, if you can call it work. He sits at his desk in the back office, shuffling paper clips all day while he's playing video poker. No wonder his uncle wants him out. He just keeps him on for his sister's sake. She's a widow, and she's at her wits end with Kelwyn, too".

"But Dad, he *is* graduating this term," put in Cara Bow, trying to be somewhat loyal to her lover.

"Yes, finally graduating, after six years, and at the bottom of his class. This is not the path you should be on, Cara Bow. Somehow, you've lost your sense of direction. Maybe it started with your high SAT score, which was unexpected. You were supposed to be a teacher, like your mother, and marry a local man and, and, and..." On and on. Cara Bow zoned out and imagined a life away from her studies. It was not a pretty picture.

Then her mother joined in, "What about graduate school, honey? With your Magna Cum Laude honors and degree in chemistry, you should be able to get a good teaching assistant position."

Cara Bow didn't interrupt again until they had run out of steam.

"I hear you, Mom and Dad, but," she gave her tummy a sad pat as she said quietly, "you're going to become grandparents in about six months. Kelwyn insists on keeping the baby." An almost palpable cloud of resignation hung over them all.

CHAPTER 3

A quiet wedding ensued at the Cooperton city hall before a justice of the peace. Judge Eden could have performed the ceremony, but he declined. He took his place beside Judy, who cried throughout the short I do's. They celebrated, if that was the right word, by driving into Green Bay and going to a restaurant that was known for their prime rib. Kelwyn's favorite. Judy had the grilled lake trout and Cara Bow finally settled on a potato chowder, as her stomach was queasy. She left the table twice to go and throw up in the lady's room. She looked at herself in the mirror over the washbowl. "How do I get out of this mess?" she addressed her image in the mirror. It did not answer back. *I still look the same*, she thought, *but nothings the same now. Nothing.* Back at the table, she picked up her paper napkin that had fallen on the floor. The others had finished their dinner.

"Let's have some ice cream," said Kelwyn. He called the server to their table and asked for butter pecan, two scoops. "And bring a vanilla for my wife. We were married today."

The Edens declined, but Cara Bow had a little of the vanilla ice cream along with a small piece of the cupcake with one candle that the restaurant manager sent along.

"We usually do this for birthdays," he said with a flourish, "but a wedding! Congratulations!" No one smiled. Judge Eden paid the bill and they left the restaurant. It was raining again. Judy Eden had held back tears during entire dinner. Cara Bow held an umbrella over both their heads as they headed for their car.

"My daughter, married, pregnant, oh Cara Bow, whatever will you do now?" She asked as her tears fell like the unrelenting raindrops.

"It's going to be alright, Mom," said Cara Bow, though inwardly she wasn't at all sure of what she would do. She felt scared. Kelwyn had merely given her a peck on the cheek and a quick embrace at the conclusion of the short ceremony. She watch him walking with the judge from the grey, courthouse room, the judge walking stiffly and Kelwyn doing his best trying to make conversation. *Its got to be alright*, she thought.

Back at the Eden house, there was a small reception group waiting, cake and punch brought in by a few neighbors. Cara Bow still felt a little nauseous and went up to her bedroom shortly after getting home.

Kelwyn soon joined her. He was tired, too. Before falling asleep on the double bed, he said he was sorry his mother hadn't been able to attend the ceremony.

"She's getting on, Caribou. She doesn't travel much anymore. I want her to meet you before my baby is born."

"You mean our baby, don't you Kelwyn?"

"Oh, yes sure. Our baby."

"Let's leave soon, Kelwyn. Tomorrow." She was anxious to get the meeting over with. Feeling constantly queasy, she wasn't looking forward to a several hour drive. I won't ride to Chicago on the Kawasaki," she said, remembering the terrible ride from Madison.

"Don't worry, Caribou, I've traded the bike for a pick-up at the Albert car dealership yesterday. We'll need it, living in Cooperton. Cooperton is pick-up country." *So, no living in Chicago*, she thought. *I feel trapped. Who is this man I married*, she wondered as she watched him asleep, sprawled on her very own bed and not even bothering to kiss her goodnight.

The next morning and several mornings after the conversation continued about how the trip to Chicago would be managed. "I'm not going to ride in a pick-up, Kelwyn," she said over breakfast, prepared by Judy. "We may be living in Cooperton, but I will not ride in a pick-up," she said again.

The judge hemmed and said she would be more comfortable in a sedan. "Look in the alley, Honey." He had bought her a shiny green almost new Volvo, a demo, only 12,000 miles. "It's a graduation present and a wedding present honey," he said. "I bought it a week ago. It's parked in the alley behind the garage. Surprise!" They all went outside to see the car.

"Oh, thank you, Daddy!" She gave the judge a warm hug. "Green, my favorite color. I'll bet Mom was in on this, too."

Judy smiled, wanly. Mr. and Mrs. Eden were trying to make the best of it, though they still had their doubts about Kelwyn. He was taking his time setting up the office that his uncle was financing.

"He'll never get an important account," said Judy to Cara Bow. "I understand his mother has been supplementing his wants for years, but he does have income from a small trust set up by his deceased father." Kelwyn's father had been a physician who practiced internal medicine and had at one time had been Chief of Staff at one of the medical centers in a Chicago suburb. His mother owned several cemetery acreages in Illinois and Wisconsin.

Cora Bow didn't realize cemeteries were a business but then thought, *of course, people are dying all the time and land isn't free. So Kelwyn's father saw the patients off and his mother planted the bodies. Makes sense of a sort.*

Finally, with Kelwyn's approval, the newlyweds headed for Chicago in the Volvo. "Easier to find parking space with a smaller vehicle," he said. Kelwyn's pick-up was the biggest truck Cara Bow had ever seen. It even had a sleeping bunk behind the passenger seat, and a gun rack behind the cab. There was no bunk in the Volvo, but Cara Bow slept most of the way as Kelwyn drove, with the hood from her sweatshirt pulled over her eyes.

Mrs. Keck lived on north Lake Shore Drive, in an apartment complex. She had a nice view of Lake Michigan from the fifth floor. "It's on the list of historic buildings," she announced as she was showing Cara Bow around the place. It was impressive, but rather dark away from the lake side. Kelwyn explained how all the apartments were laid in the same floor plan. "They're called railroad flats."

He had grown up in this very place. The long entrance hall branched out to bedrooms on one side, and dining room and kitchen on the other. The largest room was the living room on the lake side. There were three bedrooms with single windows looking out onto other buildings with seeming little space between.

"I can see right into other people's apartments," she remarked to Kelwyn.

"That's why the shades are usually drawn," he said. Lots of nosy neighbors. Our place in the outskirts of Cooperton won't have that problem, Caribou. The realtor promised we can close on it in three weeks."

Maybe that will make things better for us, she thought. They had been living in the guest room at the Eden's house since the wedding. Kelwyn had become distant since their marriage. Cara Bow found she wanted to have sex more often, even his rough quickies, mostly to reassure herself that this union was true. Her overtures were often ignored. She had to beg him to engage in the act, and then when he agreed it was grudgingly. "We don't want to hurt our baby." he said.

Something isn't right, she thought. Her doctor, Dr. Boren, had explained that sex could continue throughout the pregnancy. *Kelwyn wants this baby but not me.*

Kelwyn's mother had greeted her warmly. "Call me Elsie for now," she said. Kelwyn resembled his mother. She had the same fine hair and even the pronounced widow's peak. It had been darker red, at one-time Cara Bow noticed in an earlier picture on the grand piano cover in the living room. They called it the front room. Now her hair was a bright coppery hue, courtesy of her hair dresser. Thin though. She was going a little bald at the crown. Like Kelwyn. Her tiny wide-set eyes were cloudy green, and they constantly darted about, as though she feared a disaster was about to happen. Kelwyn must have his father's eyes she imagined. They were clear blue.

"This was my bedroom," he told Cara Bow, opening a door to a room filled with every kind of toy. Letter blocks were all over the floor, along with broken pieces of Lionel trains and Tonka trucks.

"This place is a mess, Kelwyn," she said. No attempt had been made to straighten things out since Kelwyn had left for college. There were no books on the two long shelves, only a line up of more toys and several baseball caps. Puppets hung from ceiling hooks. Strange puppets, clowns, elves, horses, dragons, pig puppets.

"Mother doesn't want anything changed. She said it makes her uneasy."

"Uneasy!" this place is a fire trap said Cara Bow.

"Don't talk so loud," Caribou," said Kelwyn, "I don't want Mother to hear you." There was scarcely room to step inside. Clothes were draped from open dresser drawers. The dresser mirror was festooned with lipstick imprints. *Who is this man*, she wondered again?

Certainly Mrs. Keck adored him. The long entrance hall was lined with framed photos of Kelwyn in every stage of his development. She thought it strange that all his early pictures had him dressed in girl's clothes. There were no pictures of Dr. Keck. Kelwyn said his father had died when Kelwyn was seven and that he didn't remember much about him, just that he had a sudden illness, a stomach ache or something, which resulted in his death in a matter of days.

Mrs. Keck took Cara Bow under her wing. "We'll go downtown to Marshall Fields and look for a layette for the baby. I know it's called Macy's now, but everyone still calls it Fields."

Cara Bow was excited about this excursion, as she had never been to Chicago. Only Milwaukee one time for a workshop in genetics. She had gone there with other students in a university van. The lectures were held in a hotel ballroom and she had not ventured outside except for cigarette breaks.

"Shopping sounds like fun, Mrs. Keck. I'm going to need some maternity clothes soon. My jeans are getting a little tight."

"You're tall, Cara Bow. You won't show for a while. I was a real dumpling when I carried Kevin."

Cara Bow could believe that. Mrs. Keck still had some of the dumpling about her.

Kelwyn went to visit with some friends while Cara Bow and Elsie were on their shopping tour. He took Cara Bow's Volvo. The women took a cab from the apartment building.

"I hear Kelwyn call you Caribou, dear. Is that a pet name?" asked Mrs. Keck.

"Just about everyone calls me that," Cara Bow answered. I don't mind. I like it."

"Well, that's a bit odd, I must say. Can I call you that, too?"

"Of course, I don't mind. What would you like me to call you?" I'm a little uncomfortable with Elsie, though it is a lovely name."

"Mother Keck would be just fine, Caribou. When the baby comes, you can call me Nana Keck."

The ride to Macy's was shorter than Cara Bow would have liked. She loved looking at the tall buildings, the people, and the lines of traffic. People walked here, she thought. No one walks in Cooperton. She felt so alive. Mother Keck was nice, too. Things would work out with her and Kelwyn as soon as the baby was born she felt sure. *This is my life now*, she thought. *I'll try my best to be more* than *fake happy*.

Macys on State street was so grand compared to the Macy's one floor store in the Cooperton mall. Floors and floors of beckoning stuff. She wanted to explore every department, but Mrs. Keck insisted on stopping in the baby layette department. "Do you have any idea of the baby's sex?" asked Elsie. "I hope it's a girl."

"No, I want to be surprised," said Cara Bow, following this with the old saw, "just a healthy child." *Why are she and Kelwyn intent on a girl baby, she wondered?* She decided not to ask Mrs. Keck. She was admittedly curious but didn't want to seem to nosy.

"Everything is going to be just fine, you'll see," Mother Keck reassured Cara Bow.

They agreed on a layette of yellow and cream. "That will do for a start," said Elsie, "and I really do hope for a girl. Girls are important in my family line." She stared intently at Cara Bow as she said this. *What family line* thought Cara Bow, *and there's that girl thing again.* She felt a chill run up and down her spine. She suddenly felt the movement of the fetus, a soft thud against her abdominal wall. The first movement. Now another life possessed her body. "I hope I'll be a good mother." she said meekly.

They took more time in the maternity department and picked out two expanding skirts with matching tops. Cara Bow couldn't imagine herself ever wearing them, but she did like the colors. Green. That was her favorite. There was a cute tiny monkey faced bauble attached to the top back zipper of each skirt. *Kelwyn will have to zip this for me. That might be fun,* she thought. *We haven't had much fun lately.*

"I like these," she said to Mrs. Keck. They're a nice heavy knit. That's good, because the baby is due in February. It's coldest month in Cooperton." *This is still not real to me—a baby—the end of my plan to go on with my studies. I hate this whole pretending thing. Maybe there's not really a baby at all.* But she had felt the movement.

When they got back to the apartment, Kelwyn was still not there, but a small black woman was seated at the kitchen table having tea.

"Caribou, this is Corky," said Elsie, "She's been with us since Kelwyn was born. She wants to see Kelwyn before you return north. Corky was a wizened old woman, but quick to take command of her surroundings. Her eyes were so alive, and she was spry as she got up and darted about from room to room murmuring words in a language that was foreign to Cara Bow. She spent an inordinate amount of time in Kelwyn's room. Finally coming to the front room, she took Mrs. Keck's hand and led her back to the kitchen.

"Will you excuse us for a bit, Caribou?" Mrs. Keck asked. "Corky wants to discuss some private matters before Kelwyn gets here."

Cara Bow waited in the living room and looked out over the lake. I love Chicago, she thought. *I'm going to live here someday.* The thought was over-ridden by the bleak reality of her situation. *Married, baby, Cooperton, Kelwyn.*

Kelwyn returned late that evening, quite drunk. Corky was still there waiting, and she gave him a warm embrace patting his face as she let go with her claw like hands. "My boy," was all she said before she left.

Cara Bow and Kelwyn slept in Kelwyn's cluttered room that night. She had many strange dreams. The fetus turned and turned. Kelwyn snored.

On the drive back to Cooperton, she tried to get more information from Kelwyn about his family. "I'm sorry there was not time to meet your uncle, what's his name?"

"He's my Uncle Ulrich, Kevin answered. "He's always been there for me. You might as well know, Caribou, I got into a bit of trouble when I was a teenager. Nothing big, except for one time when I and a few of my friends were picked up driving in a stolen car. We got caught that time. We liked to take joy rides, but we were careful to return the cars from where we took them. That time we blew a tire and there was a bit of a fender bender. Mother was upset because we were held in detention overnight—until my uncle came with a lawyer and got me out.

"There were a few shoplifting incidents at the Seven Eleven's, too. We only took some gum or cigs, something small, but I was spotted one time and stopped by the store manager. My mother had to call my uncle again to clear things up. He'll do anything for her. She's his only sister and they were very close growing up. They're twins. Not identical, you understand. Uncle Ulrich never married, and he treats me like his own son. People think I look just like him."

That's the first time Kelwyn has ever volunteered a bit of family history with me, thought Cara Bow. *He's a big talker with everyone else but not with me.* Cara Bow found that thought provoking. *He has an interesting family that's for sure.* "What about Corky?" She asked, "She seems so close to you and your mother."

"Corky's always been around," said Kelwyn. "She practically raised me, and she raised my mother and uncle, too. She must be a hundred years old. She has her own family, but I've never met them. She never talks about them. She calls us her family. She got my mother into the cemetery business."

"Maybe you noticed the third bedroom. It's hers. She stays overnight from time to time. She keeps the door locked, and I've never been inside her room, but I've been curious. Tried to open it with a credit card a few times, but it didn't work."

Another bit of information to ponder over, thought Cara Bow. *Mrs. Keck thinks my nickname is odd. Odd hardly describes Corky.*

They stayed only one day in Chicago and Cara Bow was more than ready to get back to Cooperton. They left early in the morning, after reassuring Elsie that they would certainly return soon. The parting was a little uncomfortable as Elsie complained over and over again that Kelwyn seldom came to visit and he never stayed long enough.

"That's Caribou for you, Mother," said Kelwyn. "Always wanting to be going somewhere."

Cara Bow was surprised by Kelwyn's remark, making her the bad guy. She decided not to make a fuss in front of Kelwyn's mother. She didn't want any argument about her return plan.

"Kelwyn, let's go back through Madison. There's some books I've left in the sorority house that I'd like to pick up."

"Really, Caribou? When will you have time to look at those old texts? You're going to be busy with the baby and the new house."

"New house?" laughed Cara Bow. "It's not a place I'd have chosen. Sure, it looks manor-like from the outside, but the inside is a rattle trap fix-up."

"Well, it'll soon be ours, Caribou. I want to get out of your parents' house."

"And I want my books," insisted Cara Bow. "I have to have those books. I paid for them and they're mine."

"Okay, okay. We'll go that way. I can show off the Volvo. My friends will be impressed."

Alecia was still living at the sorority house. She had to take one final required credit to graduate.

"Well, Caribou, an old married lady," she greeted her. "Congratulations. I thought you'd invite me to the wedding."

"It was a small affair," said Cara Bow," and hurriedly added as if it were an afterthought, "Turns out I'm pregnant. How would you like to be a godmother?"

Alecia laughed. "Don't count on me. When I finish here, I'm moving to LA. I'm going to be a Valley Girl for the next few years, but thanks for asking. I thought you were applying to graduate school. Guess that's on hold, huh?"

Cara Bow didn't know how to respond. She grimaced, then asked Alecia where her books were stored. Alecia had packed them in three boxes. She sat on the sorority house steps with Cara Bow and the boxes for the next two hours, talking over old times and waiting for Kelwyn to come back from his campus tour with the Volvo.

It was near dusk when he finally arrived. He'd been drinking.

"I'll do the driving, Kelwyn. Help me get these boxes into the trunk. You look a little beat"

"Hey, I'm fine, Caribou. Tell her Alecia. You've seen me like this before. I'll drive"

"Just do as Caribou says, Kelwyn. That's a good boy," Alecia said in a soothing voice. "Let Caribou drive. You don't want anything to happen to the baby, do you?" You've had your share of fender benders in the past."

Kelwyn immediately acquiesced to Alecia's soft command.

She's had to do this before, thought Cara Bow. *What exactly was their relationship?*

The drive from Madison to Cooperton was quiet. She didn't want any more information about Kelwyn's family. She had enough to process for the time being. They passed a field of sunflowers on the way still visible in the fading light. *Let the light shine on my future like these flowers*, she thought. It was almost a prayer.

It was after ten in the evening when they arrived at the Eden house. Her mother let them in, already in her night clothes.

"How was everything?" she asked her daughter while Kelwyn was carrying the bags and books up to the guest room.

"I had an okay time, Mom," she answered. "Mrs Keck is a nice lady. Maybe you'll meet her someday. She doesn't like to travel much, except to the southern part of Wisconsin where she owns a few cemeteries. One in Illinois, too."

"That's interesting, Cara Bow," she said a little taken aback. 'I've never known anyone who owned a cemetery before."

"Nor have I, Mom, nor have I. I think it's kind of creepy, to tell the truth. And you should have seen Kelwyn's old room in Chicago. That's creepy, too. It's probably a long story and I'm only now beginning to get part of it."

"Well, you look exhausted, honey. Try to get some rest. You've got a lot on your plate in the next few days with the house closing and furniture shopping. And the baby clothes."

"Mother Keck—that's what she wants me to call her—has already bought us a layette. Cream colors. She's anticipating a girl."

"That would be nice, honey. A boy would be nice, too. The judge would like that. You were not the athletic type he'd hoped for. We'll have to wait and see, won't we?"

"Yes, Mom. We'll have to wait a few more months. I'm not anxious to know either way. It will be a lively baby. The fetus is moving all the time. That's what makes me so tired. Where is Dad, by the way?"

He turned in early, Cara Bow. He has an early tee off time in the morning."

They heard Kelwyn clumping down the stairs. He helped himself to a beer and nodded briefly to Judy before pulling Cara Bow upstairs. Mrs. Eden watched, feeling helpless as he led her daughter away.

Cara Bow had a restless night. She wondered why Kelwyn had to snore so. *I'm going to get some ear plugs*, she thought. She tried to lessen the sound by pulling the covers over her head.

CHAPTER 4

C ara Bow was determined to think positively. "Yes, Mom, it's an old house, but it has good bones. And Farmer Olson, our our closest neighbor, can be counted on to take care of the small problems that frequently arose. He's that handy. Stuck drawers, leaky faucets, door knobs that fall off, and screens that need to be replaced with storm windows for the winter months. Everything, Mom, and Mrs. Olson said she would be glad to help when the baby arrives.

"I've taken care of many babies," she told me. "I've had three of my own, eh?"

Judy was somewhat mollified. She had been carping about Kelwyn's slow business set up but now things were looking better. She finished her margarita faster than usual. They were at the mall having lunch, though Cara Bow only had a few olives and a club soda. She craved olives.

"We'll still have our Wednesday lunch date, won't we?" asked Judy.

"Yes, Mom, absolutely. And I'll be able to have a margarita with you after the baby is born. I'm smoking less now, too. Most days not at all. It's the biggest sacrifice I've had to make since I've been pregnant. And thanks for not smoking around me. The smell makes me a little sick."

It would be a winter baby. "February thirteenth is the due date," said Dr. Boren. The amniotic fluid had shown one small anomaly in the amnio fluid, but it strangely vanished during the procedure. "Probably a misread by the lab," said Dr. Boren. Nothing to worry about. The baby is developing well, all the fingers and toes. It won't be a small baby, given how big it is at this stage. Are you sure you don't want to know the sex?" he asked.

Cara Bow hadn't looked at the sonogram while the cold metal camera rolled over her now rounded tummy. "No, Doctor Boren. I'll know soon enough."

It was November. The trees had lost their leaves and the new gas furnace had been installed. Kelwyn's office in the heart of Cooperton was up and running, even though Kelwyn was seldom there. He'd hired a formidable assistant. Miss Albert was her name. Darla Albert. Kelwyn soon decided that accounting was not his thing, and he had persuaded his uncle that he would do better running the business as an insurance office. Uncle Ulrich agreed, perhaps fearing Kelwyn's return to Chicago.

Miss Albert had experience in the insurance field. She came equipped with the added attraction of being related in one way or another to an extended family of Alberts. Sisters, brothers, in-laws, parents, uncles, aunts and many first and second cousins. Before long the office had a large file cabinet of insurance customers. House insurance, health insurance, life insurance, burial insurance, car insurance, rental insurance, and even pet insurance.

Kelwyn did stop by the office on occasion, certainly on Fridays to sign Miss Albert's generous check and to collect his own. He made sure to bring some small token of thanks to Miss Albert—things like a potted plant from Kmart, a set of the colored pencils that she favored, a new stapler or a small sampler box of chocolate covered cherries.

"You're awfully nice to Miss Albert, Kelwyn," Cara Bow remarked one morning over breakfast. *Was she jealous?*

Kelwyn sensed her unease. "You've seen Miss Darla Albert, Caribou. She's well past her prime. You're not jealous, are you?" he said snidely.

Cara Bow hated that tone. "Of course, I'm jealous, Kelwyn. I feel trapped in this house at times. And I'm getting so awkward with the baby growing. I've become such a balloon, only I can't float up to the sky. It's been difficult, that's all. And you've become rather distant."

"Let's talk about that some other time, Caribou. I'm late for the office."

"It's not Friday, Kelwyn. You only go to the office on Friday."

"Keeping track of me, are you? Well, don't. You'll be free soon enough when the baby is born. I'm arranging for child care."

Kelwyn had suggested the possibility of bringing Corky from Chicago when the child was born, but Cara Bow nixed that idea, saying Mrs. Olson would do just fine. "Your mother is getting on Kelwyn and she would miss having Corky." *What a stupid thing to suggest*, she thought. *Corky is so much older than Mother Keck. But she is certainly a spry one. I'm going to use Mrs. Olsen and that's that.*

Kelwyn, thankfully did not pursue that topic any longer. He spent most of his days organizing fishing hooks and lures or cleaning his hunting rifles. He had three of them, and a bow and several arrows.

"I'll be at my camp most of this month, Caribou," he said. November was hunting season in the northern part of Wisconsin. The camp was in a woodsy area west of Cooperton. Cara Bow had never been there. She'd asked Kelwyn to show her the camp, but he said she was in no condition to go tromping through the woods.

"I don't want anything to happen to the baby. You know that. I've said it many times."

What about me, Kelwyn, she thought but decided not to argue. Besides she didn't really want to go. She was not a nature girl. And, she was well aware of the season. She didn't like it. Hunters came from Milwaukee and Chicago to join the locals on their quest for a buck deer. Cars could be seen traveling back to the cities with the slain animals tied to the van roofs or splayed on small open trailers.

"There goes an eight pointer," the kids would say as the parade of dead animals passed, the men still in their orange hunting clothes waving out the windows, proudly tooting their horns.

The hunters left the camps on Saturday nights, crowding into the local bars to drink tap beer and shots of Jim Beam while bragging about their kills. They reeked of damp, soggy smells in their unchanged hunting garb.

All of the married women in Cooperton became 'grass widows' and some were among the women who sat at the tables listening to the twangy, imported guitar playing bands and joining in the stomping in the small dancing area. The bar owners were supposed to have a license for the dancing part, but a complaint was never filed. The sheriff's deputies, who were part of the scene, would not have acted on one anyway.

Cara Bow would have been even lonelier, but Alecia, with whom she regularly kept in touch via phone texts, said she was coming to see her sorority sister before leaving Madison. Cara Bow loved Alecia. They had become close during their college years. Cara Bow even dreamed about Alecia at times, in Technicolor. She would wake from these dreams all warm and happy. She had set up a portable cot in what was to be the baby's nursery for Alecia.

"You sure live in the boonies, Caribou," was Alecia's first comment after maneuvering up the bumpy gravel drive in her Volkswagen bug. She gave Cara Bow a warm hug. "I'm surprised Kelwyn wants to be here, him growing up in the big city scene."

"Being here seems to have been his long-term goal," said Cara Bow. About to cry, she shifted focus to a forced cheeriness "You look so pretty, Alecia. I've really missed you. I wish I could go with you to LA."

"That was my plan, but it's changed," said Alecia. "My dad has had a stroke and Mother wants me to stay in Chicago right now. I interviewed for a job in at a big theater company, doing PR and hitting up people for sponsorship. It's a large outreach office and I like the set up. I'm sure I'll get the job, knowing so many people from the North Shore. Most of them have deep pockets."

"Lucky you, Alecia. I love Chicago. I want to live there one day."

"That doesn't seem likely, Caribou, what with the baby and all, this house, and Kelwyn has planted his boots here with such vigor."

"Oh, Kelwyn," moaned Cara Bow, and she started to bawl.

"Hey, kiddo, what's wrong?"

"I'm not sure what's wrong, but something is surely not right. Half the time I don't know if I'm living my life or someone else's." She moved her hands over the rounded bump on her tummy and the bump responded with several hard pokes.

Alecia laughed. "Let me feel the little stranger." The stranger responded to Alecia's touch with even harder rolls and pokes.

"This unborn child exhausts me. I can't imagine what it will be like after it's born."

"It?" said Alecia. "Don't you know what sex you have tumbling inside you? What about your sonogram?"

"I don't want to know, Alecia. I know Kelwyn wants a girl more than anything. God knows why."

"Didn't he tell you about his grandmother's trust?"

"You're full of questions, Alecia. Yes, maybe he did say something. I can't remember. Come on," Cara Bow said through her tears which were beginning to slow. I'll show you where to put your things. Then we'll go out for a bite. My mom's going to join us. The judge is out in the woods, too."

She gave Alecia a brief tour, leaving out the basement and the attic. Alecia was surprised to see a mattress on the floor in the master bedroom.

"Kelwyn wanted to invest his first checks in hunting gear," explained Cara Bow. We'll be getting the bed frame next month. I do like this room. Look at the beautiful window seat. The top opens and covers a nice storage chest. It's where I keep my science books. I like to review them regularly, so I don't fall behind in my field."

Cara Bow was falling behind in everything, as was evidenced by the clothes lying about, the ironing board in the living room and the dirty frying pan in the kitchen stuck with the remains of the morning scrambled eggs. The breakfast dishes were still on the kitchen table.

"What's going on, Caribou? You always wanted everything in order at the sorority house."

"I'm not sure about anything anymore. Kelwyn is seldom here and when he is, he's on the phone to his mother about the baby. He calls Corky, too. They want this baby more than I do. I'm not getting any sleep with Kelwyn's snoring. Look at me, I'm a mess. The baby kicks so hard, like it's angry at me."

"You're being silly, Caribou. What does your doctor say?"

"Oh, you know these small-town doctors. They're just practicing here because of the fishing and hunting."

Dr. Boren says, "My friend, you're just imagining things."

The last time he said that I told him, "Dr. Boren, you're not my friend."

"Ha, ha, that's funny, Caribou. Well, only a few more months and it will be over, and you'll have a darling little baby."

"I've never really wanted to have children, Alecia. Too late to do anything about it now. Me, a mother. I wanted to be a scientist." She groaned as she felt an extra strong kick against her tender abdomen.

"C'mon, Caribou. You'll get no sympathy from me. Put on something decent. Let's get out of here, get that lunch you mentioned."

"There's a new place in the mall. We could try that. My mother said they serve a good Cobb salad. The coffee's good, too." Cara Bow dug around in the pile of clothes in her bedroom and fished out an oversized blouse and a pair of slacks with an expandable waist. She had never worn the skirts purchased by her mother-in-law. She didn't know why. She had thought them pretty at first, but this was Cooperton. *They were Chicago skirts, I guess.* She looked at herself in the full-length mirror attached to the back of the bedroom door and sighed. *I look terrible, so frumpy.*

"This'll have to do, Alecia. My bump is getting big. Kelwyn told me not to invest in maternity clothes. He just wants the one child, thank God for that."

"It's not that bad, Caribou. Just put on some lipstick or something. You're not dying, you know. Some of the other girls in our sorority are pregnant too. Remember Marsha? She's having twins and is ecstatic about it."

"Well good for her and her ecstasy. Let's get out of here. Can't keep mother waiting."

The day was sunny for November and the two friends drove the three miles to the mall in Alecia's Volkswagen. Judy sent a text at the last minute saying she'd decided not to join them.

Over their salads, and small plates of olives, Cara Bow asked Alecia for more information about Kelwyn "I've met his mother and the weird Corky. How long have you known Kelwyn?"

"Seems like forever," said Alecia. "My family lives in the same apartment complex as the Kecks. My mom and dad were friends with them before Kelwyn was born. Mrs. Keck was intent on having a girl. A girly girl who she could dress in pretty things. She told my mom that boys were such a bother. She did like her own twin though, Ulrich. Kelwyn looks just like him. And, oh yes," she laughed, "I remember Kelwyn wearing dresses in kindergarten."

"Dresses, Alecia"? *She remembered the pictures of Kelwyn in the Chicago apartment wearing dresses as a child but had thought they were a dress up for Halloween.* "You're sure you remember that?" asked Cara Bow, wide-eyed.

"Yep, Mrs. Keck wanted the teacher to call him Kelly, but Kelwyn was intent on being a boy. He wouldn't respond to that name when roll was called. He wanted to please his mother, but she was the type who could never be pleased about anything."

"She seemed to like me well enough, Alecia," protested Cara Bow. "This is crazy stuff."

"Well, yes, you're a girl, and you've taken Kelwyn on, and you're probably going to have a girl baby." said Alecia.

"It's more like he's taken me on, Alecia." Her eyes began to brim with tears again. Alecia passed her some tissue from her purse.

"Well, whatever. You'd better finish your salad. Have you been eating enough? And all those olives. You look a bit pale."

"You'd look pale, too, Alecia, if you threw up every morning. That was supposed to stop after the first three months, but the constant kicking really upsets my stomach."

Alecia nodded in sympathy and ordered another club soda for Cara Bow. "This will help," she said. "It's my go to remedy after a night of drinking." She laughed and changed the subject. "Here's something else that might interest you about the Kecks, Caribou. My mom and dad played bridge with them every Monday night until Dr. Keck died. There was an investigation or an autopsy or something like that after doctor Keck's death. I was young when it happened. So was Kelwyn. I'm not sure what he died of, only that it happened suddenly. Kelwyn was pretty upset after that."

Alecia added some sugar to her coffee, hesitating a few moments before going on. "Once Kelwyn set fire to the trash bin behind the building. He was out of school for several weeks. Mom said he was seeing a psychiatrist. I heard he was in a few scrapes with the law over the years before college. Nothing serious. He managed to get in with a rowdy bunch, wanting to prove he was a boy, maybe."

"Yes, he's confessed to his past," said Cara Bow, a few more tears running down her cheeks. "I should have paid more attention. At first, I was besotted by him. Now we barely speak, and we never have sex. He says it'll hurt the baby, but I really think he's not at all interested in me. And he snores, really loud. Did you know that? Of course, how could you? I asked him to see Dr. Boren about that, but he refused. "I think you're making that up," he said. "I never hear myself snore."

"He's really quite stupid. Why didn't I realize that before I got involved with him? You told me not to use big words, remember?"

Their lunch was interrupted by a sudden clatter of falling dishes. A server bringing their Crème Brule tripped over a baby stroller, sending the loaded tray to the tile floor. "See? babies, nothing but trouble" said Cara Bow.

"We didn't need dessert anyway." said Alecia. "I'm watching my figure."

"At least you have a figure to watch, Alecia. I'm so jealous. C'mon let's get out of here. My stomachs getting pummeled by this brat."

On the drive, back to the house, they had to cross over a railroad track. Alecia decided to go around the lowered barrier; they barely missed being struck by the oncoming train. Cara Bow, in her cheerless state, wished they'd been hit.

Alecia was curious about the small house across the road from the Kecks, a ramshackle structure. "There are two old bachelors living there." said Cara Bow. "I seldom see them. I believe they're harmless. I waved to the tall one the other day when I was outside picking up the still falling plums from the two plum trees. We haven't had a frost yet. He didn't wave back. I can't help being curious about them. Maybe even a little afraid."

"Oh, pooh, Cara Bow, I've never known you to be afraid of anything. Remember the time a mouse ran across the floor in the sorority house living room. I screamed and jumped on a chair. You took a heavy book and smacked the mouse before he could get away. Then you lifted the book and picked up the squashed thing by the tail and dumped it in the burning fireplace."

"Well I am afraid now, Alecia. Afraid I'll never get out of this house, afraid I'll never get out of Cooperton. I'm in such a quagmire" Cara Bow began to cry again.

"Now stop that, Caribou! Go and wash your face. You look a mess. And this place is a mess, too."

Alecia decided not to stay the week as she'd planned. She had begun to sneeze violently when they entered the house. "Guess I'm allergic to something in this place," she said through the sneezes. "Mold, most likely. I hope you get it cleaned up before the baby comes. I can't stay here."

"Oh, Alecia, thanks for coming all this way. Please don't go. You can stay in my mom's guest room. She won't mind. You're my best friend. I love you so much. I'm really sorry about the clutter."

"Doesn't matter, Caribou. Hey, try to cheer up," she said as she embraced Cara Bow and affectionately kissed her on both cheeks. I'll call you when I get back to Chicago. And say hello to Kelwyn for me when he returns from the hunting camp."

Cara Bow gave Alecia a jar of plum jelly as a parting gift. Alecia left through the side door, still sneezing, almost falling onto the drive from the open porch. The growing baby gave another two hard kicks. Like a ha-ha laugh.

Now alone, Cara Bow looked ruefully over her surroundings and decided to clear up the mess. Kitchen first. There was more jelly to be made. She took leaf storage bags and filled them with everything she decided was useless. Next, she called the furniture store and demanded that they bring the bed frame and dressers at once. The store had advertised no money down and no payments for the next three years. She would have something other than the black Naugahyde two-piece sofa and Kelwyn's easy chair in the living room. *And why was she so stingy? She wasn't poor*, she thought. *There was the regular monthly generous checks from her own grandmother's trust. Kelwyn didn't know about that. Time to end the charade of her dependence on him.*

Her mother had ordered a child's crib and rocking chair for the nursery. "Bring that, too," she told the sales clerk. She heard scratching on the back door. Mewmew. Cara Bow had forgotten about her. "Oh, poor Mewmew," she apologized. "Come in Kitty." Mewmew obliged, dropping, a dead swallow at Cara Bow's feet. "Good girl, Mewmew, now you're getting the hang of it."

We're going to have a baby, Mewmew," she whispered to the cat as she cuddled it in her arms. "Maybe things will get better. Kelwyn and me, the baby, and you, Mewmew. A family. She gave a deep sigh. The baby turned and kicked non-stop.

CHAPTER 5

There was little family celebration in Cooperton at Thanksgiving. The men were still in the hunting camps. Cara Bow and her mother went to the Catholic Church Thanksgiving dinner that was held yearly for their parishioners and all who were without a family. That was half the women in the town. The Kecks and Edens were not Catholic, but the parish greeters did not ask for ID cards at the church hall door.

"Hello, Mrs. Eden—Mrs. Keck. Nice to see you here. Our doors are always open to anyone who wants to enjoy a good meal." The greeter was Mr. Allen who was still principle at Morgan High School. "Cara Bow isn't it? I thought you'd be long gone from Cooperton."

"Hello Mr. Allen. No, my plans were interrupted by a little stranger." She smiled trying to make light of the situation. Mr. Allen did not smile back. He gave a small shrug and led the women to an empty place at one of the long tables. Most of the people sitting around them were Alberts. Cara Bow said hi to Darla Albert. Karin Albert, Dr. Boren's nurse, was there, too. Cara Bow found that her appetite was gone and took only a little of the turkey dressing. There were no olives.

Conversation centered around the church's current mission, which would greatly affect Cara Bow's life. They had welcomed an Armenian family who were trying to get a new start for their family in the United States. There was an old deserted farm house up the hill from the two old men's place.

That's where the family had been living since their arrival. They were the Terzians, father, mother and two young children, Davi and Ani, and a grandmother, the mother of Mr. Terzian.

Gor Terzian had been a street vendor when the protests broke out in 2011 in Armenia. Being unable to make a decent living for his family, he decided to leave Yerevan. Eventually, via England, they had come to the United States and were given refugee status, although technically they were not life threatened refugees. The Cooperton Catholic Church parishioners had taken up a collection for their entry into the United States. Rumor among the old folks pointed to some high official in Armenia being paid off. Miss Darla Albert had spearheaded the collection, as most of her many relatives were of Armenian descent.

Kelwyn had mentioned their nearby presence to Mother Keck. Cara Bow heard them exchange the news one evening when Kelwyn forgot that his cell speaker phone was on. His mother urged him to become acquainted with the family. She told him about the *Dakhanavar*, a local legend about a vampire of the Kingdom of Urater, who was supposed to have vanished from Armenia. *What nonsense* thought Cara Bow.

Kelwyn began to spend time with the Terzian family on an almost daily basis, saying goodbye to Cara Bow after the evening meal, not forgetting to give her round belly an affectionate pat. One time he returned from his pilgrimage with a compact disc of Armenian music. It was now his music of choice. He insisted that Cara Bow listen to the haunting, endless scale chants every evening before retiring. "Corky told my mother It's good for the baby."

"Corky's crazy as a bat," said Cara Bow.

Another time he brought food prepared by the old grandmother—bulgar cereal and boiled meat. "Eat this, Caribou, it will make the baby strong."

She liked the dish, it stayed down, but wondered *how much stronger does this baby need to be*? "This baby's already strong, Kelwyn. It's constant tumbling exhausts me," she complained as she watched Kelwyn hang an enlarged photo of *Rock Art on the Gagham Mountain in Armenia* over the fireplace mantle. He said it was a celestial map which would guide the baby safely to earth.

"This kids on earth already, Kelwyn," moaned Cara Bow, "pounding away with vigor."

"There, that looks nice, doesn't it, Caribou?" was his response. He ignored Cara Bow's complaint. He snapped several photos of the picture. "I can't wait to show these to Miss Albert," he said. I think I'll go right now. She'll love these."

He put on his heavy coat and stomped out the side door, not saying goodbye.

Even though it was now December, and the snow was deep, Cara Bow decided to make the trek up the hill to the old farm house while Kelwyn was at the office. She wanted to be a good neighbor to the Terzian family, who had traveled so far to make a new life for themselves. She brought two jars of her plum jelly as a housewarming gift. Davi and Ani were there, as the school had declared a snow day. Mr. Terzian was at work at the local cheese factory. The old grandmother was in a rocking chair, holding an ice bag to her forehead.

"Is she ill, Milena?' Cara Bow asked Mrs. Terzian. The grandmother had a black eye and her nose was bleeding.

"She'll be fine," said Mrs. Terzian in a heavy accent. She was seated at a table painting her fingernails with a deep red polish. "Gor was out of temper this morning before leaving for work. The grandmother failed to add the eggplant sandwich to his lunch bucket yesterday. He had to beat her, so she would not forget again." She thanked her for the jelly and asked Cara Bow to sit down.

Cara Bow declined the offer of coffee; she couldn't wait to leave. She took one more look at the grandmother, who was quietly moaning. She said her goodbyes quickly. Davi and Ani were now quiet in a corner of the room and they made a small wave to her as she left. She almost fell coming down the icy hill on the way back to her house. She recounted the incident about the grandmother to Kelwyn that evening. "Keep away from that place." Said Kelwyn. "It's none of our business. Maybe you misunderstood what she said. Their English is not the best."

"Davi and Ani spoke English clearly," said Cara Bow. "They laughed when Mrs. Terzian told me about Mr. Terzian's temper. They're becoming quite fluent in English since starting school, and they lived in England before coming here."

"I said Its none of our business, Caribou. Keep out of it. You'll only make trouble. Let the Catholics take care of it. Gor's a good guy. I like him."

That evening, Kelwyn put the Armenian CD on high volume and said to keep it playing while he was gone to the Terzians for the next few hours. He and Gor liked to play cards, not for money of course, because the new family was just getting by, but they were generous with sharing their food. Much of it was made with pork, since the parish had presented them with a few pigs to get their farm started.

The small cheese factory where Gor was employed was located another half mile to the west of the Olsen farm. It was a place of interest to Cara Bow. It's like a big kitchen, she thought when she visited one day. The weather was above freezing so the road was safe enough for the Volvo. Here she saw big copper kettles of warm milk, the milk stirred by a large electric paddle. Near the kettles was a man in a white apron. Someone of importance, she thought. He reached into the vat now and then and rubbed the milk between his fingers.

What are you doing?" asked Cara Bow. She was among a small group of people who had been let into the manufacturing section on visitor's day to view the cheese making process.

"The curd has to be just right for each type of cheese," he said in an Italian accent, "and the heat has to be shut off at the right moment or all of the milk will be lost."

Ah, science, thought Cara Bow. She was fascinated especially with the culture lab where bacteria were injected into small cartons of milk that reminded her of cottage cheese containers. Then the containers were placed into special ovens to produce the proper culture for the large kettles of milk. "Sometimes a phage infects the culture," the lab worker told her, "and then we have to borrow a fresh culture from another factory and the whole place has to be scrubbed down."

The milk intake door interested her, too. Three women waited there as the metal milk cans were unloaded from milk trucks onto a rolling steel rack. The women dipped into each can with tiny ladles and quickly tested the milk for quality. Some of the cans were rejected. *The right temperature, the right quality, the right ingredients*, thought Cara Bow. *Something to keep in mind.* Not all of the milk came in cans. Some was piped directly into holding vats from a milk tanker.

I miss working in a lab, she thought. *I'm lonely and I'm not happy. I don't love Kelwyn. Had she thought that? Yes, I hate him.* Kelwyn had added more than a few pounds to his frame since the wedding; he often went days without shaving. Hunting season was past, but the lake had frozen over, so now it was ice fishing. He rarely caught anything, but he liked the hours he spent in his little hut on the thick ice with the charcoal heater and his six packs, dropping a fishing line through the hole cut out in the center of the ice.

I wish the hole were bigger, and I wish Kelwyn would fall through and drown, thought Cara Bow. She pictured him, mouth gaping like a fish, knocking about in the cold water trying to get out, finally succumbing to the lack of oxygen and becoming frozen stiff, his eyes wide, staring, and seeing nothing through the thickness of the ice.

CHAPTER 6

There were no signs of labor pains, though Cara Bow was now so big she could only lie sideways on the Naugahyde sofa. That's how she spent the Christmas holiday season. Mrs. Olsen stopped by now and then to help her with small things, like soothing back rubs or helping her to get out of the bathtub.

Dr. Boren had cautioned her about not having the water too hot. "We don't want to start an early labor," he said. Cara Bow had heard that he would be out of town over the holidays. *He doesn't want to miss his fee if he isn't present at the birth,* she thought.

"It would be nice to have a Christmas tree, Kelwyn," said Cara Bow. "Now that we have the gas fire in the fireplace it would add more cheer to this room."

"You're in no shape to put up a tree, Caribou. Put that notion out of your head. We'll go to your folks for Christmas dinner. They'll have a tree."

"I meant *you* would put up the tree. If we can't have a real one, they have fake trees already trimmed at Walmart, Kelwyn. Let's get one of those. You just have to plug it in."

"No, it has to be assembled. It's too much work. Besides, I'm putting away some money for a pool table in the basement. Gor said he likes to play pool and we can do that while Milena has her bowling nights with the women on the factory bowling team."

Now it's Gor and Milena, she thought. *And no tree.* She felt overwhelmed and helplessly trapped. Changing the subject, she mentioned that her mother had invited them for dinner on Christmas day.

"I'm not going over there, Caribou. The judge ignores me, and your mother is just as bad."

"You just said we were going, Kelwyn. Changing your mind so fast? Let's not quibble about this. I'll go without you if that's what you want."

Cara Bow prevailed because Kelwyn didn't want her to drive on the icy roads for fear of hurting the baby. Dinner at the Eden's seemed like a lost world to Cara Bow. Crystal cut glasses, and spotless silverware. There was the usual normal holiday food. Prime rib, roasted vegetables, and a green salad. Cara Bow was given the Judge's wide armchair at the table, because of her ever increasing size.

The drive to her parent's house had been perfectly miserable. She had difficulty stepping up on the high running board step and then onto the cold leather seat of the pick-up truck that Kelwyn insisted on driving.

"It's icy and the truck has four-wheel drive, Caribou" Kelwyn had to shift his tackle box and wading boots into the bunk area behind her head, so she could get in. She wore one of his flannel shirts, as she could no longer fit into her biggest blouses. Her stretchy pants were cut down from the waist on each side into a vee. Kelwyn grudgingly helped her on with her shoes. She could no longer bend over. She had been moving around the house wearing oversized fluffy slippers for the whole week before Christmas. Mewmew loved the slippers and she liked to scratch at them. Cara Bow didn't mind.

Judy and the judge had invited the pastor and his wife to join them for Christmas dinner. Dinner was set for two o'clock as there had been a service at the Presbyterian Church that morning. The table talk centered on how darling the children had been, dressed in their angel garb and singing the carol *Come Little Children* in their tuneless high voices.

"We look forward to the day when your grandchild will be part of the pageant, Judge," said Pastor Cornwall.

That will never happen, thought Cara Bow. She had become a non-believer during her college days. She had not been to a church service for many years, except for one time when one of her sorority sisters had been married in the university chapel before a minister. It was a beautiful wedding. Her fiancé was in the air force—his military friends were there in uniform and they formed a bridge of crossed swords for the couple to exit through on their way to the reception at a pricey restaurant that had been closed to outsiders for the day.

Cara Bow thought of her wedding before the Justice of the Peace in the unwelcoming gray plastered room at city hall, with Judy crying, Norman trying to comfort her, and the awful prime rib dinner in Green Bay.

"You must be so excited, Cara Bow," said Mrs. Cornwall in a polite voice, hoping to engage Kelwyn and Cara Bow in conversation. They had been silent throughout the dinner.

"Kelwyn really wants this baby," said Cara Bow. "He's hoping for girl."

"That's unusual." said Mrs. Cornwall. "Most men want a son for their first child."

"Not Kelwyn," said Cara Bow. "All he talks about is having a girl. He's even picked out a name for her. Polly, named for his mother's mother."

Then the discussion went on about different names, how names were chosen, how names were so different these days, and how many different spellings there were for the same name. Like Kristen or Krystan, or Cristin, or Kerstin, and so on and on.

Finally, there was the traditional Eden family cherries jubilee. The flame from the silver dish reflected in the glass ornaments on the tall, real Christmas tree. Cara Bow felt the usual stomach thumping, and she excused herself from the table and toddled slowly to the downstairs guest bathroom where she threw up her entire dinner.

Mrs. Cornwall was nonplussed for several moments when Cara Bow returned to the table, looking ashen. Never one to let silence prevail for long, she broached another topic.

"Are you making a lot of friends since you've returned to Cooperton, Cara Bow? You were very popular in high school."

"I see some of my old classmates once in a while, but they've become sort of standoffish."

"Maybe it's the car you drive, dear. There are few foreign cars in this town. People here buy American."

"Well, I drive the car my daddy gave me for graduation from college and I love my Volvo."

"Oh, yes. I didn't mean to criticize, Cara Bow, dear," she said in her syrupy voice. "Not too many folks go to college from this town. Maybe they're afraid to ask you to their small doings. I'm sure things will be better after the baby comes."

"It's okay, Mrs. Cornwall. This baby can't come fast enough."

Judy and the judge remained silent throughout the interchange and Pastor Cornwall merely finished his cherries jubilee and give a small polite burp.

On the drive home, Kelwyn became upset because Cara bow had revealed the name of the hoped-for girl baby.

"It's bad luck, Caribou! You shouldn't reveal a baby's name aloud to strangers before the birth."

"I didn't know that, Kelwyn. They're not strangers. They're my family. I've never heard such nonsense."

"If Corky says it, it's not nonsense," insisted Kelwyn.

"Oh, Corky, Corky. What does she have to do with our child?" muttered Cara Bow.

"Corky knows, Caribou. You'd best pay attention," cautioned Kelwyn.

"Drive a little slower, will you Kelwyn? My back hurts when you hit a pothole."

When they got to their house, Kelwyn put on the Armenian CD and kept replaying it all through the night. Cara Bow got little rest and she had wild dreams of the vampire *Dakhanavar*. The next morning, she threw up again.

CHAPTER
7

The birth was Cara Bows first time as a patient in a hospital, not counting her own birth date. She was scared but happy that this intrusion would finally be out of her body. Being slender, she imagined herself bigger than she was. At times, she wished she had been more physically active during her growing up days. Then she would be able to combat the constant pummeling she had endured during the previous eight months.

Kelwyn had been no help. She had become a bearer of good tidings to him with his hopes set on a girl baby. There was no love lost between them. They barely exchanged words. Cara Bow longed for a boy in order to thwart him.

Her water broke on the morning of January 12th while she was preparing breakfast for Kelwyn. *It's a month early*, she thought. *Dr. Boren had said February.* The temperature outside was below freezing, and the new boiler had chosen the night before to seize up and stop sending its warmth. The gas fireplace, with its plasticized gas logs, was their only source of heat. Kelwyn had spread a sleeping bag before the hearth for himself. Cara Bow swaddled in as many blankets as she could find, laid in her usual right sided position on the Naugahyde couch. The Armenian CD was turned up at full volume. She looked at Kelwyn in his blue down sleeping bag lying before her at her feet, snoring, and she imagined herself rolling off the couch and crushing him.

She must have slept a little. Kelwyn was up before her and had started the coffee brewing. The aroma roused her from her strange restless dreams of impending doom. The kitchen was warmer, as Kelwyn had the new gas oven going and all the upper burners were giving off their blue flame. He was already dressed in his heavy flannels, intending to get to his ice hut for a day of fishing.

Cara Bow struggled to get the skillet from the drawer beneath the stove, trying to keep a blanket around her shoulders so she could stop shivering. The toast popped up before the eggs were in the pan.

"I'll have the toast right away, Caribou, with the plum jelly."

"Are you going to call the heating company, Kelwyn? I'll bet you forgot to change the filter on the boiler. You know the guy mentioned that it was important to do that every month."

"Oh, for Christ sake. You could do that little thing, Caribou. You don't do much else around here."

Cara Bow let this remark go, not wanting to get into an argument. She just wanted to get warm.

"I'll call them, Kelwyn," she said. Then she thought, *maybe it's just the battery in the* thermostat. *I'll fix the damn thing myself. I am an intelligent person, even sort of a chemist. I make plum jelly. I keep up with my textbooks. Someday...* She prepared to crack an egg into the sizzling butter in the skillet, and suddenly there were two cracks. her breaking water and the breaking egg.

"You'll not be getting your eggs, Kelwyn," she said. "Please get the car warm."

"You're starting to have the baby? I thought it was not for another month." I was supposed to meet Dr. Boren for fishing today."

"For God's sake. Just move away from the table and get the car going. Look at me, will you. My water broke, Kelwyn. Dr. Boren was wrong. It's time. Right now." Cara Bow's voice rose to a scream.

"Okay, okay. I'm going. Guess I'll have to forget about the fishing."

When Kelwyn bundled her into the Volvo she was still in her night clothes with the blanket wrapped around her shoulders. *No pick-up truck this time*, she thought.

"This is it, Caribou, my baby girl," cried Kelwyn as he gunned the motor to get some heat going. He was finally beginning to show some excitement. Cara Bow felt her first contraction as they drove across the railroad tracks. It was a strong one. *Probably a monster kid*, she thought as she moaned with the pain.

The local hospital in Cooperton was small, all on one floor, an addendum to the larger facility in Green Bay where serious cases were handled. But there was a maternity ward and Dr. Boren's office was near the hospital. The head nurse put in a call to him about an impending delivery but told him not to rush as Cara Bow Keck was only partially dilated.

There was no modern birthing room in the hospital, and things were still done in the old-fashioned way, starting with a close shave of all the hair around Cara Bow's genital area, and then the obligatory enema. I'm hating this, she thought between contractions.

Kelwyn had dropped her off at the hospital and after talking to the nurse, said, "Looks like this might take a while, Caribou. I'll be out on the ice for a few hours then, eh. Dr. Boren will be with me and he'll keep in touch with his cell phone."

What's this "eh"? The bastard was starting to talk like a native. "Get out of here, Kelwyn," she said aloud. She didn't want him around anyway. "Don't forget to get the boiler going, we don't want the water pipes to freeze," and remembering the open flame on the kitchen range, she added, "Make sure the stove is turned off."

"Oh, right, yes, guess I have to see to that now, won't I?"

"And Kelwyn, will you call my mom and tell her I'm here?"

"Well, okay. Guess I'll call my mom and Corky, too. Mother will finally be satisfied. Push that girl out of you, Caribou."

Cara Bow had her cell with her, but there was no signal available from inside the hospital. She had to rely on Kelwyn. *Mr. Unreliable*, she thought.

Once Kelwyn was outside the hospital, he called Darla Albert at the office and gave her instructions about who needed to be called. He told her to check on the boiler in the house and to make sure the kitchen burners were turned off. He missed having his pick-up on the way to the frozen lake, but he didn't want to take the time to go back the three miles to exchange vehicles.

Cara Bow had time to observe her surroundings in detail. She was lying on stiff sheets and an equally stiff and ungiving pillow. The headboard was of the old-fashioned variety, metal, rounded. She noticed that the enamel on the metal was chipped. There was a gadget that had buttons for calling the nurse, and arrows for moving the bed into different positions, and another button for turning on the overhead TV on the facing wall. *Welcome to the 21ˢᵗ century*, she thought.

The nurse who hovered over her said that she would be in at regular half hour intervals to check on her progress. She also told her that her mother had called and left a message. "She'll be in later this afternoon, after the bridge club luncheon."

Since this was Cara Bow's first and only child, she expected there to be more excitement and concern from her mother about the impending birth. *And it really hurts.* Cara Bow did not play bridge, nor did any of her sorority sisters at Madison. Everyone in her mom's bridge club were well past their sixties. She couldn't understand the passion the ladies and a few men had for this ancient game.

She sat up and noticed the bedside telephone. *I'll call Alecia.* The hospital operator told her there would be an outgoing charge on her line, that would be added to the Keck bill and would not be covered by insurance; calling long distance would be an initial $5.00 plus whatever time was recorded by the call. A dollar a minute.

"Please put the call through," said Cara Bow." My husband will take care of this brat, I mean bill. She hadn't meant to speak of her abhorrence so openly about becoming a mother to Kelwyn's child. She'd even had a brief passing wish that the baby would be stillborn, but she quickly put such a horrible thought out of her mind. The phone rang several times before Alecia picked up.

"I miss you, Alecia, and I'm in such pain," she complained when she heard Alecia's voice.

"I miss you too, Caribou. Where's Kelwyn?"

"Somewhere out on the lake, ice fishing. He's sure not good with sick."

"Having a baby's not sick, Caribou."

"You know what I mean, Alecia." She moaned at the next contraction. The pain reminded her of Alecia telling her of her dad's stroke. "How's your dad?" she asked

"The stroke was a bad one. He doesn't make any sense when he tries to talk, but he's showing improvement. I don't know when I'll get to LA."

"What about your job?"

"It's not the one I wanted, but I did get a job at the Modern Art museum. Same thing, trying to get people to donate or become a member. Most people are not eager to give to lines, circles, and splashes of paint that they can't seem to comprehend."

"I wish you were here with me, Alecia. I finally straightened the house, and now there's furniture. It still smells a little in the dining room though, from the old wood. I think it's rotting."

"You poor kid, some trap you're in. And call me on your cell phone next time, Caribou. It's cheaper."

"The cell signal is not reliable around here. The tall pine trees or something. There's one right outside my window. I've got to hang up now. The nurse is here again to poke around my bits. Please keep in touch, Alecia. I love you."

"Oww, oww, oww," she began to scream. "Stop this. Get me out of here."

She pushed aside the nurse and jumping from the bed began to run down the hall, almost crazy with pain and finally squatted exhausted on the floor and cried "I don't want this. I don't want this baby." Two strong nurses, shaking their heads at each other, helped her back into her room.

"I need something for the pain," Cara Bow cried.

"Your husband left instructions—no pain meds," said the nurse. "He doesn't want the baby to be affected by pain medication. Try to relax between the contractions, dear. Take deep breaths. Your mother is outside now, and I've put in a call to Dr. Boren."

"I want something for pain, and I want it now," she screamed, as her mother came into the room." Her mother took Cara Bow's hand and promised her it would all be over soon.

The nurse shook her head and said, "It looks like it will be a big baby."

"I don't want this kid, Mom," she whimpered when the nurse left.

"Well, now isn't the time for decision making. That time was nine months ago."

"Mom, ooh I'm pushing. It hurts. I think this baby's coming. Call the nurse back."

"That's impossible," said the nurse, when she finally came into the room. You were scarcely dilated a half hour ago."

"Well it's coming, you ninny."

And the baby made its way into the world in a sudden rush, as if it had purposely caused as much pain as possible and then decided to make its presence known. It was one-minute past midnight on January 13th.

The afterbirth arrived with a few weaker contractions. "This is strange," said the nurse. It looks like there was another fetus, a boy, but it didn't develop for some reason. Sometimes the bigger child crushes the smaller one. Too bad. You might have had twins. You have a daughter, Mrs. Keck. Nine pounds."

The baby began to cry, with a croaking screech.

Then there was more commotion as Cara Bow began to hemorrhage. Dr. Boren finally arrived, and they took her to the delivery room where the doctor proceeded to pack her torn vagina with gauze to staunch the flow of blood. She required twelve stitches.

She could hear the baby crying non-stop from the next room. *Twins,* she thought. *Like Elsie and Ulrich. That would have been a real mess.*

CHAPTER 8

Cara Bow had not entirely stopped smoking; but she had been down to three or four menthol cigarettes a day for the last few months of her pregnancy, long satisfying drags now and then during the morning light-up with her cup of coffee and then a relaxing one before retiring She imagined that the baby would be smaller because of this, so the announcement of a nine-pound girl came as a shocker. *This child has had its way with me,* she thought.

Polly was her name, as Kelwyn had insisted. They went back and forth about the name for the first two months after the birth. Kelwyn called her Polly immediately upon seeing the new born. "Polly's here at last. My mother will be so pleased."

"Polly? she asked, "That's not a name. That's what people name their parrots." *Maybe it wasn't a misnomer*, she thought. *She did have a squawky cry like some sort of bird when she flew out of me, ripping me to pieces.*

"It was my grandmother's name. My mother said she must be called Polly. Something about my trust fund. It's all set out in a will. I have to have a girl child and her name has to be Polly."

Kelwyn stuck around the house for the first few weeks after Cara Bow and the baby finally came home from the hospital. The vaginal tearing and blood loss had left her in a weakened state, and she really didn't mind the extra attention lavished on her. *I'm still Judge Norman Eden's daughter.* She used that thought as a tonic to lift her out of her glumness.

One of the nurses who had been caring for her in the hospital, had a son, Carl, who was scheduled to appear before the judge in the next thirty days on a DUI charge. No one had been hurt, but the local police had followed the weaving driver down a straight stretch of county road on which several rural mailboxes had been knocked over by the car.

When Carl was finally apprehended—his car was on its side in a roadside ditch—he surrendered meekly. He had to be pulled out of a side window, squirming like a caterpillar. He was wearing a hairy jacket made from a bearskin trophy. He was only seventeen at the time of the bear kill and it was his dearest treasure. Unfortunately, the jacket was caught on the inside door handle when the EMT's extricated him. The jacket had to be cut in two places. Carl was inconsolable when he realized his beloved jacket was ruined and had begun to blubber loudly. The EMT's had to restrain him saying, "Easy Carl. There'll be another bear with your name on it."

Carl's mother, Nurse Lois, was not a registered nurse. She was a practical nurse, one of the staff members who did the nasty work, like wet bed changing and emptying bedpans. Some of the work was nicer. She did Cara Bow's bed baths and back rubs. She took extra time, especially with the back rubs.

"I wonder if you would mention to Judge Eden how sorry Carl is about that little driving incident," she said as she applied more soothing cream. "You know, his wife has just left him and he's heart broken. That's why he had a bit too much to drink. And then there are the little Albert children." Lois was one of the Albert clan, too, and like the rest of them had all their insurances with the Keck "We've Got You Covered" agency in downtown Cooperton.

The baby could be heard crying at regular intervals from the hospital nursery. "She's hungry, Mrs. Keck. You will need to nurse her. She needs your first milk, the colostrum, so she'll have immunity from some diseases during the first three months."

"I thought you said she was fine. I saw you stick a needle into her foot for a blood draw. You said there were no problems," said Cara Bow.

"Please, just give it a try. It will be a wonderful bonding experience between you and the baby," countered Nurse Lois.

And she did try. Her small breasts had become rounder during the pregnancy. However, Baby refused to take hold. She seemed to dislike contact with Cara Bow's nipple, that Cara Bow squeezed hard to shape into something Baby could grab onto with her beak like mouth. But it was no use. Nurse Lois finally said they would start Baby on a bottle. "We'll have to bind your breasts, so the milk doesn't come back in, Mrs. Keck," said the nurse. Cara Bow was happy with this dictum.

During her few short visits to the sick room, her mother voiced repeatedly, "You were a bottle baby, Cara Bow, and look how well you turned out. Nursing isn't for everyone. You don't want to be turning heads in public. A lot of people are put off by seeing an exposed breast."

"Yes, Mom. I did try but Baby wouldn't cooperate."

"You can't keep calling her Baby," said Kelwyn as he entered the room. "Her name is Polly."

"What about my mother," said Cara Bow motioning to Judy who was leaving, Judy never stuck around when Kelwyn was present. "I'll call her Polly if you will agree to the middle name of Judy, my own mother's name. Polly Judy. We'll call her that. Kelwyn finally agreed as it wouldn't have an effect on his trust, and the name was officially entered into the record at the courthouse two months after the birth. Polly Judy Keck.

Cara Bow tried her hardest not to feel so antagonistic to Kelwyn. After all, she thought, she had once felt such mad passion for him. Surely those feelings could be resurrected. On her return home, she was surprised to see that Kelwyn had decorated every room in the house with large stalks of gladioli. It was a particularly cold January. Miss Albert must have ordered them from a warm climate she surmised, but at least at Kelwyn's request. *Maybe he does love me in some fashion*, she thought.

Mewmew was glad to see her, too. She hadn't forgotten her mistress in the six days they had been apart.

"Keep the cat away from the baby, Caribou," said Kelwyn as he gave Mewmew a little kick. "My mother said cats and babies don't mix. She's read somewhere that they like to sleep on babies' faces.

How silly, thought Cara Bow, pushing down a brain surge of resentment toward any advice from Mother Keck, who lived in her ivory tower, tomb like apartment, calling almost daily with this or that bit of unwelcome advice. "The baby lives here, not in Chicago, and I'll manage this child without a stream of superstitions that probably come from crazy Corky. And don't kick Mewmew ever again, Kelwyn." She sat on the couch and Mewmew settled into her lap. The baby began her squawking cry.

"She's hungry, Caribou," said Kelwyn. Do something. I don't like to hear crying."

"Guess I'll have to fix her bottle, Kelwyn, you could be helping with this. I'm exhausted."

"No, that's a mother's job, Caribou. You're supposed to be nursing and I know nothing about feeding babies."

Cara Bow reluctantly set Mewmew on the floor and headed to the kitchen where Mrs. Olsen had kindly fixed several bottles and left them in the refrigerator.

She began to feed the baby, but it was slow going. She was not a good sucker. However, Polly Judy was a thriving baby, despite the lack of mother's milk. The cans of Simulac were said to be an exact duplicate of breast milk. Cara Bow, still thinking of herself as a chemist, was inclined to agree. Mrs. Olsen told her to enlarge the bottle nipple holes with a needle. Then Polly emptied her bottle in record time. She ate better for Kelwyn, giving the nicest little burps after she finished. When Cara Bow fed her, which was usually at night, she gulped the fake milk quickly, too, then would give a loud bruump and erupt it all back up over Cara Bow's tee shirt. Kelwyn never took night feedings, explaining how he needed his rest for the following work day at the office.

"You're going to the office every day now, Kelwyn?" asked Cara Bow.

"Of course, Caribou, there's another mouth to feed, now."

Cara Bow knew this wasn't true, because whenever she called his office to ask him to bring home milk or eggs, Darla Albert made some excuse for his being away. Still, they weren't hurting financially. *If Kelwyn is happy with his hunting and fishing, so be it,* she thought. *It's stressful when he's around. I can't stand looking at him.*

Polly Judy was growing fast. On her first check-up visit with Dr. Boren's nurse, she had already gained three pounds. "Three pounds in three months. What are you feeding her, Mrs. Keck?" she asked in amazement.

"She loves to eat, Karin. I give her stuff from those little jars of baby food, along with her regular formula. I know the baby books say not to introduce solid food so young, but she howls if I don't give her more. Maybe it's me. She doesn't cry after Kelwyn feeds her. She just tucks into him and falls right to sleep. Cara Bow thought of that howl. The way it mimicked a strong wind was a bit unnerving.

"You're talking nonsense, Mrs. Keck. You're probably not supporting her properly during the feeding. She's a nice strong baby. Look how she kicks about. She is fluttering like a caged bird. I've never seen that before. Has she tried to smile yet? That's pretty normal for three months."

"Oh yes. She smiles all the time for Kelwyn. I'm afraid she moues at me." said Cara Bow. "She doesn't like my cat, Mewmew, either. Maybe she's allergic—to both of us."

Ignoring this comment, the nurse continued with her jabbering as she tapped Polly's tummy and checked her scalp for cradle cap. "Oh look! Her fontanel is almost closed. No worries about dropping her on her head," she laughed at her attempt at a joke, as she finished the exam.

"Let's not worry about allergies for a bit, she said. "Time will tell. I'm going to schedule her three-month immunizations for next week when Dr. Boren is in the office."

"That won't be necessary Karin. Kelwyn says no immunizations. He doesn't want any needles stuck into her. I don't agree but I haven't been able to convince him of their importance," said Cara Bow as she bundled the kicking Polly into her footed pink blanket.

She was exhausted by the sleepless nights, up walking the floor with the screaming Polly Judy. Mrs. Olsen came by every morning to tidy up.

"You have to let her cry, Mrs. Keck. She'll fall asleep eventually. Look how peacefully she's sleeping now."

Little monster thought Cara Bow. She imagined the baby was tormenting her purposely. Kicking in the womb and now kicking out of the womb. Kelwyn complained if he could not get his night's rest and insisted she would be a better mother by *not* letting his little girl cry.

"Look at the moon, Polly," she would cry along with the baby, as she paced the floor night after night with the yowling infant past the mullioned windows which made the moon's image re-reflect itself thousands of times through the many small panes.

"It's a banana moon, see? You like bananas from those little jars, don't you Polly Judy?" Bounce, bounce, up and down. She kept far away from the bedroom door where Kelwyn was snoring non-stop in the same awful rhythm as the crying Polly. *Kelwyn and Polly are in perfect sync,* thought Cara Bow. *They're enjoying the duet.*

Polly seemed to take additional pleasure in banging her wet face on Cara Bow's shoulder as they paced, sometimes stiffening and throwing her head back, causing the exhausted mother to want to let her fall and break her neck. But she always caught her in time. Eventually the siege would end with something of a draw, Polly falling into a peaceful sleep in her crib, a small triumphant smile on her lips, and Cara Bow into a fitful slumber next to the snoring Kelwyn.

The baby's resemblance to Kelwyn was apparent. Her hair, what there was of it, was the same wispy red. Her eyes, which had been blue at birth were now becoming an odd sort of yellowy green, like Nana Keck's.

Judy Eden remarked, "Green eyes are not a family trait, and you weren't a big baby either, Cara Bow. You were petite— perfect."

"She's awfully heavy, too, Mom. My back aches when I carry her around at night to stop her crying. She has a funny cry, like a howl."

Mrs. Eden had come to stay with Polly one day when Cara Bow went in for a check-up with Dr. Boren. He wanted to make sure his vaginal repair was satisfactory. That was the only time Judy had agreed to baby sit. "I don't know what's wrong with this baby," Judy complained. She never stopped crying the whole time you were gone"

Of course, she didn't cry all the time. She didn't cry when Mrs. Olsen was with her, or Mrs. Terzian. Never with Kelwyn. Only with Cara Bow or when Mewmew was allowed to be inside.

"Good news, Caribou," said Kelwyn when Polly was five months old. Mother and Corky are coming to see Polly. She will be so pleased with her granddaughter. Make sure she's dressed in something frilly. They'll by here by the weekend. Mother said she and Corky want to sleep in the nursery with Polly. I've called a furniture rental store and they're going to bring in a couple of twin beds for them."

Cara Bow expressed skepticism about this arrangement. Polly was still creating havoc during the night with her demanding cries. "They'll never get any rest, Kelwyn, and the nursery is one of the smallest rooms in the manor, as you like to call this place."

The Keck manor. True, there had been improvements, like the rail installed on the side porch and the two stone lions with the blinking Christmas bulb eyes at the entrance to the drive. The mowed quack grass front lawn didn't look too bad. There was almost a rightness to the surroundings, given the turmoil she felt inside.

"I know you can make it work, Caribou. Look what I've brought you," he said as he handed her a bouquet of daisies he had been concealing behind his back. "These were not easy to find, Caribou."

So not true, thought Cara Bow. It was May and the field to the right of the house was abloom with them. Still it was a nice gesture. Kelwyn even gave her a small kiss on the cheek as he handed them to her. The flowers were already drooping, as wild flowers will when they are uprooted. *Like me, I've been uprooted from my true goal and now I'm drooping from lack of sleep,* she thought

"The furniture delivery truck will be here this afternoon, so maybe take the dressing table out to make more space for the beds," said Kelwyn.

"My back hurts, Kelwyn. You'll have to help me," said Cara Bow.

"I have to get to the office, Caribou. Ask Mrs. Terzian to help you."

Cara Bow put the daisies in an empty tomato can and put them in the window in the nursery before calling Mrs. Terzian for help.

"Vhy couldn't Kelwyn do this, Mrs. Keck?" Milena's English had definitely improved. Her accent was barely noticeable, though she still said vhy for why.

"He said he had to leave early, Milena. Thank you so much for helping. Kelwyn's mother is coming for a visit. She's never seen the baby."

"That baby's a strange one, Mrs. Keck. She has the oddest cry. Maybe it'll get more normal as she gets older."

"Small chance of that, Milena. The doctor said it was something about her vocal cords. They're unusually thick and not close enough together."

"Vell, that's too bad Mrs. Keck. I have to be off now, you know. Gor is coming from the factory for lunch today. Grandma was sick yesterday and couldn't pack his usual lunch."

Grandma probably has another black eye, thought Cara Bow. *Gor could do well with just a cheese sandwich. He works in a cheese factory after all.*

The extra beds were delivered on time and Cara Bow took extra time to see that all was in readiness. A limousine pulled into the drive that Friday from which Mother Keck and Corky emerged, looking not at all tired. *It's only for a few days*, Cara Bow comforted herself with the thought.

Polly was in a playpen in the dining room. She was already sitting up without help, almost able to pull upright, a strong child for four months. She cooed with delight when she saw her grandmother and Corky come in through the side door. Cara Bow had dressed her in ruffled panties under her lace trimmed dress and had managed to attach a small matching ribbon to her thin hair.

"Here's my girl," cried Mother Keck upon spying Polly. "A real girl this time." She scarcely acknowledged Cara Bow's presence. Polly had been crying and rattling the slats in her playpen only moments before. Now, she was all cheery and looked the perfect baby. She gave Cara Bow an enigmatic smile as Mother Keck held her in her arms.

Cara Bow warned her mother-in-law about the night cries when she showed the two women into the nursery, but that didn't seem to faze them. "What a quaint little room," was Mrs. Keck's response. "I'm sure we'll be just fine. Thank you, Caribou. But, would you please take the tin can from the window? There seem to be some dead flowers hanging from the sides.

Quaint? thought Cara Bow. *What an odd way to describe a room with a few dangling mobiles and a large stuffed giraffe that Kelwyn had brought home one day.* The giraffe stood before the window overlooking the muddy creek and overgrown garden area and the two plum trees that were again in blossom. *Maybe this was quaint to people who had never left the city.* Cara Bow nodded in tacit agreement. "Yes, it is quaint, isn't it? Sorry about the dead flowers."

Wizened Corky opened her over-sized traveling bag and took out a gnarly looking branch and began to wave it about. She was spry, hopping about the whole domicile like a jack rabbit, mumbling incoherently. Mother Keck took over the small end of the Naugahyde two-piece couch, plopping Polly alongside her.

"She's a perfect child, my dear. You and Kelwyn must be so pleased."

Wait until tonight, thought Cara Bow. But the next two nights passed peacefully, and the only sounds came from Kelwyn's snores. Mewmew sidled out from under the bed and snuggled next to Cara Bow for the first time since Polly, the intruder, had disrupted the household. Must be Corky's branch, thought Cara Bow, and she resolved to find something similar in the woods across from the stream.

The limo driver, who had been staying at a motel in the town proper arrived promptly at one o'clock on Sunday afternoon to bring the women back to Chicago. Mrs. Eden had called and asked if the two women would like to attend church on that Sunday morning, but they had declined, stating their preference for the late breakfast prepared by Cara Bow.

Corky praised the plum jelly.

"This is different from the jelly we get in our grocery store," she said as she helped herself to another spoonful for her white bread toast. "Not too sweet. Where do you get it?"

"I make it myself from the plums off the trees in our yard," said Cara Bow. The plums keep falling, even in the cold months. I've stored several jars in our basement."

"We'll take a few jars back to Chicago," said Corky. "Elsie likes it, too, don't you Elsie?"

Elsie nodded, her mouth full. Cara Bow was relieved that the two grandmothers would not have to meet. Corky and Mother Keck had spent all of the previous day marking every hour of Polly's day with cries of delight. Polly Judy behaved perfectly, only once hitting Cara Bow with her small spoon from a jar of mashed banana.

The ladies departed with two jars of plum jelly. That Sunday night Polly again began the squawking torture, which Cara Bow now thought of as deliberate. *Deliberate, hateful, torture. This child was never going to accept her mothering.* "We're enemies now," she said to the crying baby as she carried her around the floor. "My turn will come, you little shithead."

Kelwyn managed to be away most of the weekend, pleading a backlog of insurance forms at the office. Cara Bow knew he was off fishing with Gor.

CHAPTER 9

Cara Bow would have forgotten her days at Madison except for Alecia's regular calls, texts, and emails with attachments of pictures of the world outside of Cooperton.

Polly was now one-year old, still a torment to Cara Bow with demanding cries, but all sweetness and light whenever she was in Kelwyn's presence. Did she know Cara Bow hadn't wanted her, that she now considered her a child of rape? Yes, rape. There was no question in her mind now about this possibility.

Kelwyn had wanted this girl child to keep the money flowing from his grandmother's trust. How many other girls had he tried to impregnate before succeeding with her? Was she the only one? Had he done research on her family and more importantly on where they lived, so he could reside in a place where hunting and fishing were the main male activities?

Well, that's the past now and no changing it, she thought. She missed the intimacy of sex but had become quite proficient at satisfying herself.

Kelwyn's occasional quick insertions into her vagina were merely a biological need on his part and thankfully soon over with little effort on her part.

Living more than three miles from the library in the town center entitled outlying areas to visits from the bookmobile. The bus-like van came up the Keck drive weekly. On its arrival, Cara Bow went out the side door and climbed the lowered two steps of the van into a world of children's books, biographies, science fiction, romance novels, historical accounts, politics, and poetry. The bus always arrived at two o'clock in the afternoon when Polly was finally napping after a morning of the usual torment.

The bookmobile driver, Derek Humphrey, was good looking and studly. Cara Bow noted this and began to offer him coffee and a muffin spread with her plum jelly, which soon led to another offer resulting in a lie down on the yoga mat in the center of the van and a satisfying sexual encounter.

"I can only park here for fifteen minutes" Derek said regretfully. "I'm on the clock. I don't want to lose this job. Lots of people get their books on e-readers now. The librarian is so crabby. She has to deal with the people who use their computers to get on line, and the regulars who use the magazine section for their naps."

"I still prefer a real book, Derek. Fifteen minutes is not a long time to pick out a good read or for anything really"

So, Derek made an exception for Cara Bow, stretching the fifteen minutes to a half hour or more. Cara Bow insisted on precautions. Kelwyn had told her about the vasectomy he had shortly after the birth of Polly. He only needed the one girl.

"I'll make up the time on the next few stops, Cara Bow. I think I'm in love with you," said Derek.

"I love you, too, Derek," she said, and she did love him for that short period of their lovemaking. He was an anodyne to the days of housekeeping, baby minding and loneliness. He was never in her dreams. Her colored dreams were still of Alecia.

Her chemistry books in the bedroom window seat didn't go untouched. She missed her time in the lab setting up experiments, and the long hours waiting for results. Her favorite professor, Dr. Timmer, was noted for his research on the effects of oxygenation on blood cells which he claimed was the major cause of aging.

"We turn into a pile of rust," Dr. Timmer had often joked.

She decided to set up her own lab. She began by telling Kelwyn she wanted a space in the now refurbished basement. A pool table, pinball machine, card table, and two easy chairs were Kelwyn's play room during the long winter evenings. There was one closed off area where she stored her plum jelly.

"It would be perfect for a sewing table. I can make some of Polly's pretty dresses, Kelwyn," she said. "There's a high window that opens for ventilation, too. The ventilation was important for some of the experiments she was planning, along with a fan that would keep the small space free from the smoke smell from Kelwyn's growing pipe collection and any other odor that would come from her planned research.

"It's all yours, Caribou. With the door closed I won't even know you're there."

Little by little her lab emerged. Using some of her now deceased grandmother's trust money, she ordered two lab tables, a steel cabinet, an electron microscope, crucibles, a Bunsen burner, test tubes, clamps, a mortar and pestle, carboys, scoops, stoppers with their little holes, protective glasses, and any other kind of equipment she would need to review the experiments in her textbooks. And, of course, a sewing machine.

The space became her woman cave. On Polly's worst days, Cara Bow wanted to make dynamite and blow everything to bits. Kelwyn was there most evenings with Gor and Dr. Boren. They never once tried to open the door to her secret hideaway, although Cara Bow kept it securely locked. She could hear their loud buffoon laughs, only a bit softened by the heavy wooden door. She could only imagine the chomping of the snacks they enjoyed while playing poker. And the beer drinking. During the past year, Kelwyn had become more than a little overweight but had reached a plateau of sorts in that regard.

"Kelwyn, have you ever thought of wearing suspenders?" asked Cara Bow. She was repulsed by the way his stomach hung over the belt of his pants. She had begun to wear ear plugs at night to muffle his snoring that had increased in volume with the additional pounds.

"Suspenders! Are you crazy Caribou? Suspenders aren't manly. Get that out of your head. Darla's always saying how good I look."

"You haven't been to the office for two weeks, Kelwyn. When does Miss Albert see you?" *So now it's Darla*, she thought.

"I'm going to drop by today, in fact. See that everything's is in tip-top shape. Uncle Ulrich is sending someone from the Chicago office to go over the books. Hank Fischer. I'll take him to that rib place in Green Bay tonight. Won't be here for supper," he said while hitching up his belt another notch below his fat apron of flesh.

"I'll have to call Mrs. Olsen to stay with Polly this evening, Kelwyn. I won't be here when you get home. It's my bowling night." Cara Bow had become a regular sub with the cheese factory ladies on Wednesday nights. It was a form of athletics she liked, not only because she was surprisingly good at it, but also, she liked the smoky atmosphere of the bowling alley.

Mrs Olsen liked the Keck's big screen TV and was good with Polly, who went to sleep like an angel after a snack of toast and plum jelly. Polly's night dramatics didn't begin until Cara Bow returned. Cara Bow was glad to have the night out, away from the incessantly petulant child.

"I don't know what you complain about, Mrs. Keck. You have a perfect child"

Oh, if only you knew, thought Cara Bow.

Since Polly Judy, now almost two years old, was now walking, Cara Bow didn't worry about not being able to hear her cries at night. The child now made her presence known by coming to Cara Bow's bedside at odd hours and pounding her little fists on her mother's sleeping form.

"I want some water, or I'm cold, or you need to change my bed. It's wet," she would demand in her squawky voice. She never bothered Kelwyn. Cara Bow imagined the child and father were allies in this ongoing torture.

At times, she wondered if she was being unfair in her perception of having become a victim. Kelwyn was not physically abusive. He always addressed her in a patient voice, as though she were the child, an unwanted child, now that his trust fund was assured. In her imagination, Kelwyn, Polly Judy, and Mother Keck had become a kettle of thick, poisonous stew with Corky standing over the pot stirring the mixture.

The bowling night was a wonderful respite. She liked being with these women. Ruthie was the best bowler. Strike after strike, even picking up splits. Ruthie was her own woman, not to be challenged. She let nothing go. A smallest remark, deemed to be insulting to her, was always countered with a rebuttal and a demand for an apology. Her assails could be heard across the twelve lanes, the hapless victim soon reduced to a cowering puddle of melting jello who would abjectly say, "Sorry, Ruthie."

"Okay, okay, let's get on with it. You're up. Get us a strike now, Josie. Get us a strike." Ruthie Albert was all business about the game. The cheese factory ladies always won the year end final gold cup.

I want to be like Ruthie, thought Cara Bow. She managed to sit next to her at the bar after their ten games were done. Ruthie ordered a boiler maker and Cara Bow followed suit. "Nice game, Ruthie," she said. Her words were slurred. She wasn't used to boiler makers.

"Thanks, you weren't doing so badly yourself except for that seventh frame.

The seventh frame, yes, thought Cara Bow. The men's league bowled on five of the lanes on the same night. She'd spotted Derek Humphrey two lanes over as she let go of the ball. Her ball was blue, a seven pounder. Seeing him threw her off focus. Derek, her once weekly lover. He winked and grinned as her blue ball found its course down the gutter.

"Guess I lost it for a moment, Ruthie," she said.

"That happens, that happens, don't worry about it, Hon," she said.

"Hon." The Alberts called everyone Hon. It was a term of belittlement, not endearment to Cara Bow. Another way of folding everyone into the general population. *It's demeaning,* she thought.

"How's the family, Ruthie? she asked.

"Good, good." Her answers were in the familiar pairs. "Kids are all in high school. They're never home, into after school sports, you know. I'm having to give them warmed over dinners. I like to get their meal out of the way early."

Ruthie had two sons who were star athletes, one, Louie, in baseball and the other, Martin, in basketball.

"Were they easy as babies? Asked Cara Bow. "They say boys are harder than girls."

"Never a problem, Hon. Never a problem. They slept all night right away, and they were good eaters, too. I nursed them both for two years. They're fond of boobs." She laughed loudly at her comment.

"My Polly Judy cries a lot and she still doesn't sleep all night. She's three. I think she doesn't like me."

"Why is that, Hon? Never heard of a kid not liking their Mum."

"Well, I never wanted a baby. Maybe she senses that. She's good for everyone but me. She smiles and simpers even for strangers. She adores Kelwyn, and he has never even changed her diaper."

"Never changed a diaper! Never changed a diaper! Somethings off there. Take my boys. Never needed diapers for long. The husband took care of that chore. They could whizz in the pot at eleven months, eleven months, mind you." Ruthie shook her curly head in disapproval upon hearing Cara Bow's tale of woe. Ruthie had tight curls, kept in bobby pins all day, even while working at the factory. The pins came out to revealing their glorious ringlets on bowling nights.

"I don't know, Ruthie. I must be doing something wrong. She finished her boilermaker and said she had to get going.

"Mrs. Olsen is babysitting, and she likes to get home early. She has to do the milking in the morning." She felt chastised by Ruthie's comments about how soon her boys had been trained. Polly was still wetting her bed at night. When she headed out to the parking lot she found Derek waiting for her by the Volvo, and they crawled into the back seat for a quick one. He was an expert lover. It didn't take her long to have an orgasm.

When she got home, Kelwyn and Polly were asleep. Cara Bow still felt lightheaded from the boilermaker and the meeting with Derek.

She crawled into bed fully dressed except for her shoes. She fell asleep watching the ceiling spin around. She woke as she felt the familiar punching on her arm.

"Mommy, my bed is all wet," cried Polly. Cara Bow didn't get up this time, and after a few more punches, Polly climbed into their bed and squeezed between her mother and father.

I'm going to live my own life, thought Cara Bow as she drifted off again. The ammonia smell of Polly's wet trainers was the last thing she remembered.

She had a headache the next morning. Polly had a fever.

"You should have changed her last night, Caribou. Look, now she's sick," said Kelwyn.

"Kids get fevers, Kelwyn. She'll be fine. I've given her some baby Tylenol," said Cara Bow. She'd taken some extra strength Tylenol herself.

Mrs. Terzian was coming in to clean that day. She was bringing the old grandmother along because she was getting unpredictable, sometimes wandering off. She liked to visit the two men in the house across from the Kecks. Cara Bow had seen them talking together. She decided they were Armenian, too, and that was why they didn't acknowledge her waves.

"We can't leave her alone anymore. She wanders off," apologized Melina. "Last week she brought some sticks into the house and lit them on fire in the bedroom. Gor came home just in time to put it out, but there's a big scorch mark on the bedroom linoleum. Grandma won't be in the way. I gave her a little gin before we came. She likes gin. It helps her to sleep, she says." Mrs. Terzians English was much improved.

"Where were you when the fire happened, Mrs. Terzian?" asked Cara Bow.

"I was at a school conference with Ani's and Davi's teachers. Davi is doing well but Ani has had some problems with another girl in her class. Ani broke the girl's glasses in a fight and now I have to pay for a new pair."

"I'm sorry to hear that," said Cara Bow as she settled the grandmother in Kelwyn's easy chair. She noticed dark bruising on the grandma's face and arms.

"What's this? she asked.

"She's always falling, Mrs. Keck," said Mrs. Terzian.

It looks like bruises from punches, not falls, thought Cara Bow. *Gor has been a busy boy.* She knew what a punch bruise looked like. Her own arm had little yellowish blue marks from Polly Judy's nightly jabs. *I'm a battered woman, too,* thought Cara Bow. *A baby-battered woman.*

Polly's temperature continued to rise, so Cara Bow called Dr. Boren and was told to bring her into the office at once.

"It's her tonsils, Cara Bow," he said. "See, they're all full of pus. They'll have to come out. I can have the ear, eye, nose, and throat guy from Green Bay here by tomorrow morning. Let's put her in the hospital for tonight."

A night without the crying. Cara Bow couldn't believe her good luck. Kelwyn had called from the office earlier and said he would be away that night, too.

"Polly Judy's in the hospital. She's going to have her tonsils out in the morning, Kelwyn. Maybe you should stick around," said Cara Bow.

"I have to take care of some important business, Caribou," Said Kelwyn. Make sure they do a bang-up job. Can't have anything bad happen to my Polly. My mother would be furious. She'd never forgive you."

"Forgive me? Forgive you, you mean".

"Let's not start something, Caribou. Someone's on another line. I'll call you later." Caribou heard the final click. *At least he was at the office,* she thought. *Someday I'm going to run my own life, too.* But at the moment she was stuck with her unwanted child.

When Polly was settled into her hospital crib, surrounded by an adoring staff, Cara Bow left. Back at the house, Mrs Terzian had left. Everything was tidy and blissfully quiet. She called Derek.

"Come for a drink," she said. We have the place to ourselves for the whole night.

"Can't, Caribou. I'm really sorry but I have an important library meeting this evening," said Derek.

Important meeting, she thought. *Guys and their important meetings.* She had accepted her place in Derek's little black book and tonight seemed to be someone else's turn. She spent the next several hours in her woman cave, working on an experiment which was supposed to yield a common poison. Undetectable, the book said. She gave the sewing machine a kick. Her headache vanished. She decided to vanish Derek from her life, too. *I'll no longer be an available service girl in his book,* she thought.

CHAPTER

10

Nurse Lois greeted Cara Bow early the next morning.

"What an adorable child, Mrs. Keck," she said. Those beautiful green eyes look right through me. She slept like an angel all night. The tonsil doc is with her right now, Dr. Puli. We joke about his name. He's always pulling things out of people, not just from their throat, but from their wallets, too."

"Ha ha," she responded politely. "Thanks, Lois. Which room is it?" asked Cara Bow, though she knew which room, but decided to let Lois be her guide. "How's Carl? she asked remembering his past drunken skirmish. She had pleaded on his behalf to Judge Eden at the time of Polly Judy's birth.

"Oh, that's all done with, thanks to you, Mrs. Keck. He got probation and he's been working hard at the Albert Car Repair shop. He's even worked on your Volvo.

That explained the food wrappers and beer can she'd found under the back seat after the last oil change. They'd given her a loaner, so she

71

wouldn't have to wait. She'd met her mother for lunch and it was at least two hours before she returned to the garage. *Guess the cars been out to lunch, too*, she surmised.

"He's a nice boy, Lois," she said. "Glad he's kept out of trouble."

Polly began to cry when she saw her mother. *What else is new?* Cara Bow thought.

"Why am I here, Mother. Where's Daddy?" I want Daddy, not you."

"You won't be here long, Polly. Just one more night, the doctor says. That's because of the infection. Daddy has some important business to attend to." *Important business. He wasn't there for this terrible child's birth either. He must be allergic to sickness and hospitals or whatever.*

"What's an infection, Mother"

"Some bad germs got into your throat and made your tonsils all swollen and gave you a fever, Polly. Now stop your crying. The nurse is coming in." *I think I've just described Polly,* she thought.

Nurse Lois came in with a shot she said would make Polly quiet before she was to have the tonsillectomy. Polly immediately was all smiles.

"Here she is. What a good little girl—and so pretty, too. Now this is just a little pinch," she said as she poked the needle in Polly's arm. "Dr. Puli is ready for her now, Mrs. Keck. You can wait in the visitors lounge. Don't worry, Mrs. Keck. It's a simple procedure. It won't be long."

"Thanks, Lois. I'll see you soon, Polly." She bent to kiss Polly, but Polly turned away as she scrunched up her face and spit at Cara Bow. She tried to stick out her tongue, but she was already falling asleep. Cara Bow left her to nurse Lois.

"She's all yours, Lois. I'm not going to wait. Call me if there are any complications. I'll be back in the morning."

She had had a straight through night's sleep for the first time since Polly was born. The silence at home continued when Polly came home. There were only little mewlings when Cara Bow spooned jello and ice cream into the child's bird beak mouth. *I don't need to be doing this,* she thought. *Polly is perfectly able to feed herself.* Polly sat docilely in her high chair in the kitchen. Kelwyn wanted no part in the feeding. He was in his usual spot in his easy chair, reading the local sports pages.

"What are you giving her, Caribou?" yelled Kelwyn from the living room.

It was vanilla ice cream. Polly would only eat vanilla.

"Ice cream, Kelwyn," said Cara Bow.

"Bring me a dish, too. I hope it's butter pecan this time," said Kelwyn.

Polly gave her mother a sideways rictus grin when she heard her father's voice. Cara Bow shoved an extra heaping spoon of the ice cream into the child's mouth. Mewmew came scampering up from the four steps leading to the basement door. She joined in Polly's mewling as she circled around the high chair. *Mewling and meowing. Quite a chorus,* thought Cara Bow. Polly pushed her dish of ice cream from her chair onto the circling cat. There was no love lost between the two.

Cara Bow lifted Polly from the highchair, took her into the living room, parked her on Kelwyn's lap, managing to crumple the sports page he had been reading. Now a pipe smoker, he glared at Cara Bow as he put the pipe into the ashtray on the end table by his chair. The smell from the dirty ashtray sickened her. The smoky miasma lay heavy in every part of the room. He had made a big deal of selecting various jars of tobacco from the local smoke shop. They were lined up on the fireplace mantle: licorice, spice, pine, all of them pungent, and the smell lingered for hours after his last suck on the pipe stem. Since she had finally quit smoking, even the slightest whiff of tobacco had become abhorrent to her.

"Here's your daughter, Kelwyn. I've got to answer my phone," she said, thankful for the interruption and the chance to get out of the smoky living room.

"You do that, Caribou," he said, unwilling to leave his comfort zone. "If it's for me, tell them I'm at the office."

"If its for you, I'm sure they would call on your cell, Kelwyn."

Alecia was on the other end of the line.

"Hey, Caribou, we haven't talked for a while. What's up?"

A while, thought Cara Bow. It had been almost two years. She had dropped her from her paltry list of friends. Milena and Mrs. Olsen didn't count.

"I thought you might like to know, I'm getting married in July. I want you to be my maid of honor," Alecia announced with a hint of triumph in her voice."

"Who's the guy, Alecia." She tried to keep her voice steady. "And it's matron of honor. I'm an old married woman, now. Thanks to you."

"I knew you and Kelwyn would be a perfect match," said Alecia, with no hint of regret in her voice for the fateful introduction. "I'm engaged to Tony Banya. Remember him? He was pre-law at UW. Now he's head of the legal staff in the mayor's office.

Cara Bow did remember Tony. He'd been one of her brief casual affairs before meeting Kelwyn. A nice enough guy. He had an undescended testicle, if she was recalling the right person.

"That's wonderful," said Cara Bow. "I sort of remember him, and I'd love to be your witness." She was amazed that Alecia had thought of her. She had imagined that her one-time best friend still regarded her as a special someone. "I'm excited for you. You'll have to send me the details like place, time, and dress requirements. How many will be in the wedding party?" *Maybe just me*, she thought.

"Oh, six, I think," Alecia answered. "You'll get all the details on our Paperless Post announcement. I'll want Kelwyn to be one of the guys. Tony's going to have the mayor's PR person as his best man. Mrs. Keck and Corky will be there, too. My mom's making out the list. You'll get the invite in your email. That's what everyone does now. Daddy's finally up and about with his walker. He'll walker me down the aisle." She laughed.

"I'll talk to Kelwyn about it. I'm sure he'll want to be there. Maybe my mom will take Polly Judy for a few days," Cara Bow said.

"Are you kidding me?" She's all Mrs. Keck and Corky talk about. They want Polly to be there."

That ended Cara Bow's thought of a few days away from Polly. But maybe Kelwyn wouldn't want to come. He had begun to travel less and less. He was content to drive on occasion to Green Bay with a potential client for ribs but spent most of his days fishing or hunting. And nights in the basement playing poker with Gor and Dr. Boren.

Who am I kidding, she thought. *Kelwyn would be there with bells on showing off Polly to Elsie.*

After the call ended with kiss kiss sounds, Cara Bow thought about the relationship between Alecia's parents and the Kecks. *How close were they, really? Had Alecia been part of some nefarious plot to get her hooked up with Kelwyn? Did she know about the trust fund? A girl to be named Polly? That's what Alecia had called her, Polly. Not Polly Judy, though Alecia must know Cara Bow's preference. She had written it on the birth announcements.* The thought of Alecia's possible betrayal depressed her.

She decided to take Polly Judy from Kelwyn, giving in to her natural instinct of trying to be a proper mother. "Kelwyn, all this smoke is bad for Polly. Why don't you move your pipe rack to the basement? You don't want her to get asthma, do you? I've read second hand smoke can cause asthma."

Kelwyn grumbled at this suggestion but said he would get the stuff moved on the weekend. "Did you forget my ice cream?"

"We only had vanilla in the freezer, Kelwyn. You don't like vanilla. I'm taking Polly for her bath." She didn't like this chore. Polly delighted in splashing water all over her mother as she leaned over the tub. This time, at least, she wouldn't be able to cry. An ice cream covered Mewmew followed them into the bathroom.

"I'll give you a bath, too, Mewmew," she said, "as soon as I have Polly tucked in."

Mewmew curled up contentedly licking the melting ice cream from the tile floor. Polly tried to splash water on her, too, but the cat managed to scamper from the few drops of water with an almost Cheshire cat grin on her face.

◆ ◆ ◆ ◆ ◆ ◆ ◆

Gor and Dr. Boren came over that evening for their poker game. Carl Albert's dad, Owen Albert from the body shop, was now part of the group. Kelwyn proudly showed them his treasured pipe rack filled with his assortment of pipes before they headed to the basement.

"These will be valuable someday," he bragged. The men nodded in agreement.

As soon as Polly Judy was tucked in, Cara Bow and Mewmew headed for her lab retreat. She was working on distilling alcohol from the plums she had stewing in a beaker. She could hear the men's loud beery voices discussing their latest big fish catch through the ice holes cut with a saw on Lake Wakesha.

Kelwyn's getting so heavy, she thought. The thought repeated itself. *Maybe the ice will break.* His red hair, once so appealing was now thin, like embroidery threads, plastered to his scalp with pomade. *He's like a contented bull. He has his daughter Polly, his trust fund, and his servant, me.*

She had never, until Kelwyn, followed someone else's idea of what her path should be. Her mother and father had wanted her to be a teacher. Cara Bow's mother was a teacher. She seemed to have been happy with her job at the Lincoln Elementary School. Cara Bow never heard her say a bad word about it.

"Cara Bow," she had often cautioned, "Keep away from the later grades. Kids start thinking for themselves at that level, then it's nothing but trouble."

Kelwyn wanted her to be a stay-at-home mother. Despite her education, escape from her current imagined prison seemed impossible. *I'm only twenty-six years old, younger than Kelwyn. He's twenty-eight going on sixty-two. This house is a tomb, despite the decorator's attempt, so moldy, creepy, creaky. Stop this gloomy thinking right now,* she told herself. *Find the way out. Maybe I'll look for a job,* she thought.

She decided to see the boss at the cheese factory after she returned from the wedding in Chicago.

"I'm a chemist, Cara Bow Eden Keck," she told Mr. Santini. I can help to ensure your cultures are phage free. I've lived in this area most of my life. Judge Eden is my father."

The boss, Mr. Santini, was the owner of the plant. Since he was expecting the annual FDA inspection of his factory, he thought that it would be to his advantage to employ this beautiful dark-haired girl. He had had some dealings with Judge Eden in the past in regard to a few of his needed employees who had to be excused from jail time because of some petty offense such as public drunkenness or driving with a suspended license. "We need these men, Judge. I can't let the milk go bad." And the judge would then impose a fine which Mr. Santini was glad to pay.

With the inspector coming he felt the usual angst, which wasn't good for his ulcer. Typically, he took the inspector to a good steak house and made sure he had enough gift boxes for the inspector's family. The inspection always took place during the Christmas season.

"I've got an inspection coming up next week," he said. We've been scrubbing the place down. I'm sure he'll be impressed with an actual chemist in the culture lab. I could take you on part time for now."

"That would be great, Mr. Santini" she said. "I do have a small daughter. Miss Albert, at my husband's office said one of her nieces, Donna Albert, who's a little slow but good with children, has agreed to watch Polly while I'm at work."

"Yes, I know Donna," said Mr. Santini. She didn't work out here at the plant, but she'll be a good babysitter. When can you start? We had a problem yesterday. A whole vat of milk failed with a phage. I had to send a guy to Kiel for fresh starter."

"Give me a few days, Mr. Santini," said Cara Bow, "We just returned from a wedding in Chicago and I have to finish putting up my plum jelly. It's Polly's favorite."

Polly had given a star performance as the perfect child all during the wedding ceremony and reception. "She's named Polly for Kelwyn's grandmother and Judy for my mother," explained Cara Bow.

"How darling, real old-fashioned names. Bet you call her PJ," was the response heard more than once.

Okay, PJ, thought Cara Bow. *That's what she'll eventually be called at school, no doubt.* Even Kelwyn took to the abbreviated name on occasion. Mother Keck and Corky wouldn't hear of Polly being called by an abbreviation.

Cara Bow had dressed Polly in a gown she'd managed to sew, copied from a Goya painting she saw in one of the art books she occasional borrowed from the bookmobile. A wine-colored velvet skirt, a sky blue lacy top embroidered with tiny ballet dancers, a blue velvet ribbon in her springy red hair, white socks, and black patent shoes. Cara Bow's fingers had suffered more than one needle stab during this sewing venture. She decided not to try such a project again. She thought Kelwyn would be impressed but he only said sarcastically, "Glad you're getting good use out of your sewing machine."

Mother Keck and Corky never stopped fawning over Polly. Except for the occasional photo which Cara Bow sent, this was the first time they had seen her since their visit to Cooperton. Corky was without her twisted wooden stick, but she still reminded Cara Bow of picture she had seen in the story of Snow White, a wizened old witch. Elsie actually had a cell phone with a camera and she took pictures of Polly almost non-stop.

They're desperate people, powerless people, to be pitied, thought Cara Bow. *No wonder Kelwyn is so determined to be the man he imagines real men to be. They hadn't wanted him. He was skipped over. Now they had their girl. a girl who hated her mother. Well, I'll be glad when this wedding is over.* Tony Banya didn't seem to remember their past encounter at the university. Alecia looked beautiful. Her mother cried as Alecia and her father with his walker processed down the aisle of the large Methodist church the family were members of. *Nothing like my wedding day*, Cara Bow thought again.

She told Kelwyn about her upcoming job on the drive back to Cooperton. Polly thankfully slept during the whole drive. Kelwyn took the news of Cara Bow's job with seeming indifference. "You'll be home to fix breakfast, won't you?' he asked while looking through the sports pages of the Chicago Tribune. Cara Bow was the driver as Kelwyn was too hungover to drive.

"I'll only be working two or three days a week, Kelwyn and of course you'll get your breakfast. Donna Albert will be with Polly when I'm away," she said.

"Oh good," said Kelwyn. "She's quite a pretty girl. Dumb though. I suppose she won't do any harm."

"Darla told me her cousin has managed to get her driver's license, even drives her own pick-up." She gave an inward sigh of relief at Kelwyn's unspoken approval.

The following week went surprisingly smoothly. Milena or Mrs Olsen were there every morning by nine and Polly was nice enough except for the nightly poundings.

Kelwyn stayed home until they arrived as Cara Bow had to leave earlier. She happily left the two of them together, Polly clinging to Kelwyn's leg.

On Friday, Kelwyn's check day, he mentioned to Cara Bow that he would be stopping briefly by the office, his usual day to pick up his check before heading to his hunting camp. "I'm having some wiring done for the new refrigerator.

Maybe he'll be electrocuted, thought Cara Bow.

CHAPTER 11

The next few years were busy ones. When Polly Judy turned four, Kelwyn announced his intention to take her to Disneyland. "My mother and dad took me at that age, and I still remember the trip. You can come too, Caribou. We'll take the Volvo."

Driving across several states with a fussy, crying child didn't sound appealing to Cara Bow. "I'm pretty busy at the cheese factory right now, Kelwyn, and it's the middle of winter. The roads will be bad."

"It's her birthday Caribou," he said insistently. The weather will get warmer as we travel west."

She knew Kelwyn wanted his slave-wife to be at his disposal on the journey. She stood her ground and refused. "Take Donna along. Polly likes her."

"My mother wants to come, too, Caribou," he said. What will she think if you refuse to come?

"Let her think what she wants, Kelwyn. I'm not going on this crazy trip."

Mother Keck was alone now. Corky was gone. A messenger bicyclist had hit her while crossing State Street in Chicago. Mrs. Keck had sent her to buy Frango Mints at Macys. Corky had shriveled to the size of an eight-year-old and dressed in her usual black was almost invisible in the early evening when the accident took place. At her funeral, Mrs. Keck had at last met Corky's family, a son, his wife, two grandsons and one great-grandson. No girls.

The trip was finally arranged. Donna Albert's face lit up when she was asked to go. *She should have been Polly's mother*, thought Cara Bow. Kelwyn made good use of her, she felt sure. Donna was pretty, her blonde hair worn in a long braid down her back, ear lobes pierced in many places, studded with colored glass dots, a snake tattoo running up her right arm, long fingernails, each painted in a different pattern, eyebrows plucked to a thin line. *Pretty but dumb*, Cara Bow thought. *Just right for Kelwyn, fat Kelwyn, flannel draped Kelwyn, balding Kelwyn. They belong together*, she thought. *The perfect pair.*

Cara Bow and Kelwyn no longer shared a bed. He had moved the black naugahyde couch to his basement playroom two years ago. He slept surrounded by his pool table, pinball machine, the pipe rack, and jars of flavored tobacco on a table alongside his easy chair.

She could still hear his snores through the floorboards, but they were less disturbing, more like a distant foghorn. He only appeared above stairs to eat, change clothes, and make use of the bathroom for his big dumps. He kept a chamber pot downstairs or used the muddy creek for pissing. *He's become a troll, a fat troll*, thought Cara Bow.

Polly and Kelwyn would be away for two whole weeks.

"I'll need the Volvo, Kelwyn, you'll have to take the pick-up," she said. I can't drive a stick shift.

"What about my mother?" he whined. "I can't take her to California in a truck."

"You can take it to Chicago and then fly from O'Hare. *Kelwyn is truly stupid*, she thought. "You'll have more time to explore. Donna will love it. Have Darla Albert arrange the flight and a car rental," she remained adamant. "The Volvo stays here." She had become intolerant of Kelwyn's silly ideas since working at the cheese factory.

She and Mr. Santini had been working on a plan to make use of the whey by- product in the cheese making process. It was exciting. Giulio, that's what she called him now, had been trucking the whey along country roads and dumping it in culverts along the back roads. The county board finally said this was a no-no, as the farmers were complaining about the flies which were invading their barns and houses.

His solution was to keep pigs behind the factory. They were happy to slop in the whey. The pigs also supplied bacon, ham and lard to the employees who took part in the occasional slaughter.

"Whey is used in a lot of commercial products, Giulio, chocolate, for one. Look on the labels, the next time you're in the grocery. You're a small outfit. You have to get with the times. Cooperton is not your small town in Italy. I don't know how you pass inspection"

"Dried whey, Cara'—he called her Cara. 'Not the watery stuff."

"You could build a whey drying plant," said Cara Bow. She had been reading up on the process All of the other cheese plants in Wisconsin had a whey plant or shipped the whey to where it could be processed. I'll invest in it if you agree to the idea. There's money to be made in whey."

Cara Bow hated the pigs. She'd watched one of the guys, Olivo, try to rescue a litter before the boar killed them. The boar was mean. He charged Olivo when he entered the pig pen and had a large gash taken out of his leg. It took several stitches to close the wound at the hospital emergency room. Nurse Lois broadcast the mishap to the Albert family.

One of her cousins was married to Olivo. Several complaints were registered at the town hall. It wasn't illegal to keep the pigs, but Mr. Santini finally realized it was bad for business.

"Guess I'll have to do it, Cara, build the drying plant."

"Good for you, Giulio," said Cara Bow. "You'll make a profit on the waste and you can make Olivo the manager of the whey plant. It's a solution where everyone benefits."

Mr. Santini had come to increasingly rely on her. He had been satisfied with his small business, but rules and regulations were something he did not want to be bothered with. Cara Bow Keck was happy that she was beginning to shed her self-image of a compliant weakling. *I'm on a bowling team, go to the gym, and have a real job in my field,* she thought. *Daddy must be so pleased.*

The judge had come to her house only one time and declared it a dump.

"Can't breathe in this place," he said. "All this smoke."

"Daddy, you smoke cigars," said Cara Bow.

"Outside, honey, not in the house. Your mother won't have it. Besides, Dr. Boren say I must give them up. The bronchitis, you know."

She sensed his frustration with this new dictum. "Maybe try a pipe, Daddy. That's what Kelwyn smokes. Take a puff now and then while you're in withdrawal. She loved her parents, but not their rules. However, she wished Polly would follow even one of her cautions without making the hateful face. *Maybe things will change when they return from the Disneyland trip.*

Cara Bow was in her basement lab when the pick-up truck slid back to the side porch. There had been a late January thaw, but the nights were below freezing, causing the long driveway to become a sheet of ice. The loud stomping and muffled voices above her head announced the homecoming.

"Caribou get up here," Kelwyn shouted down the basement stairs. "There's been a small accident."

She hurried up the wooden stairs thinking, maybe it's Polly Judy. But no, not Polly. Sprawled on the living room paisley covered couch— the black naugahyde now moved to the basement— was Donna Albert.

"Oh, I think I've busted my ankle getting out of the truck," she moaned.

"Why didn't you have Mr. Olsen spread salt on the drive, Caribou?" said Kelwyn.

"I thought you wouldn't be back for a few more days, Kelwyn. What happened?"

"Polly complained that she was bored, and Mother Keck got a case of food poisoning. She's not used to traveling much. You know that! She vomited in one of those little bags on the flight back to O'Hare. You should have come with us, Caribou. Donna was useless at Disneyland.

She vanished right after we got inside the gate. Took off with a bunch of people that looked like vampires. All in black get-ups.

Cara Bow looked at the moaning creature with little sympathy. "Get Donna to the Immediate Care Center, Kelwyn. Call Miss Albert and tell her to meet you there while Dr. Boren examines her ankle. I'm sure it's not too serious."

Hope I'm not losing a sitter, was Cara Bow's overriding thought. She was now almost full time at the cheese factory, except for Wednesdays when she met her mother for lunch and a round or two of margaritas. She loved her mother, but didn't want to be like her, a retired school teacher, bridge player, shopper, silent movie fan, and game show watcher. The lunches were tedious conversations that ran the same weary looping track.

"How's the slouch?" Her mother meant Kelwyn, of course. She seemed to glory in her prediction of Cara Bow's unhappy union.

"He's still around, Mom. Please don't keep calling him that. He did get his general degree at Madison and his business is doing fine." She felt some obligation to defend her choice. "How's Dad?" was her counter.

"Oh, you know your father. He's at the court house all week and weekends he sits in his chair watching golf. He rarely plays anymore. Just watches. He's starting to lose touch, I think."

"What do you mean, Mom? Losing touch."

"He forgets where things are, sometimes. One time he lost his car at the Walmart parking lot and I had to go and pick him up and drive around until we found it. It was right by the front entrance. In a handicap parking space. Lucky, he didn't get a ticket. That would have made some talk in the neighborhood. Judge Eden getting a citation."

"Oh, Mom. I'm sorry to hear that. You must be so worried."

"I didn't mean to complain, Honey. It's just little things. Let's order another margarita. I'll buy. Strawberry, this time," Judy said suddenly changing her sad demeanor, but Cara Bow could see the beginning of tears held back in her mother's eyes.

No, I will not be like my mother, Cara Bow thought. *I'm off that path for good*. Her way forward was uncertain, but one thing was certain. Her thoughts returned to the present moment. The moaning woman on the couch and her strange family. Here was the tribe she was now part of. *I've got to rid myself of Kelwyn and Polly.* Polly meanwhile began her squawky cry as soon as Kelwyn and Donna left for the emergency room. Donna leaned on Kelwyn, his arm possessively around her waist. *That's a telling picture,* she thought as she looked at the two of them departing and then down at Polly kicking at her ankle.

"Come on, Polly, lets unpack your stuff and you can tell me all about Disneyland."

"I liked *Small World* and all of the dancers. I want dancing lessons," she demanded. I'm going to be a ballet dancer." She turned in awkward circles, knocking over her bedside lamp in the process. "See what you made me do? You're a bad mother." The crying began again. In fury, her small body flailed against Cara Bow.

See what you're making me do, thought Cara Bow. *I'm so sorry you didn't vanish with Donna at Disneyland.* "Okay, Polly, that's enough. C'mon in the kitchen. You must be hungry," she said, trying to appease the child. I'll make you some nice toast with plum jelly."

Polly loved plum jelly. The offer quieted her for the moment. *Oh, you little monster,* thought Cara Bow. Polly fixed her green eyes on Cara Bow with a long stare. Was she sensing her mother's dislike?

Oh, you'll be sorry, thought Cara Bow. An idea had begun to worm its way into her chemist's brain. *Yes, you will surely be sorry.* Now, she had real purpose in her lab projects. Not the ones in her chemistry books. This project would take some focused researched.

She heard Kelwyn's truck come up the drive, this time slowly. Polly slid off the kitchen chair, toast in hand and ran to the side door to greet her father. "Mama's being mean to me," she pouted as he picked her up.

"Caribou, for Christ's sake, quit tormenting this poor kid. She's just a baby."

Yes, a baby, and so are you Kelwyn, she thought. *Two devil babies. I'm getting off this path. I've taken a wrong turn. I'm confused and at the same time I see clearly. How can this be?* Her computer brain began flashing numbers, equations, and formulas. *Maybe I'm going crazy.*

"Daddy, I'm going to have dancing lessons; I'm going to be a ballerina."

"That's great Polly," said Kelwyn. "Caribou, get her tucked in. We'll see about dance classes tomorrow. Miss Albert's got a cousin who runs a studio in the mall."

He handed Polly to Cara Bow "This trip has exhausted me," he complained.

"The trip was your idea, Kelwyn," she reminded him. "How's Donna, by the way?" she asked. "Nothing serious, I hope. I can't be driving Polly to dance lessons. I'm working almost full time at the factory."

"It's a bit of bruising. No break. No sprain. She'll be fine. Now, I'm going downstairs. Gor and Dr. Boren are coming over this evening for some poker."

"I thought you were tired, Kelwyn."

He turned his back to her as he headed down the basement stairs without answering.

Polly pushed her remaining toast against the front of Cara Bow's blouse. The plum jelly left a stain on the collar. Cara Bow put her down. "You're getting too big to carry," she said, "and you can take care of your own wash up. Here's your pajamas."

"You're a bad, bad Mother." screamed Polly. "I hate you." Her little face scrunched up and turned red as she began to hold her breath.

Cara Bow didn't put a cold cloth on Polly's face as she had frequently done in the past during these episodes of breath-holding. *Maybe she'll never breathe again*, she thought. *I should be so lucky.*

Polly managed to put her pajamas on with noisy effort and finished her wash-up, standing on a stool. A fountain of water gushed over the sink basin onto the floor as she left the hot water faucet running and the sink plug closed. The water seeped through the floor and covered the top of Kelwyn's pool table in the basement before Cara Bow stopped the flood. For once she was happy that Polly's mischief had had a pleasing result.

The next day dawned in bitter cold. Mrs. Terzian came to stay for the day with Polly. Cara Bow left for the factory and Giulio. They had become more than work partners. Giulio was a small man, but there was nothing small about him. Cara Bow loved his thick, precisely cut, black wavy hair and smooth olive skin. He had a comfortable couch in his office to which they retired for more than a quickie at regular intervals.

"You're so beautiful and tall, Cara," he would murmur as he pressed into her. Evidently, he liked tall. He said had a wife in Genoa. Cara Bow noticed her picture on Giulio's desk, a tiny, compact woman who looked older that Giulio, almost like his mother.

"We were married when I was sixteen," he explained. She's a third cousin of my father's. She was my first. She refused to come to the United States when I decided to take over the factory. It was my uncle Bernie's factory. He started the business and he wanted to return to Genoa."

Oh, those uncles, thought Cara Bow. *Uncle Bernie and Uncle Ulrich. They would make a good pair.*

The plant laboratory had been running smoothly since her arrival. Olivo turned out to be the perfect choice to manage the whey plant, which satisfied the Alberts who had been so upset by Olivo's pig bite that they had threatened to sue. The cheese produced had won many prizes at local fairs and even the blue-ribbon prize at the state fair.

Though Cara Bow's life was busy and even bearable away from the house, going home became a different kind of factory. A horror factory. Kelwyn with his sporting obsession, poker games with Gor and Dr. Boren and resonating snores, adding to the constant berating by Polly Judy, reminded her of a bad movie she needed to get out of. A cartoon in vivid color, like Wile E. Coyote and the Road Runner. *This is unbearable*, she thought. *It's a crazy quilt.*

Still, it was a full life—the weekly margarita lunches with her mother, the arrangements for Polly's piano and dancing lessons, time spent in the factory lab, the bowling team, Giulio, and Derek.

Lately, she had met her old high school classmates, Belle and Kerzy, at the bowling alley bar. They had never left Cooperton. Cara Bow recalled the time when the two girls had been prosecuted for possession of marijuana. They had been fifteen at the time.

Judge Eden had remanded them to the custody of their parents. Both girls had married into the Albert tribe and seemed to be comfortable with their expanding bodies.

"I never lost the weight after the second kid," said Kerzy, slurring her words as she took in Cara Bow's trim figure.

"Same here," echoed Belle. "I've got four now. They're all in school. My youngest, Billy is in first grade with your Polly. Kids like to hang out with her. Billy said she makes up good games."

Was this the same Polly Judy she knew, thought Cara Bow? At the last parent teacher conference, Polly's teacher, Miss Overton, had praised Polly and remarked on her beautiful green eyes.

"Do green eyes run in your family," Mrs. Keck? she almost gushed.

Cara Bow mentioned Kelwyn's mother briefly. "They're a family trait on her father's side."

"Oh, that explains it. Family is everything. Here, look at the interesting family picture Polly's drawn." Miss Overton leafed through a small stack of workbook papers and pulled out a picture of crude figures showing a man and child in a blue sunny sky setting, and a woman and cat below in a dark muddy colored area.

"She's so bright," said Miss Overton. "Look how she's drawn ears, hands and feet. Quite perceptive for a first grader. She has the hands attached to arms and the feet have shoes on them. The little girl figure is wearing ballet slippers and the man has these big boots. The woman appears to be barefoot and standing in water. Yes, interesting." The noise from the bowling alley interrupted her recollection of the conference.

"I'm glad she and Billy are friends, Belle," said Cara Bow. "Let me buy you and Kerzy another beer. Maybe we can get together sometime, Kerzy." Kerzy looked flustered. Cara Bow sensed that they would never get together outside of the regular bowling night.

Belle and Kerzy went to the Catholic church. All the Alberts did. That was a sticking point. The only place for coming together would be at the bowling alley. Cara Bow was not Catholic. She went to the Presbyterian church at Christmas time with Judy and the judge. The kid's pageant was part of the service where Polly Judy was costumed in her angel wings and Kelwyn was in the crowded aisle making movies with his iPhone. *Where am I in this crazy quilt*, Cara Bow thought?

CHAPTER

12

Her basement lab had two gunny sacks in the far corner, filled with seeds from the plum pits she had saved after making jelly. The pits hadn't been easy to open. She had devised a method of putting them one at a time in a vise, turning the vise until the pit opened a bit on one side and then completing the task with her Swiss army knife. The pit seeds were small and white. It had taken many batches of plum jelly to get enough of the pits.

Here would be her source of cyanide. She used only the good pits, the ones that sank when she put them in jars of cold water. There were two shelves in her makeshift lab for the plum jelly jars, the top shelf holding the jars with the carefully extracted cyanide. Just enough, not too much to interfere with the sweet taste of the jelly. Undetectable.

The time would come for the demise of Polly Judy and Kelwyn. First, Cara Bow needed to determine the path that would lead to her departure from Cooperton. Chicago and Alecia were her goals.

Alecia hadn't come again for a visit, despite Cara Bow's having turned her house into quite an inviting place. A designer from Green Bay had completely transformed the space, despite Kelwyn's protests. Cara Bow's bank account had grown healthy with the monies from her investment in the whey plant, and she frugally deposited a good bit of the money from her trust into the account every month.

Kelwyn spent most of the time in his basement man cave or in the kitchen, rooting in the refrigerator for whatever leftover fast food was available. Polly Judy had taken over the west wing, two rooms with the windows overlooking the plum trees and the sludgy creek.

An exterminator had rid the eaves of the swallow nests, and the wasps. There were still bats in the attic, but Cara Bow didn't mind. She thought they added to the character of the place. The moldy smell in the dining room had been impossible to get rid of, but jars of cinnamon sticks and cut lemons placed in every corner were of some help. She also added bags of unpeeled onions and a boxes of baking soda. Kelwyn complained, but Cara Bow prevailed.

"Kelwyn, you can't see these items. They're in these large pretty pots on the end tables I got at the Presbyterian tag sale. Besides, you said I could do what I want with the décor."

"Did I say that? I don't remember saying that."

"Well you did. After you came back from Disneyland. Even Donna Albert complained about the odor. She said it was affecting her sinuses. We don't want to lose Donna."

"Oh, do what you want. You will anyway. Just keep that stuff away from my poker table in the basement."

"No chance of that, Kelwyn. I've got to see to Polly's dinner. She's become so fussy about anything I serve up."

Polly Judy ate in mysterious ways. Mrs. Terzian had made her rice puddings and sloppy joes which she left in the refrigerator before leaving that day. No one saw the food going into her beak mouth, but somehow the dish of pudding became empty and the sloppy joe buns filled with tomato-sauced ground beef disappeared during conversations about her goings on at school and dance class.

Piano lessons went by the board. Her teacher, Miss Jenkins, insisted she sing the melodies of the little tunes she was to play, and it was discovered her voice could not hold a pitch, only a variation of her squawky cry. The teacher conveyed this to Cara Bow and the lessons ended, but not before Miss Jenkins was accidentally pushed from the chair she sat on while giving instructions to Polly Judy. This resulted in a broken hip, requiring a long period of recovery.

So, the piano in the dining room was largely unused until Cara Bow met Ginger at a PTA meeting. There was an immediate attraction between the two women. Ginger Sandberg's husband was the local dentist. Dr. Sandburg had grown up in the area. He had a long client list. He was the sort of man who had no problem with people who didn't pay their bills. He spent one day every month in small claims court with the miscreants. Cara Bow admired his fortitude.

Ginger was from Mississippi. When she married Dr. Sandberg, she agreed to move to Cooperstown, though she hated snow. She had spent her childhood shrimping on a barge with her brothers. She loved shrimp and she could peel them faster than anyone Cara Bow had ever seen. Dr. Sandberg, Ginger, Kelwyn and Cara Bow often frequented a local restaurant on Friday nights where the salad bar featured high piles of the pink crustaceans. The speed with which Ginger unwrapped them was a remarkable sight.

Ginger spoke with a charming southern drawl. She pronounced shrimp "seerimp." Her hobby was playing the saxophone and she persuaded Cara Bow to accompany her on such tunes as *O, Susannah,* and *Down by The Riverside.* Cara Bow readily acquiesced, as Ginger's soft beauty appealed to her. She had naturally waving, spun red- gold hair, an inviting smile, and an enticing Southern accent. It was a good end to the Wednesday lunches with her mother. Cara Bow and Ginger played their musical duets before Polly Judy returned from school.

The school bus, on rural route three, arrived promptly at 3:40 PM each afternoon, depositing Polly at the end of the long drive. Ginger's daughter, Louise, who was in Polly's second grade class, got off the bus with her on Wednesdays when her mother was there, saxophone in its case, waiting for her daughter's happy hug and wet smacks.

Wednesday was non-routine day when Polly returned. Not wanting to present anything but a perfect angel figure, she croaked "Hello Mrs. Sandburg. I'm so glad to see you and Mother having such a good musical session. Aren't you going to kiss me, Mama? I thought about you a lot today. We were drawing family pictures again. Louise drew a nice one, too."

What a fake, thought Cara Bow.

"You have such a darling daughter, Caribou. And she and Louise have become wonderful little playmates. Well if you're ready, Louise, we'll be off. Your daddy likes to have his dinner early."

But on most days, especially in winter, if she knew Cara Bow was home, she stood at the side door, ringing the doorbell insistently until Cara Bow opened the door. With a smile on her face, Polly would squint her green eyes and proceed to wet her pants.

"Hello, Mother. I'm all wet."

"Yes, I see that, Polly. Come in and we'll get some dry clothes."

"I hate you, Mother."

"Yes, I know, Polly. Let's hurry and change. You're dance class begins at 4:30. Your father is going to pick you up after class." *Yes, Kelwyn, pick up our devil child,* she thought.

"Mother, I'll wear my purple dance outfit today. I like that color so much. It reminds me of plum jelly. Everyone says I look beautiful in that color. Did Donna get it washed? I spilled my lemonade on it last week." Polly jabbered on and on in her strange, un-childlike voice while Cara Bow helped her into the little tutu and tights.

There was no time for a bath. Polly would have to be smelly for this class. *They'll think I'm a bad mother,* she thought and didn't care. She resolved to work longer hours at the cheese plant. Milena Terzian or Donna Albert would have to come sooner in the afternoons. Not Wednesdays, of course.

One evening Kelwyn mentioned, after Polly Judy was settled for the night, that he thought it was good that the town saw Ginger and Floyd out with them out and about in the community on Friday nights.

"Miss Albert is trying to get the dental insurance contract with Floyd's office. We need to socialize more, Cara Bow. There's a new insurance guy moving into town. Uncle Ulrich's keeping an eye on the business. You like our nights out, don't you, Caribou?" he said in an almost cajoling voice.

She pulled away as Kelwyn tried to put his arm around her. "I have my Wednesday bowling night, Kelwyn. Friday nights are hard for me. I'm too tired what with your daughter making non-stop demands," she said. "If you want to socialize more, take Donna."

"Don't be funny, Caribou. Uncle Ulrich says getting this business is crucial,"

"I'll see if Mrs. Terzian can sit on Friday nights, Kelwyn, if it's that important. Can't you wear something other than your flannel shirt, and for god's sake, shave. You're starting to look as old as your uncle. You're only thirty-one years old. It would help if you'd lose some weight, too."

"Don't be funny, Caribou. I need a little extra fat when I'm out in the cold weather."

"You don't need to be out in the cold, Kelwyn. Dress for the weather, for God's sake. Get a down jacket—if you can find one big enough to zip around your gut."

"You're such a nag, Caribou. Donna says I'm a handsome dude. Nice and cuddly."

"Well, cuddle with Donna, then. You sure don't with me."

"Maybe I will, Caribou, maybe I will."

"You're starting to sound like Ruthie, Kelwyn. Not good when you do it."

"Let's get back to Friday nights, Caribou. Uncle Ulrich says this is important."

Uncle Ulrich had moved in with his sister, Elsie, since Corky's fatal accident. *Together at last*, thought Cara Bow. *Dear Mother Keck, the orchestrator, the cemetery owner, the demander, the conniver and possibly the murderer of her husband, Dr. Keck.*

I'm stuck in this moldy house with an unwanted husband and child. Cara Bow felt her gorge rise at the thought of being seen around town with Kelwyn.

"Let's get together in Green Bay, Kelwyn," she said. "This town's so gossipy."

"That's the idea, Caribou. It's all about new business."

Friday nights had turned out to be not so bad. Cara Bow enjoyed hearing Floyd talk about his small claims courtroom wins.

"When you're the new guy in town, the dead-beat payers beat a path to your door. That doesn't work with me. Now, I'm getting the money up front. I'm willing to drill if they pay in green bills. That's my motto," he laughed.

Ginger's latest crazy idea was all about white water rafting. "We're not that far from the Peshtigo river, guys. I saw an article about it in the Green Bay Press Gazette. Let's try it," she interrupted the money conversation while she was peeling her shrimp.

Floyd would do anything for his Ginger. "We'll take the kids, too. Louise and Polly. That's six of us. The large raft holds eight. I hear it's safe. How about it, Kelwyn?"

Kelwyn's girth would make up for the seventh and eighth person, thought Cara Bow. She had been thinking about trying water skiing again on Lake Tioga since she had acquired new-found strength at her gym workouts. She'd only tried water skiing once, years ago. The judge had explained the whole process to her for getting up out of the water and skimming across the top of the waves. The judge himself was a star water skier.

Cara Bow liked to swim but not too far out. She did as she was instructed in the water skiing process, but she didn't have enough strength in her arms to rise. The judge had pulled her halfway across the lake before he realized she was still underwater, hanging on for dear life. She had been afraid to let go of the bar, not being that terrific of a swimmer. The judge, at last hearing her cries for help over the noisy boat engine, cut the power and the skis fell off her bare feet, but she didn't sink. She was wearing a life jacket.

Her thighs that had been pressed into the bar were horribly bruised for the next six weeks. The bruises turned a rainbow of color, blues, blacks, greens, reds, and yellows. The judge said she probably shouldn't try to water ski again which was just as well. Cara Bow hated the orange life jacket. It was so bulky. The fairy water wings she wore while swimming after that suited her just fine. Despite the gym workouts, sports were not her thing.

But she wanted to be with Ginger. Because of her sun allergy, if she wore a wetsuit, there would be no danger of a burn. *Wouldn't her mother and father be surprised to hear of her rafting?* Then a darker thought, *perhaps Polly Judy would fall out of the raft.*

Kelwyn agreed to the adventure, and a date was set for the outing—the third Saturday in April, when the water would be at its highest from the snow melt. Donna Albert came along with them in Floyd's van to keep the girls entertained in the back seats.

Arriving at the wooden shack where the equipment was rented, Cara Bow and the rest of the party were told, "No children under sixteen." *What a disappointment*, she thought.

"Take the kids for ice cream and meet us at the journey's end," said Kelwyn. Come on guys. Let's get started."

"Stay seated in the raft," the rental manager warned. "You'll get bruised by the river rocks if you sit on the raft bottom"

So, Cara Bow, Ginger, Kelwyn and Floyd took their places in the black ballooned rubber raft, Floyd in the back as the steering guide while the other three sat forward. They were told to keep paddling no matter what. The slow drift downstream was pleasant enough. Cara Bow was feeling proud of herself.

"I'm a successful sports person, now," she said to Ginger. After another ten minutes, she began to feel hot under her wetsuit. Ginger looked so comfortable in her bikini and orange life jacket. *I love Ginger*, she thought. Gazing up to the left, she spotted a look-out structure where several people were standing.

"Why are all those people there, Floyd," she called back.

"Just keep paddling, guys," he answered.

The water was flowing faster. Directly ahead were the falls.

"We're going over," cried Ginger as she dropped her paddle and crouched in the bottom of the raft, hanging on to the sides for dear life. Cara Bow joined her. As the raft flew over the steep falls, Floyd lost control of the vessel and the raft was up-ended. Kelwyn was thrown out first and then the others followed. The crowd on the look-out stand laughed and jeered as the stragglers made their way to the shore. Floyd managed to retrieve the raft. Kelwyn moaned that he thought his arm was broken.

"I heard a crack," he said.

A river rescue team maneuvered the bedraggled rafters back into the raft and sent them on their way. The remaining trip was again peaceful.

Did this really happen? thought Cara Bow. She could feel the bruises from the rocks on her butt. *And now fat Kelwyn probably has a broken arm, Polly Judy has ice cream, and I might have to play nurse.*

"This was fun," laughed Ginger. "We'll have to do this again, she said on the otherwise quiet drive back to Cooperton.

Donna and the kids played count the number of red cars passing by in the back of the van. Cara Bow inwardly resolved to never do this again, but she looked forward to bragging about her adventure to Ruthie at the next bowling night.

CHAPTER
13

Giulio told Cara Bow he wanted to open a sales distribution warehouse in Chicago. The business was expanding, and he had bought out another factory as the demand for the Santini brand product was now available at major supermarket chains.

"You'll go won't you Cara?" he asked after another smoochy encounter on his office couch. "I have to stay here. I've taken on new hires and I must keep an eye on the employees. Someone's been stealing cheese from the warehouse."

The warehouse was a separate building at the rear of the factory where the pigs had been. They were disposed of when the whey plant was finally up and running.

"I think it's Gor. Olivo doesn't trust him," said Giulio.

"I hope not," said Cara Bow. "He's Kelwyn's poker playing friend. I don't want anything to change with that group. Having Kelwyn at the supper table is about all I can stand. And Polly. She wants me to set out her food on the small table she has in her part of the house. It's a circus around the place. She only eats in the kitchen for breakfast. Kelwyn insists on that. They have muffins and plum jelly along with their scrambled eggs."

"You've often mentioned the plum jelly, Cara. I don't see it on the grocery shelves."

"It's my own recipe, Giulio. Our property has two plum trees that never seem to quit producing. I put up a batch every three or four weeks. Like another chemistry project. It's fun."

"Maybe you could let me try some, Cara. It must be pretty good."

"Maybe," said Cara Bow. "The pair of them go through it fast." She thought of the special batch infused with the cyanide from the plum seeds. The time was coming to start testing the effect on her husband and child. Polly would be the first volunteer.

How did it come to this, she thought? *Somehow, I'm the wrong mother for this child. Donna should have been the mother. They seem to love each other. Yes, love was the correct word. Have I become such a horrible person to even think of murder?* When Cara Bow returned from a day's work, if she caught them unawares, she would find Polly and *Donna* engaged in some puzzle or video game, laughing as they knocked out a villain. Sometimes they were even doing homework or putting together a special project.

They had stacks of cut out shoe boxes filled with tiny models of fantasy story figures. Super Girl or Wonder Woman, or little mermaids and ogresses. The boxes reminded her of the shelves in Kelwyn's old bedroom in Chicago. Now, Chicago was in the offing.

"Kelwyn, I'm going to be away for a few days. Chicago," she told him over breakfast. Mr. Santini wants me to look for a warehouse. He wants to set up a sales office there.

"You go right ahead, Caribou. Donna and I can handle things here. Make sure you see my mother. She and Uncle Ulrich are getting on. She told me she's ordered a head stone for one of her cemeteries, the one in Lake Forest. She wants to be buried next to Uncle Ulrich."

"Not your father, Doctor Keck? That seems odd, Kelwyn. I know she and her brother are close, but that's a little strange. Not even in the same cemetery?"

Who exactly is Kelwyn's father, thought Cara Bow: She had often remarked on Kelwyn's resemblance to his uncle. *I'd better let that idea lie. It would be too terrible, but it would explain a lot.*

"Of course, I'll check in on them, Kelwyn. I've printed out some pictures of Polly from my phone for Mother Keck's album. She abhors pictures stored in the 'Cloud'. She wants them in hand."

"You can't kiss a cloud picture," she says.

"Donna could stay here overnight while you're away," said Kelwyn.

"No problem, Kelwyn, the guest room is next to Polly Judy's. Mrs Terzian can come during the day, or Mrs. Olsen, if Donna needs to pick up groceries or something. I'll be gone at least a week."

Free rein for the pair of them, she thought. Big Kelwyn and plump Donna. Evidently, she knows how to handle him and Polly, too. Yes, Donna should have been the mother. What strange twist of fate had planted Polly in her womb, not Donna's? Corky with her spiky branch was gone, but her dark spirit hovered over this ungodly match. Yes, Chicago, here I come. I'll bring Uncle Ulrich and Mother Keck some of my plum jelly.

"Caribou, ask Mr. Santini who handles his employees' insurance plan," called Kelwyn as Cara Bow headed out the side door.

Another newer model had replaced the Volvo. Now she could afford to buy her own, instead of relying on the judge. Her bank account, separate from Kelwyn's, had burgeoned with the profits from the whey factory.

She had two stops to make before heading to Chicago. Her mother would have to miss their Wednesday lunch and the saxophone duets with Ginger would have to wait a week.

Cara Bow had been a late in life child. Her schoolmates thought her parents were her grandparents. It was her mother's mother who had left her the trust. Like Kelwyn's grandmother, she thought, only there was no crazy stipulation about having a girl named Polly.

Now retired, the Edens were not as active socially. The Judge still golfed, but now rode the cart around the course, picking up a ball along the way and carrying it to the green, if his tee-off was on the short side.

Her mother, Judy, said he was becoming forgetful, sometimes doing things like putting sugar on his eggs instead of salt. And, if the coffee was not hot enough, he would dump it on the floor.

"He fell the other day, while trying to get the row boat into the lake. Right off the dock," she said. "A neighbor boy managed to haul him ashore. He hit his head on the end of the pier. Blood was all over, but he refused to go to the ER. I cleaned him up. It was more blood than anything. There was only a little cut. You would hardly notice it now."

"That's not good, Mom. Maybe this house is getting too big for you."

The judge was seated nearby in his recliner chair, while mother and daughter discussed his health. The TV was turned to a morning news program, muted with subtitles rolling.

"His hearing going, Cara Bow. It drives me crazy, always having to shout. At least he's stopped turning up the TV volume."

Cara Bow noticed the quiver in her mother's hand, as she set her coffee cup back on the saucer, causing it to clatter.

"Is Harriet Albert still coming to clean every week?" You shouldn't be doing anything heavy. I worry about you falling. Anyway, I have a favor to ask while I'm gone. I want to leave Mewmew with you. Polly is mean to her, always pulling her tail, and even kicking her. Think you can manage?" asked Cara Bow.

"Where are you going, Cara Bow? How long will you be away?"

"Just a week, Mummy. I'll call Harriet about checking in on you and Dad every morning around ten. She can pick up anything you might need at the grocers. You and Dad shouldn't be driving."

"There's my bridge club, Cara Bow. Lately I've been hosting it here because of your father. I can't trust him alone. And my eyes. My ophthalmologist says I might be developing glaucoma, the wet kind. That's the worst, you know." Mrs. Eden sounded a little panicked.

"It's only a week, Mom, and Harriet will stay longer, if you want her to."

"Well, I guess if Harriet comes, I can manage Mewmew. How are the pair of them anyway?"

Cara Bow knew she was referring to Polly and Kelwyn, the unholy terrorists.

"No news on that front, Mom. Polly's been upset lately because her dance teacher told her she couldn't be a ballet dancer. She has flat feet. No surprise there. So has Kelwyn. Still she screamed it was my fault that her feet are flat."

"I don't envy you, honey. Polly is a strange child. But she is our only grandchild. You should never have married that man. Remember I told you that," and Judy Eden began to ramble on with her motherly warnings from years back, ending with "You should have been a teacher."

"Yes, Mommy," Cara Bow interrupted. "Where's Dad going now?" The judge had left the room wearing his sun hat, a vacant look in his eyes.

"He's always puttering around the yard, Cara Bow. He likes to pull weeds, even where there are none. We have a good lawn service person. Carl Albert."

So, that's what Carl's doing now, thought Cara Bow. *The Alberts are the weeds in this town.*

"Last month, Millie Albert, the one married to a Gleason boy, had a baby, a boy with bright green eyes."

Kelwyn has been busy, thought Cara Bow. "Where'd you hear that, Mom?" she asked.

"One of the bridge club gals told me, I think it was Meredith."

Oh, yes, the town gossip," said Cara Bow. She's that Presbyterian lady who seems to know everything, her head turning slyly at everyone who walks down the church aisle on Sundays, gathering the bits of information she quietly disseminates in her knowing voice during the coffee hour."

"Now, Cara Bow, that's not a nice thing to say,"

"I've got to get going, Mom. Thanks for looking after Mewmew. She's no trouble. I've got her in the car with her favorite pillow."

She left to collect the cat and coming back into the house she deposited her and the pillow near the fireplace hearth. The cat immediately climbed from the pillow onto the judge's chair.

"Your father won't like that," said Judy.

She gave her mother a hug.

"Oh, Cara Bow, I just remembered, Meredith thought it would be nice if you opened your house for the annual tour of homes next Christmas. It's part of the Women's Club project. They raise money for the library."

"You haven't been in our house for months, Mom."

"I heard from Miss Albert, who was told by Donna that the decorator has done a marvelous job. So French. The front entrance must be redone, of course."

The front entrance was never used. *When I finally leave, I'll go out the front entrance*, thought Cara Bow. *Until then it's the side door. The front entrance will be saved for when I'm on the correct path.*

"Not this year, Mom," she said with finality. "We still have the plastic Christmas tree. Kelwyn never takes it down. Tell Meredith I'm sorry. I'll send a check to the library fund. Now, I've really got to run. I'll see you in a week. Thanks again for taking Mewmew. I'll catch Daddy on the way out."

She saw the judge alongside the house pulling imagined weeds from the perfect lawn but decided not to disturb him.

CHAPTER 14

Ginger's house was along the shore of Lake Tioga—not far from the Edens. That was Cara Bow's next stop. The house was another fake colonial, much like the Eden's with synthetic white siding and tall wooden pillars flanking the entrance. Cara Bow had never been inside.

Waiting for Ginger to respond to the doorbell, she heard it chime 'Dixie'. She noticed the short picket fence running alongside the front windows guarding the pink impatiens. Shade flowers. *No need to protect these*, she thought. *The deer only ate the bulb flowers—day lilies and tulips.*

"Cara," Ginger cried. "What a surprise! Come in, she said, in her appealing drawl.

She was still in her nightie, a baby doll, ruffled, blue, which complimented her uncombed thick red-blonde hair.

"I'm sorry to be so early," apologized Cara Bow. "Maybe I should have left a message. I'm off to Chicago, Ginger, on business. We'll miss our Wednesday afternoon this week."

"Stay a while for iced tea, Cara." Ginger never drank coffee. Iced tea with lemon—that was the drink she grew up on in Mississippi.

"I can't stay long, Ginger," she said, though she suddenly wanted to.

Ginger's house surprised Cara Bow with its farmhouse décor. Tiny flowers danced on wall paper and every room was wallpapered. Blue glass bottles stood on window sills in the kitchen. Copper pots and pans were suspended from a wrought iron wagon wheel. Appliances were in cobalt blue and black. The gas stove mimicked a wood range.

The furniture in the living room looked stiff and uncomfortable and the dining room table was of thick wooden boards flanked by wooden picnic benches.

"What an interesting place you have, Ginger. It's lovely," Cara Bow managed to comment. *Goes well with the saxophone*, she thought.

"I'm glad you like it. It reminds me of my home down south. We were poor as church mice. Floyd wanted something more modern, but I reminded him that the woman reigns in the house. He can have all that modern stuff in his office."

She's strong, too, thought Cara Bow, *like her husband. I'm a coward in my moldy house, especially with Polly.* Her whole being trembled at the realization of what she had become. Life was passing her by, twisting along other people's paths. Kelwyn, Polly Judy, Mother Keck, Alecia, *Derek, Giulio, and the prolific Alberts.* Nothing seemed right or of her own doing. She was the reactor, not the instigator. There was her basement lab, of course, and the special plum jelly.

That was real, the plum jelly, the sugary arrow pointing to her escape. The only time her direction had seemed to be in tune with her correct path was when she was in college. Then, a huge boulder in the road appeared in the road by the name of Kelwyn.

Even before Kelwyn, there was her mother and the judge obscuring her vision. She had been wanting to escape all along, only not realizing it until Polly. *Polly wants to get away, too—from her.*

Finally, after a tall glass of the iced tea, she made her goodbyes to Ginger and as she left Cooperton, the cheese factory, the whey plant, Lake Tioga, the mall, and the moldy house, her breathing became more relaxed. Her sense of freedom was almost overwhelming. The new Volvo, a dark blue, cruised smoothly along US Highway 43.

She passed a stand of trees growing in a half-circle around a grassy swath. She imagined herself a caribou, standing on the green, a stately ruminant not moving, all at peace, the master of its domain, male and yet female. She snapped a mental picture of the scene. Here is where she could return when needing to find calm and peace.

The drive to Chicago from Cooperton was less than four hours, about 200 miles, most of it on four lane highway. Yet the freedom it promised seemed a thousand miles away. She decided to exit at Fond Du-Lac for coffee, no cigarette. That was a smoky ghost from the past. An on-and- off MacDonald's would do. The coffee wasn't bad during the morning hours.

Alecia's cell number was at the top of her list. There weren't a lot of contacts. Ginger was next, then Giulio, her mother, Miss Albert, Mrs. Terzian, Mrs. Olsen, Ruthie, and Elsie Keck. Might as well get it over with, she thought as she dialed Elsie first.

"Hello," sounded the familiar voice.

"Hello, Mother Keck. This is Cara Bow."

"Caribou, it's a bit early, isn't it? It's just past nine. Anything wrong?"

"I'm on my way to Chicago on business, calling from Fond-du-Lac. Kelwyn wants me to stop by and see how you're doing"

"Fond-du-Lac! That's not far from one of my cemetery properties. Do me a favor, will you? Drive by the cemetery guard house. The watch man is always there. Have him take you around and check out the grounds. Make sure there are no weeds by the headstones. His name is Mr. Thibedot."

"I'm running a little late, Mother Keck. It must be a quick tour."

"Thank you, Caribou. I'm not getting out much these days. Uncle Ulrich's gout has been acting up."

My plum jelly will fix that in short order, thought Cara Bow. *Two down, two to go*. The cyanide would be undetectable by the time they were found. Her careful titration would result in a swift demise. Mother Keck was always greedy with the jelly and quick to toss empty jars in the hall trash disposal.

Cara Bow could picture them slathering the jelly on their soft white bread. Elsie had complained on her last call about gaining a little weight. She was never a small person. Her fat rolls must be hanging over her thighs, like Kelwyn's apron, by now.

Having met Uncle Ulrich but once, she remembered his striking resemblance to Kelwyn. His eyes were bright blue. Here was a mystery, perhaps one that would never be solved.

CHAPTER 15

The cemetery was more beautiful than she'd anticipated—peaceful, quiet. Stone pillars signaled the entrance. Mr. Thibidot was in the caretaker's small house to the left, made of the same stone as the pillars. She tapped lightly on the narrow wooden door and he opened it at once.

"I don't know you, Miss," he said. "Are you a new hire at the funeral home?"

"No, Mr. Thibidot, I'm Mrs. Kelwyn Keck. Mrs. Elsie Keck wanted me to stop by and see that everything was in order."

"Oh, Elsie. She's not been here much. Once that I can recall when Dr. Keck was interred. Did you want to see his stone?"

"Maybe I'd better. I didn't know he was buried so far from Chicago. Mrs. Keck has a few cemetery properties closer to her."

"It was quick, as I recall. The PJ funeral home on Division sent notice that they were transporting the body a few days after he died. I had to arrange for the grave digging equipment on short notice. Cost a lot extra for the overtime. There's not too many spots left in this place. The town pays for the upkeep and there are long-term arrangements made by several families."

He does go on, thought Cara Bow. She let him run on for a bit before asking him when he last saw Elsie.

"Elsie and an old lady came with the body. There were no final prayers, as I recall. Elsie—she ordered a nice stone though. Let's drive over there. I'll show you. Here's the map of where every soul is interred in this place."

Cara Bow noticed a space heater in one corner and a two-burner hot plate on a stand in another corner of the small room. She waited as Mr. Thibidot opened a huge book on another stand in the center of the room. It reminded her of an altar ambo. Page after page listed the locations of the dead, drawings of the lot sizes, and the family names who owned the plots. Some of the lots had room for several bodies. There was only one space where Dr. Keck was buried.

"Leave your car here, Mrs. Keck. There's nobody scheduled for today. I can take you around."

They drove together in a silent, electric battery powered golf cart. Cara Bow liked the grounds with their raised granite and bronze markers. There was even a mausoleum. Dr. Keck's remains were buried near a narrow stream. Several nearby weeping willows hung over the water, their narrow leaves touching the slow-moving stream.

The stone was fashioned in a tall marbled obelisk design. Dr. Keck's name was at the base with an inscription that read, *Beloved Husband.* Nothing about being a father.

"Thank you, Mr. Thibedot. Everything looks just fine. I'll tell Elsie you're doing a great job. You've been here many years, haven't you?" He had an ancient and wise look about him.

"I've lost count, Mrs. Keck. One day I'll be listed in the book. My appointed spot is over by an unused railroad track. That's where they put the ones who can't afford the plot fee. The town pays for them and puts in a flat marker engraved with their name. There's still a few spots there. Nowadays some folks get cremated. Not too many in these parts.

It's a shame, though, getting turned to dust right away. Goes against nature."

Cara Bow recalled a part of the Halloween hearse song she and her friends sang as a child.

The worms crawl in, the worms crawl out, the worms play pinochle on your snout—and leaky bones—not a pretty picture.

She said goodbye to Mr. Thibedot. Before getting into her Volvo, she decided to stroll the path leading to Dr. Keck's marker. It was confusing. Before many minutes, she knew she had lost her way. *Damn, I'm going to be late getting on the road,* she thought. It was already past noon. It took several turns before she finally got back to the entrance. She had passed so many stones, all inscribed with family names, dates, histories, eulogies—*beloved, dear, lovely. What would be her final etching?*

She had driven past the cemetery in Cooperton many times on the drive to her parent's house, but had not given it a second thought, nor a first, truth be told. She now wondered who owned it. *There must be a lot of Albert stones,* she smiled wryly at the notion.

There were no Eden or Keck stones. Polly might be the first. Or she could lay her to rest in Fond-du-lac, next to Dr. Keck. She wouldn't take up much room. The idea of owning cemeteries was appealing.

Grandmother Genevieve Cooper, her mother's mother—her trust fund grandmother was buried in Cooperton. Cara Bow had a vague remembrance of an old woman, lying motionless in an upstairs bedroom in her parents' home. A fatal stroke, they said.

As she drove, she thought about her parents' home in Cooperton. The best families lived there. Tioga lake bordered the west side of town. Comfortable houses surrounded three sides of the lake like a giant horseshoe. The Edens had the largest house, a stately white pillared edifice. The lake was big enough for swimming, boating and water skiing. Cara Bow remembered liking to swim, but not too far out.

The contrast with her present house—she couldn't bring herself to call it a home—gave her a headache. She opened the driver's side window to let in the fresh air.

She texted Alecia that she would be in later that same day and would be staying on North Michigan at the Chicago Marriot. "Meet me there," was the message, "and bring Tony. I want to talk to him about the locations of refrigerated distribution warehouses. Eight o'clock this evening. OK?" She attached a smiley face. The GPS voice, Cara Bow called her Gladys, finally announced "You have arrived at your destination.'

After handing her keys to the valet and checking in, she lay on the bed in her room on the 6th floor of the Marriot and immediately fell into a deep sleep. She hadn't expected to sleep, but the absence of snoring Kelwyn and squawking Polly was such a relief that, before she knew it, it was seven o'clock. *Uninterrupted sleep*, she thought. *How long had that been?* "I like being alone," she said aloud to her reflection in the bathroom mirror.

She took a quick shower and donned her slinky black. Looking at herself in the full-length mirror, she thought, *I'm still pretty, my legs are great.* She turned this way and that, striking provocative poses and laughed aloud at her image.

Alecia was waiting for her as Clara Bow got off the elevator. "Tony couldn't come," she apologized. "He had a late meeting at the mayor's office. A shooting victim retained an attorney to represent him They're suing the city for a lot of dollars. The mayor has everyone on deck."

"That's okay, Alecia. I'm so happy to see you. You're looking wonderful"

Alecia was wearing a slinky black, too, and diamond studs in her ear lobes. They matched the diamond pendant around her neck. *Tony must be doing well*, she thought.

"I'm hungry," said Cara Bow. "The menu's good here, and I would love a mojito."

They ordered small plates of deviled eggs, an array of olives, thin toast with garlic butter and an antipasto along with their mojitos and a bottle of Pinot Grigio.

"I can't eat another bite, Caribou," said Alecia. "I'm watching my figure."

"So am I," said Cara Bow It took a real effort to lose the pounds after Polly Judy. Gym every day and a lot of water. My job keeps me hopping, too."

"How is Polly?" Alecia asked. "She must be getting big."

"She's a devil child, Alecia. I don't love her. I never wanted her. She's mean, hateful, tells me she hates me, blames me for everything." Cara Bow felt the tension rising throughout her body as she raged on with frustration.

"Hey, Caribou, calm down," said Alecia. "People are staring. Your face is turning red. She poured more wine into their glasses. "Polly is just a kid. She'll grow out of this phase."

"This is *not* a phase, Alecia. She's been horrible since birth and before. She's only this way with me."

"Well, Tony and I have agreed not to have kids. Tony was one of five, the baby. He said he was always picked on by his big brothers. He's not going to bring another miserable child into the world. That's fine with me. I only like fully grown people. I'd be a terrible mother."

Cara Bow wanted to ask Alecia if she had been aware of Kelwyn's need for a girl baby named Polly in order to access his trust account, but she decided not to spoil the relaxed mood created by the soft wine and the candle-lit atmosphere of the roof-top lounge. Alecia had introduced her to Kelwyn. *Maybe there had been other introductions, but she was the chosen one. The chosen one, ha-ha. Maybe I am on the right path,* she thought, *I've just not been paying attention.*

The basement chemistry lab, the cheese factory, the whey plant, all turning a profit. I'm a rich woman. Now there are the cemeteries. Five of them at least, that is after the demise of Elsie and Ulrich. I'll be following Elsie's example. She got rid of Dr. Keck. I must be more open to possibilities. Time to break out of the Cooperton bubble. That moldy house, Kelwyn, Polly, even Giulio. Her thoughts reeled after leaving Alecia, spilling over into her dreams.

They were happy dreams. She was teaching eager students in a large hall, scribbling diagrams on a dissolving screen. The figures on the screen moved in wide arcs as they disappeared into the heads of the students.

The next morning, she woke refreshed, and ordered a small breakfast from room service, a sesame bagel with cream cheese, fruit, and strong coffee. While eating, she thought about her dream and considered the notion that teaching would not be such a bad choice.

Maybe I should have been a teacher, she thought. *Life would be so much simpler.* She dressed quickly, wanting to get the morning wash up done as soon as possible. The internet listed several warehouse distribution centers and she made a few calls and set up an appointment with the Chicago Industrial Agency. The agent, Tony Peshek, cautioned her about the fees that would have to be paid to outside interests for protection.

"You wouldn't want to have a fire," he said. "Last week a whole shipment of computer paper was gone. Just like that. The fire department came, but they took their time."

"Mr. Santini will certainly agree to that," Cara Bow assured him. It will not be a problem. He's old country."

She was happy to find a building in the Fulton District with a decent office space. Part of the building had refrigeration available and was shelved for the wheels of Parmesan and Romano. Another area could be arranged for hanging the provolone. She called Giulio and he immediately agreed to the rent and extra fees.

"Yeah, I know about those fees," he said.

"Talk to Olivo about moving to Chicago to manage the center. He does a good job with the whey plant. Move Gor to management. He doesn't put up with any nonsense. She thought of Grandma Terzian and her bruises. "Olivo and his wife will like Chicago," she said. "There's are a lot of good Italian restaurants here. He mentioned once that he has cousins in the Little Italy neighborhood."

"Sounds good, Cara. Are you heading back soon? We're having a problem with the culture."

"I've another stop to make, Giulio, Kelwyn's mother. She's expecting me, and I promised Kelwyn I would check on her. She and her brother, Ulrich, are getting on.

Cara Bow had put off her visit to Elsie and Ulrich. "I'll head back in a day or two, Giulio. Send someone to Rhinelander for fresh culture."

She left the Volvo at the hotel garage. The valet got her a taxi. *Gloom and doom*, she thought on the short drive along Michigan Avenue. The jars of plum jelly, two of them, were clinking in the satchel at her side. At the Keck's apartment building, she noticed a new young door attendant. He opened the lobby door. The old door attendant must have retired, or dropped dead at his post, she supposed. Nothing changed very fast in this area.

He called up to the Keck's apartment and announced that young Mrs. Keck was on the way up.

Cara Bow stepped off the elevator into the hall and saw Elsie waiting for her outside her apartment door.

"Did you bring Polly's pictures?" was the only greeting.

"Hello, Mother Keck," said Cara Bow. It's been awhile. Yes, I have photos. Hard copies as you requested." She tried to give her a peck on the cheek, but Elsie would have none of it. She backed away as if she was going to be bit by a snake.

"Come in and keep your voice down. Ulrich is resting. He hasn't been well."

Cara Bow thought Elsie looked unwell, too. Shrunken. Her cloudy green eyes were more filmed and watery than she had remembered.

"Give me the pictures," she demanded in a whispery voice. "Turn on the bright light in the front room near the piano."

Elsie picked up a magnifying glass from the piano-top.

Why do people think a closed piano top is a place to put things? Cara Bow thought. She kept the top of her own piano open. Polly had played it for a short time, until she had pushed her teacher from the bench. Cara Bow wondered if Kelwyn had ever played on this piano.

She handed the photos to Elsie, one by one.

"She's so pretty," said Elsie, "The red hair and the eyes. Lovely green eyes. And the bow lips. That must come from your side, Caribou.

"Bow lips? Like me?" Cara Bow pictured the bird beak mouth on Polly Judy. Yes, bow lips, but thrust forward, pursed. When she talked, *squawked*, they opened and closed like a newborn bird in the nest, neck thrust forward for the mother bird dangling a worm.

When Elsie finished looking at the pictures of Polly in her tutu, Polly in her bath, Polly in the school Halloween parade, dressed like Snow White, Polly eating a rainbow ice cream cone, Polly with her friend, Louise, Polly sitting on Kelwyn's lap, Polly sitting on Donna Albert's lap, Polly pulling on Mewmew's tail, Polly, Polly, Polly—there were none of Polly and Cara Bow. Elsie didn't seem to notice that.

"Yes, she's quite pretty and talented, too. She looks so much like my mother, Polly Serkis. Grandma Polly, we called her. She didn't care much for Kelwyn—wished he had been a girl. Kelwyn did look like a girl, until I cut his curls," Elsie went on. My mother called him Kelly. Always wanted him to wear dresses. Well, now there's another Polly, and that's that. The money stays in the family."

Cara Bow heard a bedroom door open and Uncle Ulrich made his appearance. He moved slowly, leaning on a cane as he came toward her.

"Who are you, girl?" he asked.

"It's Caribou, Ulrich, you know Caribou. You met her at the Banya wedding—remember Alecia, our neighbor's daughter? Caribou is Kelwyn's wife," explained Elsie speaking loudly. "Poor Ulrich has trouble with his hearing."

"Oh yes. How's that boy doing?"

"He's fine, Uncle Ulrich. The insurance business is doing great, too," said Cara bow.

"What did she say? She needs to speak up."

"Everything's fine Ulrich, yelled, Elsie.

Cara Bow looked at the pair of them, standing together. *The funny twisted twins*, she thought. *Frail, tottering, old, yes old. Not long for this world. I'll merely be helping them along.*

"I've brought a jar of plum jelly, Mother Keck. I'll put it on the kitchen counter." She decided to leave only one jar, thinking one jar was all it would take. Then, standing in the kitchen, after a long moment, she took the jar back, her hands shaking, feeling guilt—horrified. *I can't be a murderer. This is what Kelwyn and Polly have brought me to.* She had one unadulterated jar that she had forgotten to give to Alecia and left that instead. She took a deep. He'd never seen anyone peel a shrimp that fas breath before returning to the front room where Elsie was showing the pictures of Polly to Ulrich.

"Do you have help coming in, Mother Keck?" She had noticed the thin cover of dust on the kitchen chairs and table.

"No, Ulrich and I manage fine. Since Corky died, we decided not to have anyone here poking around. There's all our private matters—my cemetery papers, five of them you know, and all of Corky's stuff. Her family didn't want any of them. I fixed a little shrine in her room. We never go in there."

"Yes, the cemeteries. I stopped in Fond-du-lac. Mr. Thibedot showed me around. He keeps it in pristine condition." *A lovely village of dead people*, she thought. "I saw Dr. Keck's gravesite. A very nice monument to Kelwyn's father."

"Oh, yes, Kelwyn's father. He died when Kelwyn was young," murmured Elsie. She and Ulrich glanced at one another quickly.

"Well, I've got to be off," said Cara Bow feeling intrusive. "You can keep the pictures. I'll send more soon." She moved to give Elsie a hug, but Elsie turned away, almost falling backward to avoid her touch.

That suited Cara Bow. She didn't want to feel the bony body. After leaving the apartment, she asked the new door attendant if the Keck's went out much.

"They never go out," said the young man, "except to the trash depository in the hall. They have groceries delivered once a week, and I leave them outside their door. They're private people. No one bothers them. You're the first visitor they've had since I've been here."

He hailed a cab, and Cara Bow asked the driver to take her to the hotel. Chicago suddenly looked messy to her. Trash on the streets and people standing outside doorways with their cigarettes.

She thought of Alecia. She had her life in order. Was she still what Cara Bow wanted to call her people? Cara Bow felt a little lost. So much time had passed since her marriage to Kelwyn. Who were his parents? Elsie and Dr. Keck? Elsie and her brother Ulrich?

Did that explain Polly and her unusual asymmetrical face? Kelwyn, with six toes on his left foot, the extra two had been surgically removed when he was still a baby. Everyone laughed at that story. He was the slow student in college, paying others to do his papers and sit for his exams. He bragged about it, too.

Now, he has Miss Albert running the office. There was no logic to this, or maybe it was completely logical. *I've got to stop thinking these things.* Cara Bow's brain was a complete muddle, except for the certainty that Kelwyn and Polly could no longer be part of her life.

Driving south on Michigan in the Volvo, she noticed that everything looked so tall and crowded. She merged onto Shore Drive, where there were five lanes of traffic, all rushing past the buildings, cars, and long trucks. *When did semi-trucks become so long? But this would still be her town and her people. Who did she know? Uncle Ulrich Elsie, Alecia, and her absent husband? That would change when I get on my real life. Starting over. She still had her Chicago dream.* Cooperton had become an impossible place to be. People there knew their roles and Cara Bow had taken on a part, too. *Like a person in that movie. The one about the pod people she had watched once with her mother. Her mother with her old movies.*

A lab worker at the cheese factory, Giulio's paramour, Kelwyn's wife— but not for long— Polly's mother. That had to end and soon. Then there was Ginger and her saxophone, her mother, Judy, and her father Norman, a judge pulling weeds. She smiled at that picture in her head.

She laughed aloud as she made an illegal U-turn on Michigan Avenue, almost causing a major crash with a floral delivery truck and headed north for the exit onto Highway 94. She caught US 43 in Milwaukee. She tooted the horn as she drove past the Fond-du-lac exit.

Kelwyn was with Gor and Dr. Boren in his basement playroom when she entered the house by the side door.

"Where's Polly?" she called down.

"She's having a sleepover at the Sandbergs" Kelwyn yelled back. Donna wanted to go to Green Bay. They opened a new tattoo place near the Krogers. She said they use a better ink. Cara Bow could hear Gor and Dr. Boren laughing. She could smell the mixture of cigar and pipe smoke wafting up the stairs.

It overcame the rotted wood smell in the dining room. *My olfactory nerves have been numbed, insulted.* She left the side door ajar to get rid of some of the smoky haze. "Time for tea," she said aloud to no one. She parked her suitcase in the bedroom near the window seat.

Tomorrow she would ask Giulio for a raise. *I'll need to have some cash on hand for new hires at the cemeteries I'll probably have to manage one day.* She was glad she had decided to let nature take its course in the demise of Elsie and Ulrich. Perhaps Mr. Thibedot would make a recommendation for caretakers. She'd taken a file from the small box under the kitchen sink at the Keck's when she'd left the plum jelly on the counter.

She put on the kettle for a cup of tea, lemon ginger.

CHAPTER 16

I t was quiet there—*sitting on his folding chair in his red Eskimo Fat Fish ice fishing tent all anchored down covering the hole in the ice.* The Ice was thick on Lake Wakesha. Kelwyn could see the Eden's vinyl sided colonial from there. *I don't think they like me,* he thought. *For sure they don't like to see my truck out here. They think they own this lake, but nobody owns a lake, I always say.*

He was sure Judy thought he was not good enough for their daughter. His musings continued as he opened a can of Coors. *When Caribou and I drove up the Eden drive on my Kawasaki, Judy made me sit in the kitchen. That's the only room in the place where I've ever been welcome. No, never welcomed, just allowed to sit there. Except for the Christmas dinners. Then I have to take my shoes off to walk on the white carpeting. They should put up a sign on the door—Kelwyn Not Welcome. The judge came to our house once and snorted "It's a dump", and Judy only came that one time, too, when she looked after Polly the time Caribou and I went to dinner with the Sandburgs.* The ice hut was good for thinking.

Now there's a nutcase—Ginger. Her and that saxophone. And that drawl. You'd think she'd learned to say shrimp by this time. Seeeremp, or something like that. I've never seen anyone peel a shrimp that fast. Floyd's okay, I guess. Darla said he's called about getting some insurance for his practice. Maybe I'll invite him to my hunting camp next fall. He'll be impressed with the new refrigerator. That Ginger is a real looker. I wonder how they ever got together. Floyd sure is lucky. I've always liked red heads. I know it's hands off on that one.

Caribou should maybe get a dye job. That would help some. But I know her. She wouldn't consider getting a boob job. Such flat little jellies. Speaking of jelly, the only thing good about our marriage is her plum jelly. And Polly, of course. Polly's such a smart kid. She asked me if I would take her to my hunting camp. She wants to learn how to shoot. I told her maybe when she gets a little bigger. I don't know what the problem is between those two. Caribou has never liked the kid. I don't think she likes me, either. Alecia should have picked someone else for our date, but time was getting short. I'm not bad looking, manly, you might say, and I needed someone to have a baby, a girl baby, so I wouldn't lose out on Grandma's trust. Well now I have few extra pounds. I know Caribou hates that. She wants me to wear suspenders. Suspenders are for sissies. But things have worked out. Elsie's got her girl, I've got my money, and I've always dreamed about being in a place that's good for hunting and fishing. Man's country. Life would be just about perfect if I could get rid of Caribou. I don't mean anything like her dying. Just if she could disappear one day. Then me and Donna Albert could get together. Polly likes Donna. Donna has great boobs.

He couldn't remember the last time he and Caribou had had any conversation other than "Don't forget to pick up Polly Judy from dance class. I'm working late at the factory." Stuff like that. *Well, sure,* he thought, *Caribou's smarter than me and I'm sure not interested in chemistry.* He'd barely made it to graduation and wouldn't have except for the student in his American history class who needed money and wrote his papers and took his exams.

Uncle Ulrich's no prize either. Mother says they're twins, and there is a resemblance, both with that red wiry hair. Except for the eyes. Ulrich's are blue, like mine. Mother's eyes are green. I remember him always hanging around. Dad didn't like him much— he didn't like Corky, either. Corky, always waving her sticks around. She'd done something bad to Dad, I know it. She and Mother. Dad was there one moment and the next he wasn't. I don't remember him ever being the least bit sick. I missed my dad. My dad took me to the Cub's games and the Bears, too. Mother didn't like that one bit. She wanted me to be part of a ballet class. She even tried to enroll me once, but the teacher said I had flat feet and not to waste money on me trying to be a dancer.

The same thing happened to Polly. She got my flat feet, and that took care of the ballet nonsense. She really put up a tantrum when she was put out of class. Her cute little trumpet mouth could be heard all the way to the Terzians. Gor and I had a good laugh about it that night at the poker table. Polly blamed Caribou and I thought Polly was going to knock her over She should have. Polly likes Donna and that's it. Too bad I didn't meet Donna first. She's dumb as an ox but good in the hay. I think Polly's going to be flat chested, too, like Caribou. That's sort of sad, I guess.

His truck sat outside the hut *where* Dr. Boren would see it. *Dr. Boren will be here in a few hours—after seeing the few patients who continue to trust him with their health issues—should have no problem parking his two-seater ILX next to me. Solid ice this year. One of the Albert clan went under with his Volkswagen two years ago. They didn't find him until Spring. Harriet Albert's son, Marky— married to one of Caribou's old high school friends, Belle. I sure know Belle, all right. We've had a few romps in the hay. That was before the drowning. Didn't seem right to keep on after the funeral. Belle's looking to get married again and that won't be me. One marriage is enough. Still, there's dumb Donna. If anything were to happen to Caribou she could move right in. Polly likes her, and Donna is easy to please. She'd have to get rid of those tats, though. They're not good for business.*

Boy, Caribou makes a fuss about the house. Always complaining about the smell. Moldy, she says. She complains about everything. My pipe rack that I finally I moved to the basement. I thought it looked good up there on the mantle. Classy. The black couch and my recliner, too. That's where I sleep now. In the basement. I don't mind. I like it. She says I snore and the noise keeps her awake. Its Polly who keeps her awake. That little girl is a real pistol. She and Caribou are as far apart as the Atlantic from the Pacific. Polly's almost a teenager now. She's been beating on Caribou from day one. She knows Caribou never wanted her. Too bad. We couldn't have this comfortable lifestyle if it weren't for the girl. I don't hear her going on about the money coming in. She's got her own money, too. From that cheese factory job. There's something else going on there, too. I've met the boss. Dirty little Italian. He had those pigs in the back once. Good thing they got rid of them or me and Gor would have had to use them for target practice. Gor tells me everything that's going on over there. Well, I don't care.

It was starting to get cold with the wind coming up and Kelwyn put on an extra insulated jacket. *I'll have to light my Big Buddy Heater. Dr. Boren likes it warm. I thought the line was tugging a moment ago but now it's not moving. False alarm, I guess. The fish are not biting today. Guess it's time for another Coors.*

Caribou made a fuss about delivering the baby, too. She kept crying for pain killers, but I made sure she didn't get anything. I had it all worked out with Lois Albert. Caribou is strong. Good hips. That's one reason I agreed with Alecia that she should be the one. I had Dr. Boren here on the ice with me and he was ready to get to the hospital as soon as the nurse called him. But Polly popped out before he got there. She was on wheels from the get-go.

I wish Caribou would take better care of Polly. She's not a bad kid. Just fussy. Sometimes I think she doesn't eat enough. Well, I only see her at breakfast most days. She eats plenty of the plum jelly, though. That's the one thing Caribou fixes that we both like. Mother liked it, too, when she and Corky were here. She's not good with eggs, though. I like mine on top of the potatoes. I remember my dad liked them that way, too. Easy over, the yolk running down right through to the bacon under the potatoes. Lately, I've been fixing them myself. Caribou only eats that no-fat stuff. Yogurt and cantaloupe and blueberries. No wonder she's so skinny. Not like Donna. Now there's a nice handful.

Polly's putting on a bit, too. Maybe it's baby fat. Judy Eden thinks it will melt away when she gets past her teen years. Judy is a fat hater. She and Caribou are two peas in a pod when it comes to eating. They sure can put away the margaritas, though.

It's getting warm now. What day is it? Friday? Dr. Boren should be happy about that. He always wants to be called Dr. I think his first name is Jack. His initials are on his office door. J. W. Boren. Maybe it's John. He calls me Kelwyn, never Mr. Keck. Maybe if I had a title of some kind. Accounting was always a mystery to me. Uncle Ulrich couldn't wait to get me out of his Chicago office. I know he watches out for me, mostly for Mother's sake. Those two are really attached. Seems like more than twinship. When I was young, I remember them talking on the phone every day. My dad didn't care much for Uncle Ulrich. Whenever he came to our apartment, Dad would find some excuse to be away. Someone sick, or some emergency at the hospital.

I guess Uncle Ulrich's okay. He always asked me how I was and patted me on the head. I didn't like to be patted on the head, but that's what he did. He did it when I was in his office in Chicago, too, as if there was something wrong with me. Now I've got my own place in Cooperton, all set up with Darla. There are sure a lot of Alberts in this town. Most of them Catholic. Caribou's a Presbyterian. She hardly ever goes to church. I never went to church before coming to Cooperton. I filmed Polly that one time in the Christmas pageant. That was before she was kicked out of Sunday School.

Caribou enrolled Polly in the Sunday School class, but Polly always put up a fuss about it. She got in an argument with the teacher about witches. It was around Halloween and on kids' costume Sunday, they were supposed to dress like angels, and Polly told Caribou she wanted to be a witch, and Caribou gave in and let her be a witch and the teacher took Polly aside and told her she couldn't parade around in the circle with the other kids. Polly kicked the teacher and told her the dakhonavar vampire from the kingdom of Urator get would get her. That was a few years back. She's too big for Sunday School now anyway. Caribou had to take her home where Polly continued to screech and say naughty words. That kid has quite a screech.

Polly got that witch stuff from Corky, I'll bet. At Alecia's wedding she and Mother carried her off somewhere. That's because Polly started to make a scene when Caribou walked down the aisle before Alecia. Caribou was wearing some sort of pretty dress, short skirt, bare shoulders, she looked good. Caribou has great legs. I have to give her that. But Polly started complaining when she saw Caribou, loud enough to disturb the others around us. More of that screeching. Sometimes I think that kid's not right in the head. She does all right in school, though. Her teachers say she a little angel. There's two sides to her, that's for sure. Well, people forgave her. She looked so cute in the dress Caribou made.

Caribou spends a lot of time in her cave. That's what I call it. Her own room in the basement. I don't know what she does in there. She says she works at making clothes for Polly on her sewing machine. I know she stores the plum jelly there. The door is always locked. Guess she doesn't want me and Polly to have more than that one jar she keeps in the refrigerator. Anyway, I don't care what she does. We don't talk much anymore. I brought her flowers when Polly was born and there was peace for about one day.

I get away as much as I can. There's no pleasing that woman. Even when Mother and Corky came for a visit that one time, I managed to be away at the hunting camp. I got my buck that year. A nine pointer. Not bad for the new guy in the territory. That's what I am. The new guy. A real guy. That buck proves it. I saw my red curls in a box Mother keeps on her dresser. I hated the long hair and the dress Mother made me wear on the first day of kindergarten. Dad took care of that. I heard him argue with Mother. "He's not a girl, Elsie. You have to stop calling him Kelly."

I'm all boy. I got in with the toughest boys and we made a lot of mischief. More than mischief. Stealing from the little kids and thumping the ones who wouldn't hand over their lunch money. We were fearsome. We even got picked up by the police one time. Good old Uncle Ulrich got me out of that jam.

I'll mention the cemetery business to Dr. Boren if he ever gets here. Caribou is all het up about that. There can't be much money in it. Once it's filled up that's about it. I heard about one cemetery owner who piled body caskets on body caskets. The police even found empty caskets dumped in a back area of the property. People were sure mad about it.

I wonder where Dr. Boren is? He's late today. I'm glad I brought along my box of tackle. It's a mess. Guess I'll get it organized while I'm waiting for my line to jiggle. My feet are starting to get numb. I've always had trouble with my feet, them being flat and all. And that surgery when I was a baby to remove those extra toes on both feet. Little extra pinkies, I was told. I had an extra little finger on my left hand, too, and that had to be whacked off at the same time. I don't remember any of it. Corky said I had a full head of red hair and I should have been a girl. I heard her tell Mother that my blue eyes were an aberration. For such a weird baby, I sure turned into a good-looking guy. I almost hypnotized Caribou at that Greek restaurant. She was an easy lay, but maybe I did get a bit rough. That's what real guys do. Donna likes it that way and a few of the other Albert girls around here, too. I don't get any complaints.

I've never touched Darla, though. She keeps that office humming. Uncle Ulrich has no complaints about my profit margin. When Darla switched the business from accounting to insurance, Uncle had nothing but praise for my business acumen. Good old Darla. She's easy to please. Yesterday, when I stopped briefly by the office, I remembered to drop off a box of her favorite chocolates. She keeps that place neat and up to date. Not like Caribou. When she was pregnant she let the house go to pot. Stuff all over the place, dishes never done. Now, Milena comes to clean and Caribou is never home much. Always at that factory. I asked her once what she liked about her job and she just smiled. "I like being in the lab," she said.

And there's Santini, too. Giulio, she calls him. She's made a life for herself with her bowling nights and Wednesday lunches with her mother. I dropped back home one Wednesday afternoon to get my bow and arrow and there she was with Ginger and the saxophone wailing away while Caribou was at the piano. I've never heard such god-awful sounds. They didn't even notice me slip out the back door. If I'd had a rifle, I'd have shot them both. Whoopee!

Floyd's okay though. Now Darla has most of his patients' dental insurance. Uncle Ulrich had no complaints. Floyd fixed that wisdom tooth that's been bothering me for a long time. Yanked it right out, along with the other three. It didn't even hurt—that is until the next day. I swelled up like a puffer ball all the way down to my chest. It was all colors, too. Mostly black and green. Caribou just laughed at the whole thing. She said I should have had them out years ago. She thinks she knows so much. Polly was good though. She sat on my lap while I held ice packs on my cheeks and said I was still the best daddy. Polly has always been on my side. I'm on her side, too. I get a kick out of her when she punches Caribou and then smiles with that innocent look.

If it weren't for Caribou my life would be darn sweet. I could have my pipes upstairs—have the run of the whole place really. I'd be sleeping in the bedroom, too, instead of on the recliner in the basement. Sometimes I sleep on a blow-up mattress if I really want to stretch out. Caribou says she can hear my snores right through the floorboards. That's a lie. She makes things up all the time. We don't have sex anymore. I don't need her since Donna is more than willing. I wish Caribou was dead. Maybe she'll fall in a vat at the cheese factory, or something will blow up in the lab or she'll fall down the basement stairs on her way to that locked room I let her have. Except for the jelly, does she think I give a damn about a sewing machine? Why can't we keep more than one jar in the kitchen. I'll bet she hoards it there.

I've been nice to her after all. When we first went to see Mother in Chicago, Mother was nice to her, too. Took her shopping and bought her a whole bunch of baby stuff. She never took me shopping except when she had me wearing dresses. Caribou was amazed at all the toys I had in my old bedroom. All boy stuff, too. Trucks, water guns, cap guns, GI Joe's, toy monsters—no books. Reading and writing didn't come easy to me. Still don't. Thank god for fucking Darla. Caribou has all those complicated science books in the bedroom seating bench. I can't figure out why she wants to keep them. Those college days are long gone. I know she wasn't happy about not going to graduate school, her being pregnant at the graduation. Her folks don't like me either. Well that's too bad for them. The judge and I would have made a good team on the golf course. Okay, I don't play golf because of a little clumsiness in my hands. The doctor who took off my extra finger when I was a baby didn't do that good of a job. I saw a picture of me in Mother's album when I was born. I wish I had those extra bits. I heard Alecia's mother laughing about it when the four of them were at their Monday bridge game. She said if it weren't for my Dad, she would have had my penis cut off, too. Dad told her that wasn't funny.

Shit, this tackle box is a mess. Polly must have been in it. She's got the hog frogs, pond frogs and swamp frogs all mixed up. This is going to take some time to straighten out. There's mostly creature lures here. I like the lizard lure the best. They're all plastic now. Some guys make their own *lures. There are classes in lure making at Cabela's in Green Bay, but I've had enough of school. The lizards are good for the Bluegill and Bass in this lake. Dr. Boren wants me to go with him on one of his Alberta fishing expeditions. He goes every year. When he talks about the fly fishing and the clouds of mosquitos, it doesn't sound appealing to me. I've never tried fly fishing. It sounds like a lot of work. Throwing out a line over and over again and those big waders. I like it right here with my case of beer and one line dropped in a hole that I don't even have to hold. Just watch for it to bob and then pull up the fish.*

He looked at his watch and glanced out of the small flap door looking for Dr. Boren, but there was still no sign of him. *I see the judge over there across the lake shoveling a path to the Eden trash bins in the alley. What kind of trash can they have? That house is so clean. Smells like Clorox all the time. Even when Caribou and I go there for Christmas dinner, you can smell it. The Cornwall's go there, too. I bet Pastor Cornwall would like to ask me why I don't go to church. But he doesn't. Too mealy mouthed. Caribou doesn't go much either. She's a funny one. She took Polly to Sunday School for a while until the teacher said she couldn't handle someone who wanted to be a witch instead of an angel. That was the end of that. Caribou and her mom go to the Catholic church for Thanksgiving dinner while we guys are out at the camp. That Catholic church is not such a bad place. They can have beer and wine with dinner. Not at the Cornwall's church. Just coffee and lemonade. The Edens serve wine at the Christmas dinner and I notice they have more than one glass. Caribou has more than her share and she's always slipping on the ice getting out of the truck on our driveway when we drive back from the Edens., I wish she would fall sometime and crack her head open.*

She always wants to drive around and show off in the Volvo. When I took Polly to Disneyland, she absolutely refused to let me drive it to Chicago to pick up Mother. How could I ask Mother to drive in a truck across the country? "Fly from Chicago," she said. "Rent a car. I need my Volvo to get to work." That's what I did. Turned out to be a good Idea, except for Mother getting air sick on the way back. Darla sure liked Disneyland. I hardly saw her. She took off with some other tattoo type people for the whole time. I'd never get a tattoo. Corky took me to a carnival once north of Chicago. She took me in the freak tent and there was a man with tattoos over his whole body. I remember him glaring at me in a scary way. Corky had her stick with her and she immediately waved it at him and he stopped glaring. I don't like to see tattoos.

I'm going to have a bite to eat. My stomachs mad at me, making all these growly noises. A half-sandwich. That'll do it. Peanut butter and some of the plum jelly. Caribou was telling me about an uncle of hers that died of eating too much peanut butter. He had a big ball of it in one of his lungs. I never know whether to believe her. I never heard of someone eating too much peanut butter. I got some stuck on the roof of my mouth once. I had to take a tablespoon to pry it off. That wasn't much fun. Even a little scary.

This sandwich is good. I'll have to wash it down with another beer. Half a sandwich. Few calories here. Caribou doesn't like my fat. She calls me "Bad Santa" sometimes. She's getting a smart mouth. Calls me other stuff, too. I'm starting to get afraid to say anything to her. If I ask for some little thing like not getting the bacon too crisp, she just rolls her eyes. That woman sure can't cook. She sits there at the breakfast table with her little cup of strawberry yoghurt and an orange, glaring at me and Polly. I think she wishes we weren't there. Polly always manages to make a mess of things. She does it on purpose, just to get Caribou's goat. They're always at it. Polly doesn't like the dress she's wearing, or her eggs are slimy. Polly quit eating cereal not long ago. She wants bacon and eggs, like her old man I guess.

Polly has her own table in another room where she has her dinner. She mostly keeps out of the kitchen except for breakfast time. Donna usually gets dinner. Donna is good at chop suey and jello dishes. Potatoes, too. Scalloped with ham are my favorite. Polly likes hers mashed. I got a kick out of seeing her stick that little spoon of the mashed potatoes into her trumpet mouth when she was a baby. She sort of sucks it in with a slurp. She's still eating stuff as if it were baby food from those little jars. Caribou makes her wear a bib. That's probably why she doesn't want to eat at the kitchen table except for breakfast. She likes her toast and plum jelly. I cut the toast in little squares for her. She likes that.

I heard a woman comment when we were at O'Hare on our way to Disneyland about what a strange looking little kid she was. Mother got upset about that and she gave the woman the evil eye and cursed her under *her breath. Something about the Dakhanavar. Ever since I told her about the Terzians and their vampire story, Mother has added it to her string of curses. I don't know why she insisted on going to Disney Land. It's no place for an old woman. I know she went with me and Dad when I was four, but I really can't remember much about it. Corky didn't come along either. He and Mother argued about that. They argued a lot.*

I've asked Caribou to keep away from the Terzians. She climbed the hill to their old farm one day. "The grandmother had a bloody nose," she said. I know Gor has a temper, but Caribou must keep out of their business. They're foreign, I told her. They have different customs. Milena doesn't think anything of it. She said it was high blood pressure. The Terzian's kids are smart as a whip. They caught on to English real fast. Milena is still a little hard to understand, but not Gor. He must have played a lot of poker in England. I caught him cheating one night. Dr. Boren said he would not play with him again. Gor apologized and said cheating was a custom in his country. I don't think that's true, but Dr. Boren still plays with us.

Sometimes I wonder what kind of doctor he is? Sort of a jack-of-all trades. Delivers babies, gives shots, fixes sprains, that kind of stuff. But if it's a real emergency, he has an ambulance take the patient to a hospital in Green Bay. "I've never been sued," he brags. Smart man, I think. Floyd's not like that. I think he likes torturing whoever is in his chair. When Polly's first baby tooth got loose, he yanked it out and two others along with it. Caribou didn't kick up a fuss about it either. I think she enjoyed seeing the blood dripping from Polly's little mouth. Polly howled like a banshee when she told me about the butchery she had endured. "I cursed him, Daddy," she said. Only six at the time and she had at least ten curses up her sleeve.

Polly's friends with Louise Sandburg, though. Louise is probably her best friend. She comes on Polly's bus from school every Wednesday to our house because that's where her mother, Ginger is. Honking away on her saxophone. It's not a little sax, either. It's one of those big ones that, almost touches the floor. She's keeps licking the reed before she blows. Even with that instrument she looks good. Floyd lucked out when he got her. Caribou says she's from Mississippi and who wouldn't guess that? Her drawl could drive you through a barn door. It's sexy. Floyd carries my dental insurance, so I keep my hands off that woman. I can tell Caribou has a thing for her.

She's always got some excuse to touch Ginger. She picks a hair off her sweater or reaches to touch her arm when she wants to point out something in the music they're playing. That's Caribou for you. She was the same way with Alecia.

The last time Ginger was here with her sax, a mouse frightened her. It ran out from under the refrigerator into the dining room, where the two of them were holding forth on Way Down in Dixie Land. Caribou told me that night at dinner. Caribou hates mice. Mewmew, the damn cat usually pounces on them, but she's getting long in the whiskers.

"Kelwyn, we're being overrun by mice!" she screamed. "I hear them in the walls at night when I'm trying to get some sleep. Scratch, scratch, scratch. Rustle, rustle, rustle. They're going to start a fire on that old wiring. Not that I would mind if this place burned to the ground."

"Polly likes the mice," I countered. She's even made a pet of two of them. She's trained them to walk up one arm, around her neck, and down the other arm."

"I'm going to call pest control," Caribou shrieked. "Ginger was frightened out of her wits."

"Do as you like. But Polly gets to keep her pets."

"Those so-called pets are responsible for the army that's running amok in our walls. All the mice have to go. Polly doesn't need them. She has her gerbils and guinea pigs. The other day she brought in a garden snake."

"Well you have Mewmew. It's important for a kid to have pets."

"Mewmew! She's lucky to be alive. Polly is hateful to her. The other day I caught her trying to drown my cat in the bathtub hot water. She just laughed when I scolded her. Poor Mewmew."

I could see there was no winning this argument. I remember the white mice I had as a boy. Sam and Sammy. Corky said she was allergic to mice, so they had to go, too. I don't believe Corky was allergic at all. She was just jealous because Dad had given them to me for my birthday. Corky never liked it, either, after my dad took me for a haircut. She and mother were in a snit about that for weeks. Dad managed to stay away from the apartment, except for Monday night bridge games. He got along fine with Alecia's parents. I don't know why he had to die. Wasn't he a doctor? One day there, the next day gone. I can't remember him being sick at all. I think

Corky did something. One of her spells. Mother never seemed to miss Dad. She told me he was buried in one of her cemeteries. Fond-du-lac. Caribou said she saw his headstone.

Caribou's getting all hyper about owning cemeteries. Hasn't she got enough to do working at the cheese factory?" Gor says to let her be. She's not bothering our poker games.

"I guess you got the dakhanavar in her blood, playing all that music when she was pregnant with Polly," he said with a particularly evil grin. "The guys at the factory get a kick out of her when she parades through the cheese making vat room with Giulio. She's a tall one and he's a short asshole. They've always got their heads together about something."

I see Dr. Boren's van pulling into his parking spot. He's got one saved. The town lets him put his Reserved for MD sign there. I guess that's not a bad idea. A guy in the next ice shack had a heart attack while he was pulling up a big one. One of the Alberts—Nutty, they called him. He didn't make it despite Dr. Boren's propping him up and all that other stuff he does.

Kelwyn waved to Dr. Boren as he was crossing the ice to his hut. "Hi Doctor. Glad you made it. Maybe the fish will start biting now. It's warm in here and the beers cold."

CHAPTER 17

A lecia called Cara Bow with the news. "They're both dead," she said. The building manager found them.

"What happened Alecia?"

"They haven't been out of the apartment for some time. The only visitor they've had was you, Caribou, a few weeks ago."

"Yes. They were stumbling about a bit. Mrs. Keck had cataract surgery a while ago, but the doctor told her there was evidence of macular degeneration. The wet kind. She had to stand right in front of me to see who I was. Of course, she knew it was me by my voice. I think she was trying to see if I had gotten fat or something. That's funny. She was more than plumped out once, but she had lost a lot of weight. And Ulrich was struggling, too. I don't think they should have lived alone. Ulrich had one of those plastic things stuck in his nose. It was connected to his oxygen tank."

"Well, their grocery order was left outside, and the manager reported it to the police when he got no answer after knocking several times. This is funny. They were asleep in the same bed."

"Really. Why am I not surprised? I've always suspected there was a peculiar attachment between those two. Even apart from them being twins and all."

"Yes, well I guess they had been dead for at least a week. My mom called me with the news. Oh, and the police found a paper in a file cabinet that said they wanted to be cremated. It's funny though. They weren't that old. I forgot they were twins until I read the obit."

"That's awful, Alecia. Maybe Kelwyn and I had better come down there."

"They took the bodies to the morgue for an autopsy. I haven't heard anything more. Mom said it might have been a suicide pact."

"Suicide! That's a possibility, I guess. I'll have to tell Kelwyn. Let me know if you hear anything more. Text me the number of the morgue. I'll give them a call."

"Will do, Caribou. I'm awfully sorry about this. I hope Kelwyn doesn't take it too hard."

"I'm certain he'll by okay. He won't want to have his outdoor stuff interrupted. That's all he ever cares about. That and his poker games. His emotional intelligence can be scored at zero beyond those activities. We rarely talk anymore. I'm so unhappy, Alecia, to tell the truth. Many times, I've regretted our meeting. I know you had a hand in this, but how could you know the outcome?"

Cara Bow was glad she had at last been forthcoming about Alecia's scheme to get her and Kelwyn together. She must have known Kelwyn's goal of having a girl, in order to have access to his grandmother's trust fund. Alecia and Kelwyn had been childhood playmates in their apartments fenced in back yard. Alecia had heard the talk at the Monday night bridge games. Well, that was water under the bridge. *Bridge, bridge, bridge.* The words jumbled in Cara Bow's brain. She paused for several seconds before listening to what Alecia was saying.

"...always been sorry, Caribou. I know you wanted to go on to grad school. Maybe you still can."

"I'm thirty-four years old, Alecia. I've given up on that dream. Life's not all that bad here, except for the devil child, Polly. Kelwyn leaves me alone, but Polly...we'll talk about that another time. Right now, I'm going to call Kelwyn with the news. Thanks again for calling. Love you."

"Love you, too. Bye now."

Alecia's picture vanished from Cara Bow's cell. Yes, she did love Alecia.

Kelwyn did not pick up when she scrolled down to his number, so she left a message. *Your mom and Uncle Ulrich have died. Do you want to go to Chicago?* She went down to her lab glad that she had changed her mind about the plum jelly. *Goodbye, Elsie.* Cara Bow felt a little remorse about Uncle Ulrich. He wasn't a bad guy. Maybe Elsie wasn't either, but they were looming figures in her belief that she had been used.

Before she unlocked the lab door, she remembered Mewmew. She hadn't seen the cat since returning to the house. The hated house. She called, "Here kitty, kitty, kitty."

Mewmew usually unballed herself at Cara Bow's summons but this time there were no skittering paws to be heard running down the steps. *That cat's getting old. Maybe she's deaf. I'd better see where she is. See if there's food in her dish.* She noticed the litter box had not been used on her way back up the steps. But Mewmew was no where to be found in all of her usual escape from Polly places.

It had started to rain, so Cara Bow put on her mackintosh and went out the side door, still calling. "Here kitty, kitty, kitty. Here Mewmew." She walked around the back of the house, past the large gas drum and down the short path to the murky creek. Through the rain drops she spotted a gunny sack in the shallow water, tied with a red ribbon around the neck of the bag. Her heart sank. She pulled the dripping sack from the water and undoing the red knot she forced herself to look at the cat with her little pink ears, its eyes still open, a distressed grimace frozen on its face.

"Polly, what have you done," she screamed. "Oh, Mewmew, Mewmew. You poor thing. None of this is your fault. I should have escaped from this place long ago." In shock, she carried the sodden cat in her arms to a small tool shed that had once been Polly's play house. She took down a shovel from the tool rack and carried it with the cat to the side of the house. There, between the two plum trees, she began to dig into the wet earth. When the hole was deep enough, she took a flowered scarf from around her neck and wrapped Mewmew's body in it. *Here you go, Mewmew. I won't forget you. I'll have my revenge before I leave this place.*

At the supper table that evening, she casually asked Kelwyn if he had seen Mewmew. "No, Caribou. Why do you care about that mangy creature, anyway? I saw Polly playing with her after breakfast this morning. She likes to pull her tail.

"Where is Polly, Kelwyn? She wasn't here when I came back today."

"Oh, yeah, I forgot to mention. Polly's on some sort of sleep over at the school. I signed a slip, so she could take part. They're camping in the gym. Can you beat that? TV, pizza and a scary movie. Getting close to Halloween, you know. Of course, what would you know? You're gone every day to the plant. Donna's one of the chaperones at the gym. Polly will be okay."

Cara Bow looked at Kelwyn sitting across from her at the table. His belly had expanded to the extent that he couldn't get close to the table. He slobbered as he ate. Bits of food fell from his mouth onto his flannel shirt. He chewed with his mouth open. *How did I ever think him handsome*, she thought? She thought of Mewmew, probably tormented by Polly before being tied into the gunny sack. *Why is Polly so sadistic? Who is next on her list? Was Louise safe*? She would go to see Ginger tomorrow and get some feedback about their playtimes together. First, she would call Giulio and tell him she was not coming in tomorrow. He wouldn't be upset. The business was running smoothly with Gor and Olivo taking over most of the daily duties.

"Yes, I'm certain Polly will be just fine, Kelwyn. Kelwyn we need to talk about something else before…"

"Not now, Caribou," he cut her off as he wiped a napkin across his face. The guys are coming over in ten minutes or so. We've got a game going, and I'm ahead as of last night. The stew was good, Caribou.

You're turning into a pretty good cook." He got up from the table and sounded a loud burp.

"You shouldn't eat so fast, Kelwyn." The stew was out of a can. "Dinty Moore," she said. Donna opened it before she left. It was warming in the crock pot when I came home."

"Well, it was still pretty good. Not as good as your plum jelly, though. Polly and I finished the last jar in the refrigerator this morning. The store room was locked. Make sure there's more for the morning, will you?"

"Oh yes, there will be more, Kelwyn, I put up a new batch just a few weeks ago. Those plums never seem to stop falling, do they?"

Kelwyn didn't answer. He let his belt out another notch as he headed for the basement. She didn't have to let Gor and Dr. Boren in as they came in the back-shed door. They both had a key, and she heard them laughing as they went down the steps.

The next morning, she slept in until nine o'clock and would have slept longer if the bedroom door hadn't opened and Polly rushed in and jumped on top of her.

"Oh, mommy, I've missed you," she cried.

"Polly get off me!" Cara Bow felt she was being smothered. "You're too heavy. You're not a baby anymore. Don't you have school today? Where's Donna?"

"No school today because of the sleep-over last night. It was a lot of fun. No one really slept. They showed two scary movies, and everyone was screaming a lot when the zombies started eating people, but I wasn't scared one bit," she crowed with her squawky voice. She took her time getting off Cara Bow and managed to twist her mother's hand in a painful position during the process. She pulled all of the covers with her as she dropped to the floor, laughing.

Cara Bow held her patience. This is not the time she thought. There are things to be arranged before she would put her plan into action. The plan had become clearer in her dreams.

"Mother, can I go with Donna to Green Bay, today? She wants to take me to the zoo."

"Yes, of course," said Cara Bow. *The zoo would be a perfect place for you*, she thought. "Now let me get up. We'll pick out something nice for you to wear. There's your new jeans with the flower patch on the pocket."

Donna clattered up the drive in her battered, green pick-up truck. She had a picnic box in the back held in place with bungee cords. Polly climbed eagerly into the passenger seat and she and Donna waved at Cara Bow, who was standing on the side cement porch. *Maybe the truck will crash or something* Cara Bow thought. *Maybe I'm losing my mind.*

After showering and dressing, she called Ginger. "Hey, Ginger," she said. "Today's Wednesday. Are you coming with your saxophone? You'll have to bring Louise with you because there's no school."

"No school? Of course, there's school. Louise left on the seven-thirty bus this morning."

Cara Bow decided to say nothing about Polly's tale. "Oh, yes, I forgot. I slept in this morning. I don't know why I said that. Two-thirty, okay? I'm having the usual lunch with my mother."

"Sure, Caribou. I missed you last week." Cara Bow could picture Ginger in her pink baby doll pajamas, her curly red hair mussed. *Ginger is someone I will miss*, she thought.

Noon found her and Judy at Applebee's with their usual strawberry margaritas. Her mother looked wan.

"What's up, Mom?" asked Cara Bow, concerned. "Have you been taking your vitamins?

"It's your father, Cara Bow. The judge is getting worse. He wanders off at the oddest times. Last evening, he fell on that little hill slope down the block and his face was all bloody. A neighbor called me over. Norman refused to let me take him to the emergency room. "You take care of it," he said. "I don't want Dr. Boren to see me like this." I had to wash him and put some iodine on a few cuts. He likes iodine. Iodine on everything."

"Oh, Mom. You can't go on like this. You'll make yourself sick. You and dad need to go to some nice retirement home. Darla said there's one not far from here, in Green Bay. In fact, there's even a view of their small pond from every apartment. Kelwyn mentioned that he saw dad taking out the garbage when Kelwyn was in his ice fishing hut. He said not only was dad putting garbage into the can, but he also explored the neighbor's garbage can."

"I remember, Dad did bring in a small wicker basket and I asked him where he got it, but he said he didn't remember. He doesn't remember much anymore. Once he peed in the hall closet thinking he was in the bathroom. Harriet Albert cleaned it up but said she wouldn't do this sort of thing any more. I don't know what I'd do without Harriet." Judy looked desperate. Her eyes welled up as she ordered the second margarita.

"Mom, I'm meeting Ginger at two-thirty, so I've got to go. Are you all right to drive home?"

"I'll be fine, Cara Bow. I used the new Uber service they have in Cooperton. I'll Uber back. I don't like to leave the judge alone for too long. Check with Darla Albert and get me some more information about that retirement place. A man did stop by our house while I was in the front yard weeding the pansies the other day. He wanted to know if I wanted to sell the house."

"That's a good sign, Mom. Let's get you some relief."

"What would people say, Cara Bow? We've always lived in that house. You grew up there."

"What can people say, Mom? That's what those retirement places are for—and I would feel better if you and Dad were in a safe place. I'm going to do a lot more traveling now."

"I understand, Cara Bow. Don't think I don't know what goes on in your house. People talk, you know. Pastor Cornwall stopped by the other day and said he saw Polly throwing rocks at passing cars. And Kelwyn and that Donna Albert. You've not had it easy in your marriage."

So, people talk, thought Cara Bow. *Let them. Talk dies down after a while.*

CHAPTER 18

"This is the last time I can sit for you on Wednesday nights, Mrs. Keck," announced Milena the following week. "We're moving."

"Moving! When did this come about, Milena?" Cara Bow had begun to think of Milena as more of a friend than housekeeper or baby sitter. Of course, Polly was big enough to stay by herself, but Cara Bow didn't trust her to be in the house alone when she and Kelwyn were away. She and Kelwyn had argued about this, but Kelwyn was not one to focus too long on the subject of child care.

"Gor wants to go to LA. We have cousins there. Davi and Ani are getting big now and Gor says they should be more familiar with our own culture There's a lot of Armenians in LA, and we would be able to go to our own church. The Catholics have been nice to us, but we've always gone to an Armenian church."

"The Alberts are mostly Armenian, I think, Milena."

"That's what we were told when we agreed to settle here, but that's not true. Their folks migrated from Hungary. It's not the same. The kids are excited to go. Ani said Cher is there. And there are a lot of Armenian restaurants around LA. Gor's cousin owns one. He told Gor he could have a job in the kitchen."

Cara Bow laughed inwardly at this. Gor, in the kitchen. He couldn't even fix his own lunch. Grandma Terzian had died of a hemorrhage not long ago. The funeral was held at the Catholic Church. There were only a few mourners in attendance. Cara Bow and Kelwyn had both gone. The priest had read quickly through the ritual mass. Cara Bow was glad Gor had no one else to beat.

"The Terzians are moving, Kelwyn," she told him the next morning at breakfast. "I'm going to lose Milena. They're moving to LA. I won't leave Polly alone while we're away which is most every day. I'm only here on Wednesday afternoons when Polly gets off the bus."

"Christ, we have Donna and Mrs. Olsen, Caribou. Don't get yourself into a lather. Milena is rarely here anyway. Damn, that means Gor won't be here either."

"Oh, Gor, Gor. What will Giulio do with Gor gone?"

"That's not our problem, Caribou. I'll have to find someone else for my poker nights. Owen Albert hasn't been reliable either. Too much work at the body shop, he says but I think he's having problems at home with his wife. Damn. Maybe Dr. Boren can find someone."

Polly was silent during this exchange. "I want some more toast with the plum jelly, Mother," she said. And fix me another egg, too."

"Say please, Polly. You always say please to Donna."

"Ok, pleeeeze," she said dramatically.

"Leave the kid alone, Caribou. She's hungry," said Kelwyn.

"She's had two eggs already, Kelwyn." She wanted to stuff a dozen eggs down Polly's throat, remembering the terrible end of her beloved Mewmew.

Polly began to kick her shoe hard against the table leg. *I'll fix the egg*, thought Cara Bow. *At least we're on a different topic.*

"Hurry and finish your breakfast, Polly. The bus will be here in ten minutes."

"Why can't you drive me, Mother, Louise's mother drives her every day."

"I have to get to work, Polly, you know that. The bus is for kids who live too far from school. Now, get your coat on. It's chilly today."

She decided on a whim not to go into work that day. Everything was running smoothly there, and she needed time to think. Like a phoenix from the ashes, a cloudy plan had begun to form in her mind. *When I leave Cooperton, they'll find that lab in my jelly room.* That's how she referred to her lab space. The Jelly Room.

"Kelwyn, would you take the Volvo today? I need the pick-up to load a new desk for Polly's room. She's falling behind at school. I want to fix up a better place for her to do her homework."

"Sure, Caribou. You know I like to drive your car." What time do you want it back?" Kelwyn was surprised by Caribou's offer. He thought she must have reconsidered her continued touchiness about Polly's behavior. Kelwyn was already out the door at the offer.

Why doesn't Polly rag on Kelwyn? Cara Bow thought. *Kelwyn goes right by the school on his way to the office. He could have driven Polly. He's probably not going to the office. Oh, well, I have my plan. Time to get out of this quagmire.*

She had all day. She dressed in jeans and an old flannel shirt of Kelwyn's. Piece by piece she began to dismantle her lab equipment in her basement room and put it into the pick-up. The tables were too heavy for her to move. She decided to leave them, the only twice used sewing machine on one table and on the other the colored thread and extra needles, along with the extra sewing machine attachments. I'll pick up a few patterns and some cheap fabric at Walmart. To fill up more space on that table.

When all was dismantled, except for the plum jelly, of course, she drove the truck to the cheese factory. It was near closing time by the time she got there. Giulio was still in his office, looking glum.

"Hey, Giulio," she said. "I picked up some stuff we need in our testing lab. How about helping me unload. Why the long face?"

"You didn't come in today, Cara. I have bad news about Gor."

"I know about the Terzians moving to LA if that's what you mean. I'm sure one of the other guys can take over his job."

"Not only that, Cara. My wife in Parma is not doing well. I have to return to Italy. I don't know how long I'll be gone."

This news gladdened Cara Bow's heart. She had been wondering how to tell Giulio that she was planning to leave, too.

"Giulio, not to worry. When I was straightening the papers on you desk, I noticed the letter with the offer from that company in Canada. They want to buy your plant. It's a good offer. I'll get a return on my whey plant investment, too. You must take them up on it. This is the perfect time. Your getting on in years and you've been complaining about your bursitis. The warm weather in Parma will fix you up in a hurry. I'm sorry to hear about your wife.

She had mixed feelings about this absent wife. Her romantic encounters with Giulio had been satisfying but she was somewhat concerned by her occasional feelings of guilt. She never saw herself as a homewrecker. A murderer maybe but not a homewrecker.

"Thank you, Cara. I'm sure she'll be all right but the family, you know. They have to come first. We've been good together, haven't we? I'll miss you."

"And I'll miss you, too, Giulio. Now come on and help me take the stuff from the pick-up into the lab. The microscope is much better than the one we have now. I got the stuff on eBay for a good price. You can repay me out of petty cash." With Giulio gone her tracks would be covered. No one would ever know that she had been working on a lab in her basement. Things appeared to be falling neatly into place.

That night at dinner, she had ordered pizza. Both Polly and Kelwyn loved the stuffed pizza from Gelsomos. Polly as usual ate in her own space in her corner of the house.

"Did you get the desk?" Kelwyn asked.

"I found one at the furniture store that was closing, Kelwyn. They said they would deliver it, so I didn't need the pick-up after all. It'll be here by the weekend. Polly has a special project to complete by the end of the semester. She and Darla will have their own space to get it together. It's about the history of Cooperton."

"That's good, Caribou," he responded, his mouth full of pizza. Cara Bow looked away from the food being masticated in his open mouth.

"There's something we need to talk about, Kelwyn. I want to go back to school and finish my masters. That means I'll be leaving you, Kelwyn. I want a divorce."

"A divorce! What about Polly?"

"I've thought about that, Kelwyn. Polly hates me." She didn't tell him about the demise of Mewmew. He'd never mentioned anything about the absence of the cat. "You can ask Donna to move into this moldy place. Polly likes her, and I know what's been going on between you two. You have your money and I have mine. We can make this simple."

Kelwyn pretended to be alarmed by the suggestion but not for long. He finished the pizza with a can of Miller and said, "Well if that's what you want it's okay with me. Gor and Doctor are coming over tonight for some poker. Guess I'll be able to move my pipe rack back upstairs when you're gone."

You do that, thought Cara Bow. *Maybe you'll burn this place down.* That was easier than she had imagined.

"See if you can get some info from your mother about the history of Cooperton for Polly, will you? I don't think Donna will be much help with that project," he said.

"I'll get right on it Kelwyn. Enjoy your evening." She felt a coolness as she spoke the words. Freedom was in the offing.

CHAPTER 19

"The house is being sold," was the first thing her mother said when she walked in the door. Your father has become impossible. Always pulling weeds, making funny noises."

"Funny noises, Mom?"

"Clucking noises, Like a chicken." Judy tried to make the sound, her lips moving quickly as she pushed air through them. "Buuck, buuck buuck" she managed to say.

"That's kind of funny, Mom," Cara Bow couldn't help a small laugh at the sight of her mother's face all squinted up as the sound continued.

"It's not funny, Cara Bow. He even walks along the road around the lake lifting everyone's trash can covers to see what's inside. He gets lost, tries to get in the wrong house—the neighbors are locking their doors. We've never had to lock our doors in this town."

Cara Bow could see the distress in her mother's face. "This must be hard, Mom. You've always lived here. I grew up here. Where will you go?"

"There's that assisted living place in Green Bay you mentioned. Right on the water. I've got to be near water. They weren't sure about taking us because of your father's odd behavior, but I assured them he wouldn't be a problem because I would be with him at every moment—and we have the money, you know. We wouldn't ever be on Medicaid or whatever it is that happens when the money runs out."

"That sounds good, Mom. The reason I stopped by today was to tell you I'm leaving Kelwyn and Polly and that house."

"Well, I warned you, didn't I? And our only grandchild has never warmed to me. She's a funny one."

"You don't know the half of it, Mom. When I told Polly and Kelwyn I was leaving she said, "You'd better go before I kill you. Daddy and I hate you.""

"I don't know what to think, Mom. Sometimes I've wanted to kill them both. It's better that I leave. Kelwyn has Donna Albert for a playmate and Polly likes her. Poor Donna. She's so dumb"

Cara Bow watched out the window and saw the judge kneeling on the grass with a scissors. In his hand.

"What's he doing, Mom?'

"Cutting the grass. Can you believe it?"

"Oh, Mom!"

Judy shook her head. "And Harriet Albert, you know, our maid, she quit last week. She complained that your father follows too close behind her and she can't take the funny noises he makes."

Cara Bow noticed that her mother was not dressed in her usual put together self. She was still in her night clothes at eleven o'clock in the morning.

"It's Wednesday, Mom. Our Margarita day. Come on. Get dressed There won't be many more of these."

"I can't leave him, Cara Bow. It's sad."

"Yes, it is sad, Mom" She turned and walked through the house to the screened in porch off the kitchen. Tioga lake was calm. Smooth as glass. A family of ducks was parading silently along the shore line. She saw a red-winged blackbird fly from one branch to the next in the thick summery leaves on the many shade trees—a few evergreen firs, but most of them deciduous. In her mind she compared it to the quack grass lawn in front of her own house, and the long drive to the side porch guarded by the two ugly stone lions at the start of the drive. *It was never my house. I never wanted to be there. I got lost. How many years has it been. I was always an intruder in that place. I'm thirty-four. Nearly thirteen years. Polly is eleven. A terrible mistake. It's made me consider murder—Elsie and Ulrich. Now I run cemeteries. I'm going mad thinking about it. My brain is rattling. I need to leave quickly. Like my mom and dad, moving to Green Bay. I need to find my people. I hope it's not too late.*

"This is the beautiful part of Cooperton," she said to Judy, who had followed her to the porch. You've been lucky, So many years living here. But you're right. Selling the house. Beginning a new sort of adventure. Think of it as an adventure. Making new Margarita friends. I'm going to Chicago. Alecia's husband says there's an opening in the Medical Examiner's office. Criminalistics. I'd be a lab assistant, part time. I'm going to apply for grad school classes at Northwestern. Maybe I'll be a teacher one day, like you wanted. A professor even. I'm not poor either, Mom. I have Grandma's trust and my investment in the whey plant is really about to pay off. This is the right time for both of us."

"That's good, Cara Bow. With our move and the money, we'll need for the assisted living center, there probably won't be anything left for you when we're gone."

"Oh, Mom, don't talk like that."

"It's true, Cara Bow" she sighed. Now, can I get you something? Tea?" I've got herbal, or how about a Margarita right here. I have the mix on the kitchen counter. There's a bottle of tequila on the bar." She began to pour the tequila in a tall glass, maybe a bit more than usual, then shook the ice basket in the freezer and added it to the glasses with the tequila mix.

"Sorry it's not strawberry, Mom. Cheers"

"Yes, cheers, Cara Bow." Judy began to cry.

"No tears, Mom. This'll be a good move for the Edens; you'll make new friends in Green Bay. There's bridge. That's always an in for you."

"I'm sorry you never learned, Cara Bow."

"We all stare at our phones, Mom. It's different now. Alecia says they have game nights at their condo. Sometimes they go on for a whole weekend. She says Tony is always playing hearts online. In between clients, that is. No one plays bridge."

Judy adjusted her robe that had fallen open, then ran her fingers through her short grey hair in an effort to pull herself into a semblance of her former confident manner. Cara Bow embraced her and kissed her cheek.

"There's something you can help me with, Mom. Polly has to do a project on the history of Cooperton. I know there was great-grandpa Cooper. Why was the town named for him?"

"Your Great Grandpa and your Grandpa were Coopers. Great Grandpa emigrated from Holland, where he apprenticed as a Cooper. I think his name was Kuyper, but immigration wrote it as Cooper. Times were tough when he emigrated to this area and started his business. There was a lot of lumber available and with the Germans who started the breweries around Milwaukee, there was a need for his barrels for their dark beer. He did well. Most of the town was employed in his shop. Cooper, Hooper. The name was interchangeable. Barrel makers. Then the steel barrels came in and wooden barrel making died out except for fine wines. There are no wineries in these parts. There's remains of the old plant a few miles west of here."

"Kelwyn mentioned the boards he used to build his hunting hideout. He said it was just lying around one area. That must have been part of the old Cooper plant. I'll tell him. He'll like the connection to this area. He'll never leave. He and Polly and Donna and the Dakhonavar. I never told you about that. It's not important anymore, Mom. Cheers again. Let's have another one." They drank their Margaritas in silence sitting on the porch enjoying the quiet view.

"I'm going to say goodbye to Dad now. Don't worry, I'll come back to visit often in Green Bay.

"Are you still making your plum jelly?' Judy asked.

"Not lately, Mom. I've been so busy. It's about gone." She knew there were two shelves of the pretty jars in her basement workroom, now just a sewing room, empty of the lab equipment.

She left and went to sit on the grass by the judge, who was continuing his grass clipping with the small scissor.

"Hey, dad. Looking good."

The judge looked at Cara Bow with a sideways glance and began to make *buck, buck* chicken sounds.

"It's me Dad, Cara Bow, your daughter" His funny sounds continued. Cara Bow gave him a fond pat on the shoulder.

"No one wants those girls, they're pot heads," he said, as she got up to leave. "Keep away from them, you hear?"

Cara Bow thought he was recalling his days on the bench, maybe Kerzy and Belle. That was so long ago. The friends were only fifteen or sixteen she remembered. She recalled that their parents wanted them to be sent to a home for delinquent girls. *They turned out just fine—married to Alberts, working at the factory, raising little Alberts.* She thought it would be an enlivening time for her parents at the assisted living center. Most of their friends had passed on. Her own childhood friends had become strangers to her now, except for the bowling nights. She'd probably never become a teacher, her mother's wish; she would never be her father's idea of an athlete. She sensed her father had wanted a boy. Things seemed to be coming to a head. It's this town. *This town has slowly poisoned me. Leaving will purge the infection.*

CHAPTER 20

T*he town should have been called Albertville*, not Cooperton, Cara
Bow thought as she drove from her parents' home. She decided
to drive around Tioga Lake for a last time. A twelve-mile drive
There were only a few houses on the opposite side. Mostly summer
places with small wooden fishing or boat docks. She thought of her
forbears—Immigrants. Her mother's had been Scottish. Their wise
investments had caused a small pile of money to become a hill, then
almost a mountain. Cara Bow's trust meant a life of ease should she
wish, but her restless nature deemed otherwise. She had always kept
her trust a secret from Kelwyn and had been specific in naming most
of the trust to benefit her chemistry school in Madison at her death. It
was revocable and after the divorce that could change. It would never
go to Polly—the devil child.

Well, Cooperton was the name, but few if any knew of the origin.
Certainly, the judge knew at one time. Not anymore. His world had
become very tiny. A pair of scissors and a blade of grass.

And the Alberts. Where had their tribe come from? Cara Bow didn't know, but thought it was probably from one of the Baltic states. Kelwyn's secretary had mentioned once about a grandmother who had been born in Canada. The Alberts. Or, maybe they emerged from raining alien pods. She laughed aloud at the idea. There were so many of them. Perhaps someday the name of Cooperton would vanish and Albertville would be the victor.

The houses on the opposite side of the lake were tucked into the woods, barely visible, ramshackle. An old row boat without oars was tied to one of the short, grey-board docks. She stopped the car and got out in front of one of the dirt drives. She thought she saw movement behind one of the raggedy curtains, but then all was still. *Just Be Kind.* It was a small sign posted at the head of the dirt drive. A funny sort of sign. The red and blue lettering reminded her of ancient hieroglyphics. All angles and staggered on the white background. *Just Be Kind.*

She liked the sign but wasn't sure of the message. *People say kind all the time,* she thought. *Kind of bad, kind of nice, kind of terrible. Kind, sort, ilk, Sort of nice. Ilk*—she'd tried to find a word to rhyme with ilk once in a creative writing course in her first year at university. Silk worked, bilk, milk, almost quilt.

She stood for several minutes, oddly at peace musing about the sign and thought she might ask the owners what they meant. *It would be kind of them to tell me what they meant by their sign.* She laughed at her effort at humor; it had been so long since she found anything very funny.

She walked the short dirt path to the house where the curtain had moved and knocked at the old door. No one came. *Must have been the wind,* she thought. She hit the Amazon app on her cell and looked for a similar sign. There it was. She put it in her cart. *I'll post the sign in front of one of the lions at the hated house when I leave.*

She passed the Cooperton Mall as she continued her drive home. It's so tired looking, she thought. Only last week the J.C. Penny store had vacated the premises. Sears was long gone, and she imagined Macy's and Carson's would soon go, too. The last time she had been there with her mother, the place had echoed with gloom. The wig shop was still there and a jeweler. A video game store occupied one building arm. A traveling strange animal show had been set up in the center area near the now defunct merry-go- round. A few children stopped to point at the armadillo and the boa constrictor. The animals looked as tired as their keepers, as tired as the few shoppers who were looking lost in the vast empty space—*as tired as I am*, thought Cara Bow. *I'm 34—too young to be tired.*

An ambulance was in front of the small house where the two men lived across the road from the Keck house. A small crowd had gathered. Farmer Olson and Mrs. Olsen—Cara Bow never knew them by any other name— and Olivo, who was on his way home from work, and Donna, Polly Judy, and two of the Olsen boys.

She pulled into her long drive and after parking, walked back to see what was happening.

"What's happening, Olivo?" she asked.

"I don't know, Cara Bow." Olivo was one of the few people who still called her by her given name. "I saw two EMT guys go into the house with a stretcher. Do you know who lives here? It's right across the road from your house."

"Two men, Olivo. They keep to themselves. I tried to make contact one time by waving to the taller one, but he just turned away and walked back inside."

"I know them," said Mrs. Olsen. They've lived here as long as I can remember. Their name is Becker—Emil and Fred. I looked it up on the tax roles years ago when I helped out at the City Clerks office. They have the same birth dates. They're twins, not the identical kind," she laughed. Their birth place was listed as Rhinelander, Wisconsin. I don't know how they came to live here in Cooperton."

The EMTs came out of the small house carrying a man on a stretcher. It was the shorter one. The tall man stood silently at his door, a confused look on his face. Another car drove up. It was Dr. Boren.

"Dr. Boren, why are you here?" asked Cara Bow.

"I've been looking after these two for some time. Social Services is concerned that they're not getting a proper diet. They're in their nineties. The last time I saw them, I thought they were both in the beginning stages of dementia. Emil has high blood pressure. They do have a landline and 911 got a call a short while ago and had to trace the call because they only heard unintelligible sounds. Looks like Emil might have suffered a stroke. Why don't you see if there's anything you can do for Fred?" Cara Bow was hesitant.

"Go on, Mother, go on." Polly was gleeful as she watched the unfolding drama. "Go on, go on. Maybe Fred will do something bad to you. Maybe he'll stab you or hit you on the head with something. Maybe he'll…Donna had the sense to put her hand over Polly's mouth.

"Take her inside, Donna, this is no place for a ten-year-old." The bystanders looked on at the taunting child in surprise.

"This is not the Polly I know," said Mr. Olsen. She's such a little angel. Everyone says so."

Cara Bow overheard the comment. "Well, now you know," she said, embarrassed by the outburst, then tried to cover for Polly. "Polly's not been herself lately. I'm not sure why. I think she misses our cat, Mewmew. She walked toward Fred as the ambulance pulled away with Dr. Boren following in his own car.

"Let's go inside, Mr. Becker," she said, gingerly taking him by his arm. The man hesitated, then turned and they both went into the house together. Cara Bow was surprised by the sight that greeted her eyes. The small front room was beautifully appointed with a grey camel back sofa and two black and white striped recliner chairs. A lamp with a plain maple wooden base with a white shade was on a small end table between the two chairs. A small bookcase was behind the sofa. She noticed in a quick glance that they all seemed to be children's picture books. The walls were painted a clean white. Everything was clean. *Someone has been looking after these two,* she thought. *How did I not notice that? Someone must come while I'm at work. What else don't I know?*

"Please sit down, Mr. Becker, I'll bring you some tea. Would you like that? My name's Cara Bow Keck. I'm your neighbor across the road."

Fred gave a timid nod but said nothing. Cara Bow went into the kitchen and found a box of green tea bags on the counter. A black tea kettle sat on an electric stove. The stove was amazingly sparkling. There was no microwave, so she filled the kettle with water and left it to boil.

She was curious about the third room off the kitchen—a bedroom with a double bed, dresser and several hooks on the walls on which hung various items of clothing. The walls were also painted white. A photo of a pretty woman dressed in clothing from another time was on the nightstand. Their mother, she imagined. What had happened those years ago? How did these men come to live in Cooperton? She knew this would always be an unsolved mystery. Like the mystery of Elsie and Ulrich, twins, maybe murderers of Dr. Keck, maybe parents of Kelwyn. She looked out of the bedroom window and noticed a rabbit hutch in the back yard. There was no sign of rabbits. Why was the hutch there?

The water on the stove wasn't boiling yet, so she walked out the screened back door to investigate. There were rabbits. Five of them, not moving, lying on the straw bed. A closer look told her that their necks had been broken. *Polly,* she thought. *Mewmew and now the rabbits. Is this what had caused Emil's collapse? Is this why she was so gleeful? Is this what she wanted me to see? Why does she like to see others suffer?*

She heard the kettle's whistle and hurried back into the kitchen. She fixed the tea in a beautiful turquoise ceramic mug. There were two of them.

"Here's some nice tea Mr. Becker," she said as she carried the cup into the front room on a tray on which she also put some butter cookies that she had found in one of the cupboards. Fred didn't respond. He had fallen asleep in one of the recliners. She left the tea on the nearby table and quietly left the house. The people standing around had gone now that the excitement was over. Only Mr. Olsen remained.

"Oh, Mr. Olsen, I'm glad you're still here. There's a problem in the back. A rabbit hutch, but the rabbits are dead. Please see to cleaning them out of their cages. Mr. Becker is in no shape right now to take care of it."

Mr. Olsen agreed to the chore. "I'll get some sacks from my farm and send my boys down Mrs. Keck. How do you suppose that happened?"

"I don't know, Mr. Olsen. Do you know of any other mischief that's been going on around this area?" She had an innocent look on her face as she responded to his question. She knew, but she didn't acknowledge that she knew Mr. Olsen knew who the culprit was. *Now to see about Polly,* she thought.

Polly and Donna were again playing one of their endless games when she walked in the side door. *What would be the point of confronting her about her wicked behavior. That's what she wants me to do so she can deny it. I'm leaving soon.* The calmness that overcame her near the two old cottages on Lake Tioga and now the simple house across the road continued to work their magic on her. She was calmly resolute as she dialed the local Social Services number and spoke to a man named Robbie Albert.

"Yes, I'm aware of those two," he said. The county has been trying to get them out of that house for the longest time. They want to put up a storage barn there for their winter plows. The town even started condemnation proceedings at one time, but someone intervened, an old woman, don't remember her name, she's not from these parts. She had an attorney with her. I don't know what was said but the town was unable to go ahead with the condemnation."

How funny, thought Cara Bow. *The town wanted to condemn a perfectly good, well kept, little house, but ignored the moldy, creepy place across the road.* "Mr. Albert," she said, "probably Mr. Becker shouldn't be alone in his house. Maybe your department will see to it that the town takes action and see to it that he has a caregiver during the day while his brother is in the hospital. There's nothing wrong with that house. The town will have to find somewhere else to put up a storage barn. You are *Social Services,* aren't you? You'll have to be more social and serve." She had never felt more powerful.

"Uh, yes, of course, Mrs. Keck. You're right I'll get on it first thing tomorrow." He sounded flustered. "Maybe there's been some mistake. That was the old town council. I believe they are looking at another property now."

"Fine, Mr. Albert," Cara Bow softened her stance. "I know you'll do the right thing." The sign *Just Be Kind* was having its effect on her.

CHAPTER 21

Look at them over there—making a big deal over an old guy. I took the laser pointer from Miss Hill's desk drawer at school. She likes to flash that thing around, pointing at words on the chart. She calls them pronouns. That's a laugh. Nobody cares about pronouns. I hate to read, anyway. Mother knows that. She buys me those stupid graphic books for third graders. I keep a stack of big kid graphics stuffed under my mattress. Mother never comes in here. She has Donna taking care of my room. Donna and I like to turn the pages and look at the pictures. I like the pictures where someone is getting shot of hanged of chopped up. Donna doesn't like reading either. Our favorite thing is the X-box games. Daddy gets me those. I've got all the Soul Caliber games

I like to point the laser at the old guys—or at their window—anytime I see them. I flash it around, just like Miss Hill. I'd sure like to have one of those green laser pointers like I saw one time on the TV. The tall guy came out one day and shook his finger at me. He didn't realize who he was dealing with. I had to teach them a lesson. The rabbits got fur all over me.

Dumb animals. Mewmew didn't though. But she sure made an awful noise when I stuffed her into the sack.

Mother didn't say anything, but she knew all right. She's afraid of me. They all are. Louise is, too. She stopped coming on Wednesdays after school. Mrs. Sandburg leaves early with her saxophone. She and Mother sure make some awful sounds. Mother wanted me to take piano lessons and she made me try for awhile until Miss Jenkins had that fall. I fixed her. Mrs. Sandburg makes some lame excuse for leaving early— like a hair appointment of having to pick up an order for her Floyd.

That leaves me and Mother until Donna comes. Mother hightails it to the basement. I don't know what she does down there. She says she's making me a dress, but I've never seen it. I pound on the door, but she doesn't let me in. I'll find a way to get in there one day. I spend a lot of time in the attic. She never goes up there.

I thought Louise and I were best friends She didn't like the idea of me having the laser. I warned her she'd be sorry if she told anyone. Now she sits with that stupid Susie Albert. They come to school wearing the same thing and they have the same thing to eat at lunch. I tried sitting with them, but they don't talk to me. They just whisper and giggle a lot.

Louise is in ballet class with Susie now. I hated ballet class and I'm glad the teacher said I couldn't be in it. Now I'll have to teach Louise a good lesson She'll be sorry.

The ambulance is leaving now and Mother's having a discussion with a guy from the cheese factory and Mr. Olsen. Mr. Olsen is pointing and looking toward our house. I don't care. I changed by sweater with the rabbit fur on it. I didn't like it anyway. I like the sweatshirt I have on now. The black one with the caribou applique. I'm going to make Dad take me hunting next Thanksgiving. Maybe I'll get to shoot a caribou. I look good in this color.

CHAPTER

22

Still Wednesday—it had been a long day—her mother's decision to sell the house, *Father is in no way able to take part in the decision*, she thought. *Poor Mother* The ambulance across the road, meeting with Fred—not Emil—he was not conscious, the entrance into the small house and the terrifying discovery of the dead rabbits.

As she drove to the town bowling lanes for a last night with the cheese factory girls, she thought about the sickening discovery. *Had there been other times that Polly had wreaked her sly evil nature against some innocent?*

She recalled the incident when Mrs. Jenkins, the piano teacher, had somehow fallen and broken her hip during Polly's last piano lesson. Even further back came the many memories of her gestation, the vicious kicking, the many nights spent walking an unappeasable baby, the poundings and bruises she had suffered. *I really tried to be a good mother to a child who hated me, even aloud. So many times, Polly had uttered spitefully, "I hate you, Mother, hate you, hate you"*

She knew that most kids said or thought those words without actually knowing the hurtfulness of the words. She, herself had even uttered the words under her breath at her own parents at times when something she wanted to do was forbidden. Certainly, she had hated her father, the judge, when he insisted she try to waterski. *But Polly, she meant the words. Cara Bow knew it. Polly wanted her dead. Maybe Kelwyn, too. Kelwyn was so dense, in love with his hunting and fishing. He was still useful to Polly and Polly played him well. Maybe she should warn Donna. Dumb Donna.*

Donna was with Polly that evening while Cara Bow spent the next few hours at the bowling alley. Kelwyn hadn't come home for supper. He'd left a note in his barely discernable scrawl, saying he was taking a client to Green Bay for dinner at his favorite rib place. Was the client a female? Cara Bow didn't care. She thought it was probably his divorce lawyer. Cara Bow was not going to fight the divorce, nor was Kelwyn. She wanted the split to be done with as fast as possible.

Kelwyn could have the proceeds from her partnership in the whey factory, the cemeteries—they were a losing proposition anyway as they began to fill up—the hated house—everything except the Volvo and her substantial portfolio, in a private safety deposit box in a Green Bay bank under her birth name. He could especially have Polly. She would gladly declare herself an unfit mother. *Just Be Kind.*

The lot at Hotdog Lanes was almost full when she pulled into a remote parking spot. Fortunately, the lot was well lit as she was afraid her roiling emotions might cause a stumble on the graveled pathway.

"Hi, all," she called, her lips wide with a smile that didn't reach her eyes.

"You're late, Caribou, you're late," grumble Ruthie. Come on, hurry. You're almost up."

Cara Bow quickly changed into her bowling shoes, took her blue ball from her bag and put it on the deck behind Belle's rainbow-colored ball. She sat on the bench, waiting for her turn. It had been a long time since she'd quit, but suddenly she craved a cigarette. Smoking was no longer permitted at the alley, but she remembered the haze of smoke that had formerly enveloped the atmosphere. Threads of the odor still could be smelled if one walked too closely to the walls and the cushions on the benches had never been updated. *Why did I think it was so bad?*

As she watched Kersey and then Belle pick up their strikes, she thought she was going to miss this bowling night. She looked over at the men's lanes and realized she hadn't seen Derek there for several weeks.

"Did I miss something, Ruthie?" she asked. "Where's Derek?"

"Have you been sleeping, Caribou? Derek got married! He's married. He and his wife moved to Green Bay. Everyone was surprised. Derek has been in every woman's panties in Cooperton for years. We all knew he was in yours, too, Caribou. We all knew."

Cara Bow failed to be taken aback by this statement. She felt no guilt. "Yours, too, I'll bet, Ruthie" she said. After a beat she asked, "Well, who was the lucky lady?"

"Would you believe it Caribou? Our town librarian. She got a job at the main library in Green Bay. Derek probably saw his chance to leave Cooperton for better pickings—and leave that damn book truck, too. I think he got a job at the Fox Valley paper mill. Funny, when you think about it, all those rolls of paper going into library books. Paper? Books? Get it? Get it?" Ruthie gave Caribou a playful punch in the arm.

Cara Bow was surprised by this bit of logical thinking. But then Ruthie saw life as it was and responded accordingly—no one messed with Ruthie.

"Okay, you're up, Caribou. Get us another strike, get us a strike."

Yes, I will get a strike, thought Cara Bow as she chalked her fingers before inserting them into the ball's three holes, swung the ball behind her and took the three running steps to the foul line, bent and let the ball fly. It did bounce once or twice on the way to its target, but ten pins fell as if by magic. *My new power,* she thought. *There's no turning back.*

An elated Cara Bow sat at the bar after their team took the game and ordered a boilermaker in a confident voice. *I've found my voice,* she thought. As a teenager, she remembered reading Dune and the character, she couldn't remember the name, who used *The Voice.* Now she knew what that was. A surge of determination surged through her body as she downed the drink.

Belle looked at her in surprise. "You usually take an hour to finish one drink, Caribou. What's got into you. Your strike?"

"Yes, the strike. I'm leaving you guys on a high note."

"I didn't know you were going anywhere."

"I'm getting a divorce, Belle. I'm leaving Cooperton. I'm leaving Kelwyn. He's making no protest. He'll never leave Cooperton." It seemed funny to be talking about Kelwyn as though he was already removed, cut off, lopped off, in a foreign place, non-existent.

"No way, Caribou," Kersey joined in. "Where are you going?"

"I'm going back to school, Kersey. My life was interrupted years ago. I've been marking time, running in place. Now it's time to start moving again"

"What about your folks? Cooperton has always been their home. Yours too, Caribou. And Polly, What about Polly? She's been having trouble in school, I heard. She hit my nephew with a bat. She said it was an accident—she didn't know he was standing behind her when she swung the bat," said Belle. "She apologized. She's a good kid, but my nephew had ten stitches in his forehead at the emergency room."

That was no accident, thought Cara Bow. "Polly's going to stay here," she said aloud. Kelwyn's insistent that Cooperton is the best place for raising her. I'll visit regularly," though she knew she wouldn't. "Donna Albert's always available for Polly when Kelwyn is away. She even has her own room next to Polly's if Kelwyn's gone overnight."

Kersey and Belle looked at one another knowingly. Cara Bow saw the look but didn't care. She ordered another boilermaker.

Ruthie came back from the other end of the bar where she had been back-slapping one of the guys on the men's' bowling team. She came in at the tail end of the conversation.

"Leaving us, Caribou? What about your job at the cheese plant? What about your job?"

"That's about to change, Ruthie. Maybe you've heard. Some Canadian company wants to buy the business. Mr. Santini is going back to Italy."

"We've heard the rumors. We're nervous about our jobs. We're nervous." Belle and Kersey nodded in agreement.

"I doubt there's anything to be anxious about, girls. Mr. Santini told me they're not shutting down the factory. They'll still need workers, and where will they find them? Forty, fifty miles away? No, your jobs are safe. Let's have another round, I'm buying."

The bartender turned up the volume on the radio. Country Music Awards was in its last hour and an air of harmony surrounded the crowd. A few of the guys asked Belle and Kersey to dance. The room seemed to move in slow motion as Cara Bow left her drink unfinished on the bar, got off the bar stool, tipping sideways just a bit as she left the Hotdog Bowling Alley for the last time. No one said goodbye or even noticed her departure.

CHAPTER

23

The drive home was harrowing. A rain storm started almost immediately after she left the Hotdog. She'd planned to take her time because of the boilermakers but the rain fell so heavily that the wipers on the Volvo could not keep up. Her headlights barely cut through a few feet in front of her. The ditches on either side of the road where the cheese factory had once dumped its whey were rapidly filling up and beginning to overflow the main road.

She saw a crossroad before a small bridge and decided to pull off and stop until the rain let up. She had never been on this road before. Instead of stopping she continued slowly on. The road cut through tall trees on either side and zig-zagged around several curves before coming to a dead end. Before her was a small house, wooden. The rain had become a drizzle. Her curious nature made her want to see the house closer.

She stepped from the car onto soft, muddy ground. She almost fell at the first footfall, but then steadied herself and slogged through the mud the short distance to the house. She used her cell phone flashlight to light the way. The first thing she noticed was the etched sign above the door. *Men Only—Log into #Kelwyn.*

This must be Kelwyn's hunting camp, she thought. It's smaller than I'd imagined. She tried the door handle; the handle was in the form of a single antler tine. The door was open. A switch near the side of the door lit up the entire interior. She was amazed. The room was fitted out to resemble Kelwyn's bedroom that she remembered seeing in the Keck's Chicago apartment. Shelves along one side of the room were filled with toy trucks, Ken dolls in soldier garb, GI Joe dolls, Superman and other action figure dolls, robots and robotic remote-control sport cars. It was a tweener boys dream play pen. *Had Kelwyn stopped at tweenerdom?*

On another wall was a gun rack holding several rifles. It looked as though Kelwyn hadn't been in the camp for a while. A spider had spun its web across the one window. She brushed it aside and was surprised that she could see the surrounding area. The switch by the door had evidently activated the flood lights around the camp. As she looked out, another pair of eyes looked in. It was a deer, *probably a male*, she thought when she noticed the small furry buds behind the ears. It was early spring. *Kelwyn's fall kill during the hunting season, when the deer's buds became antlers.* The deer was young, still sporting a few white spots on its coat.

Cara Bow and the deer locked eyes for several moments. He seemed to be trying to impart a warning to her. *Get out fast, Cara Bow, before your buds sprout to the kill stage.* She took the warning. *Yes, she would get out fast, out of the strange hunting camp, out of the moldy house, out of Cooperton.*

I'm still young, she thought. She was eager to begin her real life. The first thing she would do would be to reclaim her given name. *No more Mrs. Kelwyn Keck. Cara Bow Eden, once again.*

Still a little drunk, she took down one of the rifles from the rack and aimed it at the cot on the other side of the room. She pulled the trigger. The gun was loaded, and she fell back as the gun rebounded against her shoulder. She had never fired a gun before. The bullet pierced the pillow. The deer at the window gave a start at the sound and ran in fast graceful leaps back into the forest.

There you are Kelwyn, something to remember me by. She laughed aloud as she left the camp, stopping to run her hand up and down the wooden siding. *My great granddaddy's cooper* plant, she thought. She went back to her car thinking she would have to have the car cleaned from all the mud before leaving Cooperton.

Continuing on was easier because the rain had completely stopped. Her head lights picked up the glistening water reflections of the tree leaves. A hedgehog crossed her path one time and another time a baby rabbit.

Except for the faint snores coming from the basement, the house was quiet. Donna was sleeping over that night, so Polly would stay put. She fell quickly to sleep but was rudely awakened by a hard punch. It was Polly.

"Mother I was afraid of the lightning and thunder before when you were away. I want a drink of water. Donna won't wake up."

"You're big enough to get your own drink of water, Polly," Cara Bow mumbled in a sleepy voice. You know very well where the kitchen is."

"But it's dark, Mother, the lights went out."

So they had. Cara Bow reached for her cell and lit the way to the kitchen. Polly followed her. Cara Bow didn't see the foot stool that had been moved from its usual place. She tripped and began to fall forward but managed to stop the fall by grabbing on to the arm of the nearby couch. Her phone slid across the room in a loud clatter on the wooden floor. She heard Polly laugh in her hooty cackle. She turned to lash out at her, but Polly was gone. But for the phone light across the room everything was dark. She limped carefully across the room to the phone, picked it up, and shone it around the room. The picture of The Rock Art on the Gagham Mountain in Armenia on the fireplace mantle seemed to take on new menace as Cara Bow muttered "Damn Dakhonavar."

She winced as she fell into bed again. Her shoulder was stiff the next morning when she woke. She grabbed her robe and went into the bathroom for Tylenol. When she reached the kitchen, she was greeted by the sight of Kelwyn, Polly and Donna sitting at the table eating eggs and toast slathered with plum jelly.

"There's coffee on the counter, Caribou. You slept in this morning. Donna had to fix breakfast," complained Kelwyn.

"You'd better get used to it, Kelwyn, I'm leaving after the weekend. I've told you that several times."

Kelwyn ignored her remark and continued eating. Polly looked at her in mock sympathy when she saw Cara Bow wincing as she poured her coffee. "Will you be gone long, Mother?"

"Long enough, Polly Judy. You know your father and I are getting a divorce. Polly, do you know how the footstool got in the middle of the living room floor last night? I almost fell."

"Are you hurt? Probably it was Donna. We were playing hide-and-seek. She must have forgotten to put it back in place after our game."

Donna looked at Polly in surprise. "We weren't playing that game, Polly. We were working on the shoe box doll house for your history project."

"Donna, I said we were playing hide-and-seek. You seem to be mixing up your days. We did the shoe box thing two days ago. Tell her, Daddy."

Though he had no idea of what was being discussed, Kelwyn immediately said. "Polly's right, Donna, you forgot." A befuddled Donna rose from the table and began to clear the dishes away.

You've got a lot to learn, Donna baby, thought Cara Bow. She reflected briefly on the idea of leaving her some sort of warning note but thought better of it. Donna had made her bed, just as she had those years ago. *Had she really been captivated by this overweight, dense man? Had she been that gullible? Look at him, all flannelled up, ready for another day of fishing or hunting.*

"Have you been to your hunting camp, lately, Kelwyn? We had quite a storm last night. You probably didn't hear it from down stairs."

"The camp's fine, Caribou. It's weathered storms before, Why the sudden interest? Anyway, it's none of your business."

"You're right, Kelwyn, it's none of my business" After a pause she said, "Kelwyn, I'll be packing my things today. I picked up some boxes at the U-Haul. Small ones that will fit in the Volvo. You can throw out anything I leave behind."

"Where will you be staying, so I can send the divorce papers to be signed?"

"Send them to Alecia. I'll be staying with her and Tony for a while until I find my own place. I left her address on your pool table downstairs. Maybe I'll move into your mother's apartment. Alecia told me it hasn't been sold or rented yet. It's part of her estate you know. You wouldn't mind would you?"

"You can have that place, Caribou. I never want to go there again. I'll transfer ownership to you in the divorce settlement."

Cara Bow hadn't been serious when she mentioned staying at the Keck apartment, but the idea didn't seem too farfetched. It was in an expensive area and it had a great view of Lake Michigan. *I'd have to have an exorcism there first.*

It was a good question, though. *Where would she be living?*

CHAPTER

24

A s her chemistry texts took up a good bit of the car's trunk, she determined that only five small boxes would fit into her car. Four in the back seat and one on the passenger seat. She could put her overnight bag in with her texts. That was the first thing she packed.

No sooner had she started to put the boxes from the U-Haul together, than her cell rang. It was her mother.

"Cara Bow, our house was only listed yesterday with the Albert Cozy Home Realty Agency when two people made an offer. Right at this moment they're in a bidding war. Of course, we'll accept the highest offer."

"That's great, Mom."

"Cara Bow, your father and I are planning to move over the weekend to the Skylight Assisted Living in Green Bay. They have an opening and if we don't take it they'll give it to someone else. I need you to help us, Cara Bow. The house closing won't be for several days."

This would complicate Cara Bow's leaving date, but she couldn't let her parents down. She could hear the panic in her mother's voice.

"Mom of course I'll help. I'm on my way over." She thought quickly. Her own packing would have to wait. She decided to take her overnight bag—she had packed enough to tide her over for the next few days or however long it would take. *Just Be Kind*, she thought.

When she arrived at the Eden house she noticed the For-Sale sign had already had a sold sign pasted across the front of it.

"They sold it, Cara Bow, The Agency sold it! We accepted the offer. It was so fast."

"Relax, please Mom, the closing won't take place right away."

"You'll need to be here for the closing. Your father and I won't be here in Cooperton."

"Mom, I'll speak to the agent. I'm sure he can arrange to have the closing in Green Bay."

"Not a *he*, Cara Bow. A *she*, Laurie Albert. She's a new agent."

"Whatever, Mom, *she*, Laurie Albert. I'm sure Miss Albert will arrange for a Green Bay closing. Who bought your home?"

"A young couple from Green Bay. They have two small children. Laurie said they want to live in Cooperton. They think being out in a smaller town will be a better place to raise their children. I think the mother was an Albert girl." Judy was close to tears, thinking of leaving her home.

"You need to calm down, Mom. Where's Dad?"

"He's still upstairs. It takes him a long time to dress."

"Well, if we're going to be off today, I'll need to see to your things. What are you taking?"

"Harriet Albert agreed to come back for one last time. She packed most of our clothes and toiletries yesterday. We won't need much. Everything is provided at the Skylight—paper towels, toilet paper, bath towels, furnishings, all that stuff. I haven't been there, Cara Bow, but I saw the pictures of the place on line when I put in the application. It's a beautiful place. Oh, there is one thing. I'd like to take the clock on the mantel. It doesn't work but it was your Grandmas."

Cara Bow looked at the clock. It had a polished mahogany case and a gold metal strip around the stippled white face. The hands had pointed to twenty minutes past five o'clock as long as she could remember. As she lifted the clock from the mantel a key fell to the floor.

"Look, Mom. The key. Maybe it just needs to be wound."

"No, best leave it. That's the time someone dear to us died. It was around the time you were born. You didn't know him, but he meant a lot to your father and me."

"Ok, Mom, I'll be careful with it. I'll put it in the trunk. There's room for it with my books. They'll keep it from shifting as we drive. Now I'll check on Dad." Just as she said it she saw her father come down the staircase. He was still spry. He was wearing his golf sweater and cap.

"Norman, let's get going. Cara Bow can't wait all day. You look nice, Honey, so handsome," said Judy as she went to him and kissed his cheek.

That's what love must be like, thought Cara Bow. *I'd like to have that someday.* She and Judy took Norman's arm on either side as they went to the Volvo parked in the circular drive. Their bags were already in the car. Judy sat in the only space left in the back seat. Norman sat in the front passenger seat.

"Buckle up guys. We're off." Cara Bow was careful with the pickup on the gas pedal. She wanted everything to go smoothly.

"It's a good day for golf," said Norman, "It's not too hot."

Cara Bow had put the address of the Skylight Assisted Living Center on her Google GPS. No one said anything on the drive to Green Bay. The judge fell asleep and Judy was busy on her phone, texting friends.

The first thing Cara Bow saw as she drove up to the wide doors were the yellow daffodils—the first spring bulbs to bloom after the snow drops. There were still small patches of rotting snow, but the walks were well maintained. Rose bush plantings were on either side of the drive.

"We're here, Mom, Dad."

"It looks nice, doesn't it Norman? Like a fine hotel."

"Oh yes, the club house," said the judge. "Let's go in. I don't want to miss my tee-off time."

A porter came to unload their bags and then pointed Cara Bow to the parking area. "We can't have cars parked here for long. The van need this space. It comes several times a week to take the residents where they want to go. No one here has their own car. And there's the ambulance, too." She looked a little shaken as she mentioned an ambulance. Cara Bow gave her a reassuring hug.

Perfect, thought Cara Bow after she parked her car and walked into the spacious lobby area. The facility was well named. A skylight topped a small dome and bathed the area in a soft glow. Comfortable furnishings in soft upholstered yellows were placed around a fireplace and other areas featured seating in the same colors around small tables. Several shelves of books were in another area. A carrel with a computer was near the desk receiving area.

She went to the desk receptionist and asked, "Where are my parents, Mr. and Mrs. Eden.

They were supposed to wait for me here. I don't see them."

"They're already in their apartment, Mrs. Keck. Your father was tired, and your mother wanted to get him settled. I'll take you to them."

Cara Bow passed a large dining room as she followed her guide. It looked inviting with the tables for four set with a fresh flower vase in the center of each table. The cloths were of the same colors as those in the lobby area. The building had a circular hall and the attendant stopped at door #23. The names Judy and Norman Eden were post on a plaque alongside the door.

"I'll leave you now, Mrs. Keck. Please stop at the front desk before you leave. My name is Julia. You'll need to sign a few papers."

Cara Bow tapped lightly on the door and heard her mother call come in.

"Welcome to our home, Cara Bow. Isn't it pretty? Just like the pictures I saw on line. Look, we have our own backyard.

"It is lovely, Mom. I'm glad you and dad are here and safe. I promise to visit often. We'll still have our margarita lunches."

"I know you will Cara Bow, and we can visit on our phones. And the schedule of activities lists bridge three days a week. Your dad and I will be fine." She seemed intent on wanting Cara Bow to be reassured that all was good.

"Mom can I sleep in my old room tonight? It's awkward being in the same house with Kelwyn." She didn't mention Donna and Polly.

"Of course, dear. The house closers aren't coming until next Tuesday. Take anything you'd like before everything is sold or given to the Good Will store"

"Thanks, Mom. I still have my key. Say goodbye to Dad for me. I've got to get going."

On her way back through the circular hall, she noticed a bird sanctuary and she stopped a moment to gather her thoughts. There were many varieties of birds but only one canary. Hopping and pecking and flitting about, not able to escape from their glass enclosure. "Am I doing the right thing?" she mouthed to the canary. The canary sang its sweet song of approval.

She stopped at the desk and left her contact information with the attendant. The drive home in the Volvo was faster. Dark heavy clouds were ahead in the western sky and the rain began as she pulled up to the Eden house. The furnishings were still there. She saw the indentation in the easy chair where her father always sat with his morning paper. She decided to explore the house the next morning. She was exhausted. In what was once her bed, she fell into a heavy, dreamless sleep.

There was still coffee in the kitchen cupboard and after a strong cup, she started to look through the drawers. Most of the stuff in the drawers were piles of old bills and scribbled reminder notes. In the upstairs bathroom she smiled at the neatly organized shelves of her mother's cosmetics and compared it to her own one drawer at the Keck house, where there was a mess of little-used lipsticks and eye shadows. In her parents room the drawers had been emptied except for one drawer on the bedside table. A few small bottles of hand cream and a small album with a rose embossed on the leather cover. There was a picture of a new baby on the first page; the birth date was the same as her own. March 1st, the same year. The next page was one of her mother and father holding the baby. Baby Jeremy Eden at three weeks was the caption beneath. The rest of the album, only a few pages, was blank.

She was perplexed. *Who was this child? Had she had a brother? Was she a twin? She remembered her mother wanting the mantel clock, with the time frozen at twenty minutes past five o'clock. Had she been the undesired child to survive. Was this why her father had often pushed her into activities she hated? Soccer was the worst and of course her father's disappointment at her failed water skiing adventure.* Her thoughts whirled. She wanted to get back into the car and race to the Skylight Assisted Living Center in Green Bay then thought better of it. Her parents decision not to tell her about a brother would be let lie. She took the album with her as she left, but that was all.

She decided to visit the cemetery where her grandparents and great grandparents were buried in the family plot. The obelisk stone marker had begun to crumble at the base of the foundation. Yes, there it was—a tiny almost unreadable marker. *Baby Jeremy Eden. So, I was a twin. Twins seem to haunt me. The twin male fetus in the afterbirth when Polly was born. The twins across the road from my moldy house. Was Kelwyn a twin? No matter. Life was full of mysteries. All this will soon be in the past. I'm beginning a new life. The right life. A life interrupted. I'm on the correct path.* Her cell buzzed. It was Ginger.

CHAPTER 25

"Caribou, where are you?' Ginger's soft drawl was unusually fast.

"I'm in the car, Ginger. I'm on my way home."

"Pleeze, pleeze, you've got to get over here right now, Caribou. I'm very upset."

"I'm coming, I'm coming Ginger." *I'm beginning to talk like Ruthie,* she thought. *What could have happened to upset normally placid Ginger?* She turned the car in the direction of Lake Tioga from which she had just come. She hoped the meeting with Ginger wouldn't take too long as she still had errands to run and she wanted to be out of Cooperton on the next day, Monday. She passed the Presbyterian Church as she drove and saw Pastor Cornwall greeting parishioners as they left the church after the nine thirty services She hadn't been to the church since the previous Christmas day. There was the usual Nativity pageant, without Polly Judy, as she had been asked not to take part three Christmases before when she—by accident she insisted—managed to drop the star

172

she had been holding over the manger set in which a real baby was laid. The star tangled with the tiny lights on the plastic tree and the whole set began to collapse as if in slow motion, part of the set, the cardboard camel, fell on the baby before the Mary actor could stop it and the baby had to be taken by ambulance to the emergency room where its small arm had to be placed in a splint, as an X-ray showed the tiny arm bone was broken.

"I was supposed to be Mary, Mother." complained Polly as they drove home from the church. "They should have let me be Mary. Then my arm wouldn't have been so tired that the star I was holding fell. It was an accident, Daddy, wasn't it an accident?"

Kelwyn, who was always reluctant to attend church looked up from his phone where he was playing hearts and said, "Yes it was, baby. No more of these damn Christmas pageants."

"Yes, no more, Kelwyn. Mrs. Cornwall won't have her again. She said that to me as I was helping to clear up the manger mess in the sanctuary." That Christmas dinner at the Edens with the Cornwalls in attendance was especially quiet. And it was the last time the Cornwalls were invited to the same table with the Kecks.

Ginger was waiting for her at the door before Cara Bow had time to ring the *Dixie* tune doorbell. She looked disheveled and her face showed signs of having been crying. Louise was standing behind Ginger peering out from behind Gingers night robe.

"Gosh, Ginger, what's wrong. You don't look at all well." Louise began to cry.

"Louise, honey go into my bedroom. I have to talk to Mrs. Keck alone."

"Daddy's still asleep in there, Mommy," Louise blubbered through her tears. "I want to stay by you."

"That's okay, honey. He was out late last night—an emergency with a patient who had an abscessed tooth. Just curl up on the chaise. Pup-pup is in there. He'll keep you company." Pup-pup was their toy Pekingese. The Sandburgs also had a Pit Bull mix, Lorelei, who they kept caged when she was in the house.

"Ok, Mommy," her crying became less vocal as she went upstairs to her parents' bedroom.

"Ginger, what is this about?" Cara Bow asked when Louise was out of hearing. She was becoming alarmed. *Had someone died?*

"Oh, Caribou, honey. Come upstairs. I have to show you something in Louise's room."

The room was a masterpiece of wreckage. The bedding had been pulled to the floor. Clothes had been pulled from the sliding door closet, drawers were emptied, but most appalling were the many Barbie dolls. Their heads were twisted from their torsos and strewn randomly about.

"What ever happened, Ginger? Who did this?"

"Caribou, it was Polly. I don't know what got into her. Louise said Polly told her there was an ugly ghost somewhere in the room and they had to find it. I don't know why they had to destroy the dolls. Louise's Barbie collection was handed down to my mother from her grandmother and then it came to me. I thought it would be nice to keep them on the shelves in Louise's room. She's never played with them. She knew they were treasures."

Cara Bow didn't know how to respond. She knew it had been Polly showing her true colors. She took a shaky breath. "Why was Polly here, Ginger? I've been in Green Bay helping my parents get situated in their new place."

"Kelwyn called Lloyd yesterday and said Polly wanted to go to a sleepover here. I didn't know anything about it nor did Louise—but how could I say no? They're best friends."

"Didn't you hear anything. Ginger? It must have been quite a racket."

"No, our room is at the other end of the hall from Louise's. Lloyd got in late and I was already asleep. I'd taken an Ambien because I have a hard time falling asleep when Lloyd isn't here. And it was raining last night. The noise of the rain hitting the windows was so loud. Maybe that's why I didn't hear anything."

"I'm so sorry Ginger." *Why am I apologizing for Polly?* "Where is Polly now?"

"I called Kelwyn and he sent Donna Albert to pick her up at once. They left here shortly before you came. Polly was laughing and giggling in her funny way. You know how her lips protrude like a trumpet mouthpiece—oh, sorry, Caribou. That wasn't a criticism. It's kind of cute, you know?

"Can I speak to Louise, Ginger? I want to find out exactly what happened."

"I'll get her, Caribou, but you mustn't upset her anymore than she already is!"

"I'll be careful," said Cara Bow. *Just Be Kind*, she thought. *Yes, I will be kind.*

While Ginger was getting Louise, Cara Bow explored the room further. She noticed Ginger's saxophone case under the stripped bed. The case had been opened and it looked as though something had been poured into the instruments bell. She touched the liquid and the odor told her it was urine! She quickly picked up a cotton t-shirt from the messy clothing pile and wiped the horn dry as best she could. *Ginger must never know of this final insult.* She closed the case as she heard them coming along the hall.

"Honey, what happened?" said Cara Bow softly.

"I don't want to stay in this room, Mama," Louise said still clinging to Ginger's robe.

"Let's go downstairs, shall we?" We can talk there," said Ginger.

Sitting in the sunlit kitchen, it seemed to Cara Bow that what she had seen upstairs was a dream—a nightmare. Louise plunged right into the tale of the drama that had taken place the night before. It spilled from her in a non-stop gush of words.

"Polly came last night. Her daddy dropped her off. I didn't know she was coming, but maybe I forgot. Mama made us popcorn and we watched a movie, *The Little Mermaid* on Netflix and then Mama said it was time for bed and Polly didn't have any night clothes with her, so I said she could use a pair of my pajamas and then she began taking my things out of the closet and throwing them around and she said there was a ghost in my room, a dakabar or something like that. *The Dakhonavar,* thought Cara Bow. The stream of words from Louise

175

faded as she mentally cursed the supposed phantom....... "and then she pulled the sheets and blankets off the bed and she said the ghost was in the Barbie dolls, and she started to break off their heads and I was scared and said I was going to call Mama, but she smacked me and said she would pull off my head too if I left the room, so I ran into the closet and finally fell asleep there, and I don't know what else she did."

Cara Bow thought of the saxophone. There was a sudden silence as Louise, exhausted from the terrified recital of events, put her arms tightly around her mother's neck.

"She didn't touch my saxophone did she, Louise?" asked Ginger in a weary voice.

"I don't know, Mama. I think it's still under my bed."

"That's enough now, Louise. We'll put it behind you. I'll fix you some breakfast." Ginger automatically pulled the box of Cheerios from the cupboard and poured milk and cereal into the bowl painted with Ariel, The Little Mermaid.

Louise, having spilled every last word about the incident, seemed somewhat calmer as she began to eat the cereal and Ginger and Cara Bow left her with pup-pup. Ginger said, "Don't worry Louise, honey. After you finish breakfast we'll dress and go shopping for some new things."

The two women went into the rose wallpapered living room and sat across from one another on the matching patterned upholstered uncomfortable straight chairs. Both appeared to be shaken.

"They can't be friends, anymore, Caribou. Louise will have to get a new best friend. She's been talking lately about Susie Albert. They're in the same grade at school." Cara Bow started. *Could this have been the impetus for the wreckage? Had Polly resented another person coming between her and Louise* ? She knew Polly defended anything with a passion she claimed as hers. Cara Bow remembered the time when Polly was only four years old. Kelwyn had brought Cara Bow a gold compact for her birthday. He seldom remembered her birthday but that time he had brought the gift all the way from Disneyland. Polly screamed and said it should be hers, and she grabbed it from Cara Bow's hand and tried to smash it with her little foot on the floor. Cara Bow had laughed at the display of jealousy. Later the compact disappeared from her dressing table. But overriding all the little, often hurtful things was the terrible loss of Mewmew and the rabbits with their broken necks.

"Of course, they can't be friends, Ginger. Not after this. But Ginger, I hope this won't affect our friendship. Even though I'm leaving Cooperton."

"I know about the divorce, Caribou. I'll miss you a lot. And our Wednesday afternoon duets. I love to play my saxophone."

"I'm sure you'll keep it up, Ginger. You never know what opportunity will present itself. I read in the Press Gazette that someone from the university in Green Bay was starting a community band. It's not that far and I'm sure they will need saxophones. You could stop and see my parents, too, once in awhile at the Skylight Assisted Living Manor and let me know how they're doing."

Ginger's face began to light up. "I hope they have a jazz band, too, Caribou. I love to play jazz."

Cara Bow wondered how that would go. Not being that musical herself except for the little tunes she picked out from her John Thompson book and the easy medleys she played with Ginger on her out-of-tune piano, she still recognized that all was not exactly as musical as it should be.

"Yes, jazz, Ginger," she said. "You'll have a lot of fun. But getting back to Louise's' room I'll see to it that someone comes and cleans everything up. My mother's maid, Harriet Albert, is looking for another place. The bill is on me. I'm so deeply sorry about the Barbies. I'll look on line for a doll maker/repairer in the area. Maybe the heads can be restored to the bodies."

And what about my head, she thought, *will it stop spinning? How can I leave this place with the monster child at large?*

"I have to go now, Ginger. I hate goodbyes. I'll call you when I'm in Green Bay visiting my parents. We could meet there, you know."

"I'd like that Caribou. I don't know your folks very well, but I'd be glad to stop by."

"My dad's demented, so don't expect much from him. It's pretty sad. I don't think he even knows who I am or where he is half the time."

As she said this, Cara Bow brushed her hand against her purse where the small album was tucked in a side pocket. She had decided to get the truth about the baby, Jeremy, before her mother began to forget, too.

"That will be so good, Caribou. I sometimes wish I could leave, too. I miss Mississippi. The winters are so long and cold here, but I know Lloyd will never leave."

"Well, 'til we meet again then, Ginger. I love you."

"I love you, too, Caribou." The two women rose and moved to each other, embracing warmly. "Be off now, I've got to check on Louise. Lloyd will be up soon. He'll be furious about the room. He'll probably take his dental insurance out of Kelwyn's office."

"He should, Ginger. He should." She heard Ginger close the door quietly behind her as she left.

CHAPTER 26

S
he realized she was hungry as she left Ginger's and she pulled in to the McDonalds for a mango smoothie. Instead of the drive thru, she parked and went inside. She recognized the man who took her order. It was Louie, one of Ruthie's sons.

"Welcome to McDonalds, Mrs. Keck. What'll it be today?"

"I'd like the large mango smoothie, Louie. I didn't know you worked here."

"I'm the manager, Mrs. Keck," he said proudly. "Someone called in sick today so I'm working the counter—I started at the counter and worked my way up."

"The manager, Louie. That's wonderful. Congratulations. Your mom must be very proud." *High school baseball star to management at McDonalds. Quite a feat.* "And your brother, Martin, what's he doing?"

"He's working at the cheese factory. He drives the milk truck route every morning to pick up the fresh milk cans from the farmers. Some of the farmers have holding tanks, but the old timers still use the milk cans. He wants to be a semi driver and he's saving money to go to drivers school in Rhinelander. There's my mom sitting over there. You're orders coming right up."

Cara Bow took her smoothie and went over to join Ruthie who was finishing off her fries.

"Mind if I join you, Ruthie?' she asked.

"Sit down, sit down, Caribou. I didn't think I'd see you again after our last bowling might. You made that strike, remember? The girls are still talking about the way that blue ball bounced down the alley. They're still talking."

"Ruthie, I'm glad to see you alone. Your sons are doing so well. You must have done everything right. I don't know what to do about Polly. She's been acting out in awful ways." She didn't elaborate about what had happened at the Sandberg's. That news would travel fast enough. Nor did she say anything about the loss of her cat. It was too painful to say out loud.

"You worry too much, Caribou. Worry's a bad thing. A bad thing. You'll make yourself sick. Polly's just a kid. Kids do crazy stuff sometimes. She'll be better when she gets to Chicago. Different school and all that."

"She won't be with me, Ruthie. She wants to stay here with Kelwyn. That'll be hard for me, but I understand. She has so many friends here. *It won't be hard at all,* she thought. But she didn't want to be seen as an uncaring mother in Ruthie's eyes. I'll try to have her with me during summer vacations. *No, I never want her near me. She wants to kill me. She's a monster.* "Donna Albert will see to her needs. Polly likes Donna."

Cara Bow finished her smoothie and said, "I've got to go, Ruthie. Thanks for your encouraging words."

"No problem, no problem, now you take care, Caribou."

Caribou stopped at Walmart before returning to the Keck house. The Walmart was not a supercenter, but they still carried fabric. She needed a few pieces for her now sewing room in the basement. JoAnne Fabrics had closed their store in Cooperton two years before.

The Sunday Walmart crowd was its usual busy time, and she had to park some distance from the entrance. The Walmart greeter directed her to the fabric area. She saw several bolts of brightly printed cotton. On another table there were neatly folded pieces of fabric ends listed at one dollar a swatch. She selected several of them and then turned to the nearby Simplicity pattern catalogue and chose a few patterns for twelve-year old girls. Polly was eleven but big for her age. Thinking of dinner, she went to the fresh fruit section and got an orange, then went to the dairy section and chose a plain yoghurt. After checking out at the self-checkout, she hurried to her car. It had started raining again. She drove the familiar route to Kelwyn's house—across the railroad tracks where she had once wanted to be run over and finally turned into the long drive—past the quack grass lawn—where the overgrown grass had turned the lawn into a wild looking field.

It was past six o'clock and she had much packing to do. The past two days hadn't gone according to plan A. First her mother's call and the sudden move to Green Bay, then the album with the picture of an unknown Eden baby, then Ginger's call.

She was relatively calm when she went in the side door with her bundle of fabric. She could hear chattering from the kitchen, Kelwyn and Donna, she supposed. Polly was there, too. The remains of a pizza was in the center of the table.

"Caribou," said Kelwyn, "I didn't expect you back today. There's one piece of pizza left. Are you hungry?'

"No, Kelwyn. I have my food here" She held the brown bag from Walmart in front of his face. *As if he cares whether or not I'm hungry.* "Kelwyn, the grass needs cutting. Hasn't Mr. Olsen been here to take care of it?"

"I'll have to find someone else. Mr. Olsen said he was too busy to take on the job anymore. I don't know what's got into him. He's been avoiding me since the guy across the street was taken to the hospital. Caribou, Polly's been telling Donna and me about her friend Louise. She said Louise made a mess of her bedroom last night when she was there for a sleepover. Donna had to pick her up early this morning and Polly was very upset."

"Yes, Mother, it was awful. I'm not going to be friends with Louise anymore am I Daddy? You won't make me, will you Daddy? I don't like

Louise anymore. Donna can tell you. I was crying and standing outside when Donna came." She looked sideways briefly at Cara Bow with a triumphant crooked smile then turned her green eyes on Kelwyn.

"No more friends with Louise," said Kelwyn as he took the last slice of pizza. "Donna, bring me a beer, will you?"

An obedient Donna went to the refrigerator and took out a Coors. She took one for herself, too. Donna and Kelwyn snapped back the top of their cans in sync.

Look at them, thought Cara Bow. *This house festers with an aging agent.* Kelwyn's hair was now in little wisps—he was at last wearing suspenders, *and Donna, poor Donna is caught in Polly's web.*

As if on cue Polly said in her honky commanding voice, "Come on, Donna, I want to play our Star Wars game. Right now. I want to play now."

Donna reluctantly left the kitchen with Polly. Polly was slapping on Donna's rump as they went, like a mule driver slapping his mule. *Her turn now*, thought Cara Bow.

"I'm going to get my things, Kelwyn. I won't be sleeping here tonight."

"Good riddance," said Kelwyn as he finished his beer. "Get me another one will you Caribou?"

"Get your own beer, Kelwyn. This slave is declaring freedom."

She headed for the basement with the fabric. She closed the door, sat in her *sewing room* and ate her orange and yoghurt. She left the orange peel on the floor. She heard the back door open and Dr. Boren calling, "Let's get the game started, Kelwyn. Owen Albert is on the way."

She passed Dr. Boren as she went back up the basement stairs. They didn't greet one another. *I'm already a ghost to him*, she thought. In her bedroom she noticed that the clothes she had neatly piled on the bed were now strewn about. *Polly*, she thought. *Well this is the end of it.* She began to put the boxes from U-Haul together. She could hear Polly and Donna making bang-bang noises as they played their Star Wars game.

CHAPTER 27

She's going, thought Kelwyn. *This whole thing was a mistake from the beginning. Her and her snooty ways. And her mother and father. I'll be glad to be rid of them, too. Polly doesn't like them either. Some grandparents.*

He started downstairs to join Dr. Boren.

Dr. Boren is happy here in Cooperton—all the hunting and fishing and his wife doesn't care one bit. She's got her quilting clubs and canasta clubs and all that stuff she does at the church. A regular church lady—making those flower decorations and hanging banners and putting out the coffee and cookies after services. She probably thinks the place would fall apart without her. I think she's got her eye on Pastor Cornwall, too.... Why couldn't Caribou be contented here like Mrs. Boren.

Things will be better around here without Caribou sticking her nose in. I'll be able to sleep upstairs and have my pipes on the mantel. Donna doesn't mind. She never says much. Her and her tattoos. Now she has a bunch of spiders crawling up on one leg all the way to her big butt. What do I care. She wants Polly to get a tattoo, too.

On her neck, too. Just a little garden snake. She hasn't said anything to Polly about getting one. I put my foot down on that idea. No tattoos until she's sixteen. With Caribou gone, I can show Polly and Donna what a great dad I am. Donna had better not interfere. So far Polly hasn't said anything bad about Donna, but Donna had better realize she's replaceable.

There's a lot of women after me in this town. Just last week Dorrie Albert came into the office to get car insurance, and she was making eyes at me. Dorrie. She a cutie— underage—but I looked at her application and saw that she'll be eighteen next month. I'm a real catch—college grad, business owner, house owner and not that old. Good looking, too. Yes, Donna better be careful.

Doctor Boren says I need to go on a diet, I need to lose at least one-hundred pounds. He's a fine one to talk. He's got quite a gut himself. I like my gut. It's a real man's gut. I'm not a girl, not a girl, not a girl.

Mother once told me I was a twin. There was a twin sister who didn't make it. Her heart was outside her body, she said—something like that. She's buried in one of Mother's cemeteries. My cemeteries now, I guess. I'll have to put Darla in the office in charge of that.

Darla wants me to hire someone else on. She said she can't keep up with the incoming clients. Now with the cemetery stuff, I'll have to consider that. Maybe someone part time. No one wants to work these days. The Terzians are gone—Gore was a good worker I'm told but those Alberts, except for Darla, and now she wants me to put on someone else.

I wish Uncle Ulrich was still alive. He'd know what to do. He had that accounting business. I wonder what became of that when he retired and moved in with Mother. Twins, together 'til the last. I heard they slept in the same bed. That's not surprising, I guess. Twins are like that. I wonder what my twin would have been like. A girl. Then I wouldn't have had to wear those damn dresses. Wait a minute—a girl. She would have gotten the trust money. Where would I be? Now its mine. It's damn good she died, and I had Polly.

I suppose the money will go to Polly when she turns twenty-one. I think the trust lawyer said something like that. But I know my Polly. She'll take *care of her old man. We're a team. Caribou might have liked to be part of the team and she could have if she'd been nicer to me and Polly.*

Polly this and Polly that. Always complaining about Polly from the very beginning. I never understood it. And me too. Kelwyn this and Kelwyn that. "Kelwyn, you snore—Kelwyn, for God's sake shave, get rid of the scraggly beard—Kelwyn shower more than once a week—Kelwyn you're getting too fat."

Fat, am I? She doesn't know what fat is. I've seen some of those people at the Walmart in those riding cars. Now that's fat. I'm just manly, that's all.

Now Donna's fat, but I like fat girls. Caribou is too skinny. Eating her yoghurt. She won't touch a piece of bacon. All that white chicken with no skin on it. And that kale. Well, now I'll have a decent refrigerator. A man's refrigerator. Donna likes the same stuff I do. Tacos and pizza and brats. She fries up a good pork chop, too. Sometimes I'll take her to my rib place in Green Bay if she behaves. She'll love it.

Caribou's giving me everything in the divorce settlement—even the profit she gets when they sell the whey plant. That was one good deal she made. The whey plant. Half owner with that Italian, Giulio. Gor told me that she and Giulio used to go at it. I'm not surprised. She sure wasn't giving me anything. I heard he was going back to Italy. He's got a wife over there. Imagine that! I wonder if Caribou knew about it. I think there was some other guy too, on those bowling nights. That doesn't matter to me. She was easy to please when I first met her. She gave me Polly. I'll always be grateful for that. I told my lawyer to deed her my mother's place in Chicago. That's a nice thank you. It's in the Gold Coast, too.

Well I wish her the best. God knows, I've tried. She never understood me. I hated that place in Chicago ever since my dad died. I never want to see it again. I like it here in Cooperton. Just last week I caught a whole mess of smelt. They were running on the Peshtigo river. Caribou wouldn't cook 'em though. Mrs. Olsen came and fried 'em up. I must have eaten at least fifty, heads and all. Polly had her share, too. Then there was Caribou with the damn kale. Well, to each his own, I guess.

"Coming, Doctor Boren. Here's Owen, too. I'll cut the deck."

CHAPTER

28

"I *can't stay here tonight. I'm afraid, afraid of my own child.* Cara Bow had finished packing her few things into the five boxes. Some of clothing she left because they had been cut with a scissors or knife. *Polly.* All was quiet now except for a Law and Order program Donna and Polly were watching in the living room and the faint murmur of voices from below. The lights were low except for the glow from the television that was reflected in the leaded glass of the windows.

She began to take the boxes out one at a time to the Volvo. She cut through a back bedroom, so she wouldn't have to see Polly again. *Poor Donna*, she thought again, as she heard Donna cry out. *Polly must have done something to her.* After the boxes were in the car she decided to drive back to her parents' house for the night and then leave early the next morning for Chicago. *My last night in Cooperton, in my childhood home, on Tioga Lake.* Her bedroom in the Eden house looked over the lake, but only faint gleams reflected from a quarter moon revealed the presence of the water. She stood looking out her window and thought she saw a small light coming from one of the cottages across the lake. She felt the sense of peace envelope her again as she looked out. *Who lives there*, she wondered? *Someone good*, she supposed, *maybe giving her a signal that it was all right to be leaving Cooperton.* The light quavered a few times and then went out. *Cara Bow Eden. That's who I am again. A grown-up Cara Bow.*

She turned back the cover on her bed and suddenly remembered she had once shared it with Kelwyn during the time before Kelwyn had insisted on buying the mold house—that's how she thought of it—a mold house. Mold that crept into the skin and began a terrible aging process. Kelwyn had absorbed the bulk of it. Kelwyn, the troll, spending all that time in the basement. And she had been affected by it too, turning her will into mush. Only her time at the cheese factory, and the girls—Ruthie, Ginger— their utter innocence had kept her from completely giving in to the house's spell.

And Polly—was the evil in the house now concentrated in her daughter's body? Certainly, there was evil. Mewmew, Louise, the rabbits and who knew what else. Her mother must have felt it, too but she could only express it with off hand remarks over their margaritas—"How's the slouch"—"There's something wrong with that child, always crying."

Cara Bow decided to sleep in her parents room that night. She found a few bottles of pills left in the medicine cabinet. An Ambien. She took one and fell almost immediately to sleep. This time she dreamed. There was a baby in the dream, smiling, its little arms and legs waving about—happy. And there was another figure in the dream, a man crying. She tried to recall the dream when she woke the next morning, but it was already frizzling away. *Nine o'clock.* She had overslept.

"Caribou are you on the way?" It was Alecia on her phone.

"I'll be later than I thought, Alecia. I overslept. I'm in my parents house right now and there's someone at the door. I'll have to call you back."

"We're the Groves, Mrs. Keck. Your folks hired us to close the house. People won't be coming through until tomorrow, but we'll have to get everything in order—priced to sell. We'll be here all day. People like to get in early for the best things. I imagine there'll be a lot of folks—the Edens have been here for years. They've been town leaders, we were told. Mr. Eden was a judge?"

The Groves were an innocuous looking couple They stood outside the front door looking hesitant, not expecting to find anyone there. But they had rung the doorbell to be sure.

"Your mother mailed us the key. I have her permission letter here. We drove over from Green Bay," said Mr. Groves.

Not Alberts, thought Cara Bow. *That's refreshing.* She read the letter and recognized her mother's handwriting. "Come in Mr. and Mrs. Groves. I won't be here long." *This was it then. The house is really sold, about to be emptied.* Since her parents had left all the furnishings the house had still been a home to her. *Will anyone remember that the Edens had once lived here in Cooperton?*

"Well, you can get started then. I'll just take a quick shower and grab a cup of coffee before I go." Her brain was in a spin. *Was she really leaving Cooperton? Would she ever return?* She thought not.

But there were still some things she had to take care of before leaving. While sitting in the kitchen with her coffee—she had used an instant coffee bag—she called Alecia.

"Sorry about before Alecia. The house closers are here. Mother didn't mention that they were coming before tomorrow."

"I understand, Caribou," said Alecia.

"There's another thing, Alecia. I'd like to stop being called Caribou. I'm going to answer to Cara from now on. Cara Eden. No middle name either. Just an initial if I need one on applications. I've already sent an application to three colleges in the Chicago area."

"Ok, Cara it is," she laughed. Tony says your job in the crime lab is in the bag. How long will you be staying with us, Cara?" She laughed again.

"I'm serious, Alecia. If I'm putting you out by staying with you, I can go to a hotel. You did offer once." Cara Bow was surprised by Alecia's sudden seeming reluctance.

"Kelwyn gave me the Keck place on Michigan in our divorce settlement. I'd by crazy not to take it. I guess I will. At least until I sell it. I'll need to rent some furniture for the time being. Can you get me the numbers for some local home stagers?"

"I checked on the apartment last week, Cara Bo…, I mean Cara. It's been cleaned and emptied. I don't know why you wouldn't want to stay there. It's prime real estate—the Gold Coast and on Lake Michigan."

"Too many memories," said Cara Bow. "Too many memories." *Ruthie again. I'm going to miss that lady.*

"I'll have to cut out now, Cara. I'm at work and I see my boss coming in. Drive careful. Tony and I will see you later tonight then."

Cara Bow gazed across Lake Tioga. The two cottages, partly hidden by the spring foliage, showed no sign of inhabitants. The light from the previous night puzzled her but that would have to remain another unsolved mystery. There was the one other important errand to see to before heading for Chicago—and her people. She hoped they were her people, Alecia and Tony and their friends. She knew she couldn't count on it but if things didn't work out she would find her niche. Perhaps at school. That was where she had met Alecia. She was at last at the end of what seemed to her, looking back, a peripatetic existence. A rootless purgatory.

She headed in the Volvo for the Keck house. The first thing she noticed was that Donna Albert's pick-up was not in the drive. She must have taken Polly to school. She knew Polly didn't take the school bus often anymore. The bus driver made her sit alone in the front seat. She had complained to Cara Bow that Polly was a troublemaker and she wanted her close by. None of the other kids would sit next to her. *Don't have her too close*, thought Cara Bow at the time.

The side door was unlocked. The landline was ringing when she entered but she didn't answer. Hesitantly, she began to walk from room to room. She observed the still black and white uncleanable asphalt tiles in the dining room and could still smell the familiar moldy odor from the oak side cupboard. Kelwyn had already moved his pipe rack and tobacco canisters to the living room mantel. Next to the mountain picture on the mantel he had also mounted the stuffed body of a great white owl. The feathers looked tired and a closer look revealed tiny black insects nestled among the feathers.

She checked Polly's room and saw the two mice she liked to have running up and down her arm in their cage. She'd let them live. *Maybe they're related on some level.* The room next to Polly's where Donna usually slept was absent of the usual clothing she kept in the closet. Missing too, was her array of makeup and hair sprays and the cheap perfume she kept on her end table. Cara Bow recalled the missing truck. *Had something happened that broke her tolerance for Polly's antics?* She saw a scrap of paper left on Donna's pillow. *Polly put a mouse in my bed,* she had written in her barely readable cursive scrawl. *I quit, Kelwyn. I'm not coming back!*

So now just Kelwyn and Polly in the house. Polly would have to ride the bus again if Kelwyn wouldn't drop her at school. Word spread rapidly among the Alberts. Who would want to be part of the unholy duo? Not Mrs. Olsen. The Terzians were gone. Well that's no longer my problem. I've broken out of their bubble and the bubble has closed—sealed again. Closed the two of them in. It was easier than I'd thought. Why did I wait so long? Was it my parents moving? Was it Giulio going back to Italy? Was it Derek getting married? Yes, all of that, she thought and something more, too. She at last felt grown up. She was going to catch up with Alecia, with all the girls in her sorority whom she read about in the yearly sorority magazine, listing their marriages, careers, travels. *I have a lot of catching up to do. Twelve years behind, on the wrong road.*

Off the kitchen, there was another door leading to the attic. She had opened it on occasion but never ventured up the steps. The musty draft wafting from above had put her off. But now, she decided to brave the demons and go up. *I'm going to see everything that exists or doesn't exist in this hated house.* The steps were worn and creaky. At the top were bare floor boards, all loose so she had to step carefully. There was only dim light that came in to the space from the owl window—no sign of a switch or bulb, so she used her phone flashlight.

She scanned the area slowly. There were a few broken lamps on the floor and a table missing one leg. One area of the attic in a far corner was cloaked in stygian darkness. She could just make out a small stool. She made her way carefully to the area. Yes, it was a stool tipped on its side. She shone the light up toward the roof beams and saw a row of bats hanging from the rafter. And a rope. The rope was over the rafter and hung over the stool, a noose at the end of the rope. She shivered. *Who had died here? Who was so desperate to escape the house and whoever lived here before the Kecks? Why was the realtor so anxious to sell the house to Kelwyn so cheaply? Stop thinking these things.* She squeezed her brain into submission. She stumbled over one of loose boards and fell on one knee as she headed for the stairs. On the floorboard she found one of Polly's barrettes. The light from the window shone through the dust that had arisen as a result of her fall. She coughed repeatedly as she rose and made her way quickly to the staircase and almost ran down the steps.

She closed the door at the bottom and then made her way to the basement. Her new sewing room was a picture of innocence. The sewing machine, the patterns, the fabrics, and the two shelves of plum jelly. "Goodbye, little room," she said aloud. You have your work cut out for you. She went back upstairs and took a last look at what had been her prison for the past years. *Time to go.* She left by the never used front door. The swallows had returned but they did not go through their usual swooping threat as Cara Bow headed for the plum trees that were already in blossom. She took the extra set of house keys from her purse and placed them in the tall grass between the two trees. "Goodbye, Mewmew," she said. This place is all yours now."

As she headed back the drive to the main road, she noticed an official looking car in front of the two old brothers place. She stopped and asked the driver what he was doing there. We got word from my boss at Social Services that we were to do a house check on the Becker place every day. Emil's home from the hospital and I guess he's doing pretty good. Fred had a fall a few days ago but he's all right, too. The town provided him with a walker. Robbie Alberts inside right now. Cara Bow decided to park and way goodbye to Fred and Emil. She knocked, and Robbie let her in.

"Hi, Mr. Albert. Just thought I'd stop to see my neighbors."

"Come in, Mrs. Keck. Fred was asking about you. He wanted to thank you for the other day."

Fred was in the kitchen with his walker nearby, fixing a cup of tea. "The tea's for Emil," he gestured toward the bedroom. "He has to rest up for a few more days."

Cara Bow left him to his task. "He's not much of a talker, is he?" she said to Robbie. "I'm glad you're seeing to their welfare."

"Glad to, Mrs. Keck. A lot of folks have been helping. Casseroles and stuff like that. Mr. Olsen brought a couple of rabbits for the hutch in back. I don't know what happened to the other ones. I guess they ran away. Emil likes rabbits."

"I'm so glad the men are being looked after. I'm leaving town, Robbie, but I'll keep in touch with you." She probably wouldn't but she wanted to keep him on his toes. "You're a good man, Robbie."

"Goodbye, Fred." She walked over to give him a hug, but then thought better of it and patted him on the shoulder. She gave Robbie the hug instead. Robbie looked pleased and his lips turned up in a half smile.

CHAPTER 29

F *ree, free, free.* She drove with the windows down on the Volvo and felt the wind in her hair as if it agreed with her parting and was helping to push the car even faster. Red lights flashed behind her and she pulled over and stopped in a turnaround as the police vehicle pulled up behind her. She hadn't yet reached Highway 43 South.

"License and registration please, Maam," the young officer said. He was holding an official looking pad in his hand.

Cara Bow reached in the glove compartment for her registration. She felt a sudden jab in her hand as she did so. A jackknife with the blade open was on top of the folder with the necessary document. She stifled an ouch. *Polly, getting in her last goodbye.* She handed the registration along with her drivers license to the officer.

"Looks like you've cut yourself, Maam," said the officer when he noticed the spot of blood on the registration."

"One of those dang paper cuts officer. The bleedings stopped already." *Not a good start.*

"Maam, you were ten miles over the limit. It's fifty-five here. You have to be careful. A car hit a deer on this road just last week."

Cara Bow gave the officer her best smile. "I'm sorry, officer. Sometimes this car has too much pick-up and I don't realize how fast I'm traveling. I promise to be more careful."

"I'll let you go with a warning this time, Missus. You're not far from 43. The limit's 70 then. Careful on this stretch when you return."

"I sure will, Officer. Thank you." *I'll never be on this road again.*

Her finger was beginning to bleed again. The knife blade had been sharp. She felt every muscle in her body relax when she reached US Highway 43. She took the first exit south and stopped at a McDonalds to wash her hand and wrap her finger with a paper towel. Looking into the glass over water wet sink she saw a new Cara Bow. A free Cara Bow. She smiled. *I would purr if I were Mewmew,* she thought. She ordered a mango smoothie and started south again on US Highway 43 leading to Milwaukee that would merge onto Highway 94 to Chicago. As she neared Fond du Lac she decided to pull off thinking maybe Mr. Thibidot was still around. She had liked talking to him and was disappointed to find another man in the grey stone building at the entrance.

"Where's Mr. Thibidot?" she asked.

"He's buried over there by the tracks, Missus. He died last year. I'm his son."

"You're his son?" Then she recalled the notice she had received about his passing. "I'm sorry Mr. Thibidot. Will you be taking over for him?"

"You can call me Benny, Missus. My dad mentioned that you'd stopped by one time before. He said you were nice to him."

"He was a good man, Benny. I'm glad you're taking over for him. You should know that Mr. Kelwyn Keck will see to things now that his mother is gone."

"I guess you didn't know, Missus. The town sees to things now that the place is full. There's just a space left by my father's grave for my mom and me. That was promised to us."

"I'm glad, Benny. Well I'm just going to walk around for a bit and then I'll be off."

She looked at her phone and saw that it was almost three o'clock. As she neared Doctor Keck's marker, the sun had already begun to cast its shadow across the tombstones. It was not yet summer daylight savings time. "Well, goodbye, Dr. Keck," she said as she placed a few flowers at his headstone that she had picked from another gravesite. "Everyone here is dead and I'm sure they don't mind sharing." She laughed as she walked back to the Volvo.

CHAPTER 30

She felt increasingly liberated as she continued to drive South. Most of the trees had opened their buds along the way. Spring green. That special green that only lasted a little while until the dense summer foliage takes over creating the stacked layers of dark green one couldn't penetrate with the eye. She kept tilting her head back looking in the rear-view mirror to see if she was really there. The past was becoming a distant cobbled, swirling dark grey. She was in the moment. She glanced to her left and saw the silver birches turning in the wind, their silvery narrow leaves reflecting a rosy glow. *Friendly,* she thought. *Nature is friendlier here.* She tried to find words for the freedom she felt but couldn't. Then she remembered the words from a song she had downloaded to her car CD player. She turned it on and began to sing along with the tune. *It's All Right.* Her singing was tuneless, but her uncertain ear, fostered by the years of piano playing on her never tuned piano and playing along with Ginger's loud stuttering saxophone, inured her to the dissonance between the soothing voice on the CD and her own tone-deaf singing. *It's All Right.*

Milwaukee came into view and the GPS warned her to keep left for the merge onto highway 94. She passed the Italianate steeple clock with the green roof and the American flag high above, flying in the south wind. The clock's time matched her car's clock on the instrument panel. Four thirty. *This clock keeps up with the times,* she thought, *not like my parents' mantle clock—stuck at twenty minutes past the five o'clock hour—the hour her twin brother had died. Was it in the morning or the afternoon?* She now felt certain it had been her brother. *No need to question mother,* she resolved again. *No need to bring up what must have been a terrible sorrow for Judy and Norman.* She wondered what he would have looked like. She only had the few pictures in the small album she carried in her overnight bag. His face could barely be seen, cradled in Norman's arms. *A baby, looking like every other baby. Why were there no baby pictures of me?*

Highway 94 was slow going. The beginning of rush hour traffic. She'd almost missed the turn-off from Highway 43. She would have gone straight off north again to Madison—the moving forward happy days in her life—until Kelwyn.

She breathed slowly until her thoughts came back to the moment and the song that was still repeating itself on the CD player. *It's All Right.*

She pulled off at an exit with the McDonald empty yellow eyes for another mango smoothie and a grilled chicken sandwich. While she ate, she went to Google maps and put Alecia's address into the search engine. North Dayton was the street name.

There were three highway tolls as she drove at last in Illinois. Six Flags—Gurnee Shopping Mall. She took the Edens expressway exit to downtown Chicago. Though it was spring, the winter sun still held sway and twilight now covered the busy area. *Not much further,* she thought, *another nine miles.* But it was another hour before she covered the miles because of the now even busier rush hour traffic. This is not something I want to be part of everyday, she thought, remembering the three or four miles she drove around Cooperton and the thirty-mile drive to Green

Bay on lightly trafficked road.—a drive that could actually be done in thirty minutes. She'd mentioned the traffic problem to Alecia in one of their frequent telephone exchanges.

"Tony and I don't have a car," she'd said. We're only a short walking distance from every sort of public transportation here from Lincoln Park to the downtown loop. If we need a car, we call Zipcar. We only keep our bikes in the garage. It's a one car, but there's room for you to park there when you come.

So, no car. No Volvo. Another reminder of the past—gone. At last Alecia's address was spotted. The house was on a corner lot. It was a sort of funky looking place. She couldn't determine the style of architecture. Three stories high. She drove around the corner to the garage entrance. The garage door was open. After maneuvering her car in—she had to get out of the car first and move the two bikes to one side as they were on their stands right in the center.

She went through a short breezeway to the back door. There was another door open to the backyard of the house and she heard voices coming from that direction, so she went through the open door to a lovely landscaped outdoor seating area. Alecia and Tony were seated near a smoldering fire pit.

"Cara," she cried. "You made it. I've been practicing you name. Come on we've saved a chair for you." There were at least six chairs around the fire pit.

"We're expecting friends over this evening. They want to meet you. Tony, fix Cara a Mohito, will you, please" Tony obliged and handed the cold drink from the well-stocked bar to Cara Bow.

"Hi Cara," he said as he gave her a light peck on the cheek. I haven't seen you since our wedding. It's been quite a while. Six years. You haven't changed much. Getting prettier." Alecia gave him a funny look.

"Alecia, I'm so tired. It's been an exhausting day. Do you mind my skipping your party?"

"Oh, no Cara. What was I thinking? Have you had anything to eat?"

"Yes, I had something not too long ago on the road."

"Finish your drink then and I'll take you to our guest room. We'll talk in the morning. I have the day off from the museum. Do you want Tony to carry your bags for you?"

"It's just the one bag, Alecia. My overnight bag. That will carry me through the next few days. I have some boxes in the car, so I closed the garage door. I'm not sure how safe it is in this area."

"The neighbors have had a few UPS packages taken every so often. We have our packages sent to Tony's office. He picks up our mail from a safety deposit box at the downtown post office once a week."

They went in the back door through a laundry mud room and into the kitchen.

"How about a cup of chamomile tea and a peanut butter cookie. That will help you sleep."

"Sleep will not be a problem, Alecia. The mojito has done the trick. Love your kitchen, by the way." Cara Bow had redone her kitchen in Cooperton but in comparison to the modern design before her, the Keck kitchen was a design failure, swallowed up in the miasma of the mold smell from the dining room. The Banya kitchen had no upper cabinets. Just glass shelves on either side of the galley style kitchen. They were filled with the latest gadgets. The bottom cabinets had a beautiful copper top with wooden cutting boards skillfully inserted. A skylight cut through to the top floor illuminated the entire scene.

"I'm glad you approve, Cara. Our designer says it's the latest European kitchen style."

"Wow, you must love to cook in this space, Alecia."

"I don't do much cooking," said Alecia, a bit sheepishly. "It's for show, you know. Most of our dinners come from the microwave or we order in or eat out."

Cara Bow thought of the stacks of plastic fast food empty containers in the Keck kitchen. Her house keeping skills had never improved. *I'll have to get a housekeeper in my new place*, she decided then and there. I'm going to be busy with my new job and taking courses at school, plus I want to have some fun. She had to give Kelwyn credit for not complaining about the mess, but he and Polly were after all the main cause of it.

"Let's get you settled, Cara." She almost added Bow but caught herself in time. "You look dead on your feet. I'm afraid the guest room is on the third floor Can you make it?" she laughed.

The third-floor bedroom at the top of the house was really a converted attic. Beautifully appointed. The A-frame ceiling gave it a welcoming feel—like an embrace. Her first move would be a good soak in the square tub with soothing jets. She was reminded of her first trip to Cooperton with Kelwyn and the warm bath her mother had prepared for her.

Sleep, sleep, sleep. The last thing that drifted through her brain before falling off was the image of the basement sewing room, once a laboratory that had been her salvation during the long years as Mrs. Kelwyn Keck and the mother of Polly Judy. It was empty now but for the little-used sewing machine, the material she had purchased at Walmart, and the few patterns. Emptied of all else except for the two shelves of plum jelly glowing with promise from the light of the one small window. She had left the door to her retreat unlocked. *Just Be Kind,* she thought as she fell into a deep dreamless slumber.

CHAPTER

31

Sitting out here on Lake Tioga in my Ranger—there's my boat trailer on the boat launching pad—I have time to think. The Walleye are biting. "Ho, there's another one". They're going after the minnows. I really love fishing. Why couldn't Caribou understand that?

She's gone at last. It's just me and Polly now. Polly seems happy and so am I, I guess. That Polly. In my ashtray this morning I found a clay doll with pins sticking in it in every part of the body. Where does she get these ideas?

It never felt right with Caribou. It was always Kelwyn this and Kelwyn that. She thought she was smarter than me, but she never said it. I could tell. Nothing I did pleased her. I'm glad Mother and Uncle Ulrich weren't alive to see us getting divorced. I think she sort of liked Caribou. Although, she probably would have divorced Dad if he hadn't died so suddenly. They were always arguing about something, mostly about me.

"You've got to get him out of those dresses, Elsie. His kindergarten teacher called my office at the hospital the other day and said kids were making fun of him. She said you hung up on her." I can't remember how that ended but Dad did get me a haircut. Mother saved my curls in a small box. I found the box in her bureau drawer one day when I was looking for some cash. Well, I've plenty of cash now. Plenty of it. The money from the whey plant sale, the house with no mortgage, and best of all my trust money. I'll be glad when the divorce is final. December my attorney says. Caribou's got Mom's apartment—true I hated that place after Dad died—and the cemeteries. They're mine, too. Darla Albert can handle that business. I'll really have to get her another girl in the office and give her another raise, too. Well, I can afford it.

I don't know why Donna up and left. We were good together. Caribou said I was too rough during sex. Donna didn't care—she liked it that way. At least she had a little meat on her bones. I never saw anyone as skinny as Caribou. Even after Polly was born. Three months of yogurt, orange slices and rice cakes and she was bonier than ever. The Alberts, now, know how to eat. That's for sure. I'll have to try and get Donna back, at least over summer. It'll be a problem once school is out. No Mrs. Olsen or Milena. I might have to hire someone from Rhinelander or Green Bay. Polly says she doesn't need anyone, but I don't want any of those county Social Workers butting in. Maybe there's some summer camp. I'll get Darla to look around for me.

When I return home, there's some county person across the way almost every day at the two old guys' shack. They'd probably like to see what's going on over here now that Caribou's gone. Probably looking to pin child abandonment on me. A lot of people are probably jealous of me because of my successful insurance business—being an outsider and all that. Darla seldom pays out. She's smart at finding ways to make the other guy responsible for a house fire or accident, so the new agency across the street has to pay up.

I'll have to do something about the grass. And that damn sign, Just Be Kind. Mr. Olsen says he's too busy, but he's not too busy to stop across the street and clean the old guys rabbit hutch. Who knew they had rabbits? I'll probably have to hire the Albert Flower Power service to do the work around the place. They already took care of the landscaping around the office. It's pretty nice. The swallows are back building their damn nests, so I suppose the wasps will be next. Caribou hated those swallows. The plum trees are *in bloom. No plum jelly this year, I guess. The tree blossoms are all falling to just one spot between them.*

That Polly, sometimes she acts out a little too much but so did I at her age. She's more like me than Caribou. She has Caribou's lips, though maybe they're a little more pronounced. Caribou called them beaks. "Shut your beak," she would yell at her. That Polly, when she wants to do something, she does it.

Only two more months of school and Polly's out for the summer. She's having a rough time. She went after Ruthie's youngest kid Billy during recess with a baseball bat two days ago. She said he was a bad pitcher and she struck out every time she was up because he deliberately threw grounders. Kid stuff. The teacher said he had to have ten stitches on the back of his head. Polly said it would have been a lot more if they could use wooden bats instead of the silly plastic ones. That same day she went after Louise, too. She managed to tie her up to the tether ball pole. It's too bad they're not friends anymore. Floyd threatened to pull his dental insurance group out of my office. He hasn't done it yet though, thanks to persuasive Darla.

But what am I going to do about Polly? She wasn't allowed back in school for two days. I had to leave her in the office with Darla. Darla said she would quit if I ever did that again. What am I supposed to do, chain her up or something? I'll bring Darla today's catch to calm her down. She loves Walleye.

I've been feeling tired lately. Doctor Boren says its my blood pressure and I need to lose weight. He thinks I'm pre-diabetic. He's probably right about the weight. My fishing boat rim almost drops to the water line where I sit next to the outboard motor.

This sure is a nice little boat. I got it second hand from Harry Albert's widow after Harry had a stroke. He was young, too. Just a little older than me. "Obesity killed him," said Doctor Boren.

There's another boat on the lake going fast, pulling a water skier. Their wake is going to ruin fishing for today. It's getting toward three o'clock anyway, so I'll have to head in to pick up Polly. I can leave my boat at the landing. I used to be able to tie up to the Eden's dock but now they're gone and there's already someone else living there. I'll have Darla call them about house insurance before that new guy across the street gets his nose in.

Polly doesn't like it when I'm late. She could ride the school bus, it's the law but the driver refused to stop in front of the house. She'll only stop a few blocks over before the tracks, so Polly has to walk a bit if she wants to ride the bus. She complains her feet hurt. She wears special shoes for her flat feet. "It's all Mother's fault—the flat feet," Polly says. Now with Caribou gone and Donna gone it's up to me. Hell, I'm tired. Maybe I shouldn't have agreed to keeping Polly here. She's a real handful. Strong, too. Yesterday she said she's old enough to go to my camp during hunting season next November. She wants to learn to shoot. No one's ever been out there but me. It's my sacred place. I built it myself. I said no but she started punching and kicking me so finally I agreed. She's stronger than I thought. I'm a little afraid of her. Silly to think that way She's just a kid. Big for her age, though. Maybe chains are not such a bad idea.

I miss Caribou. Can't believe I'm thinking that. It was good once. All this thinking hurts my brain. Guess there's just time for a beer at Ronnie's Tap before I pick up Polly.

Epilogue

It was a month before the Keck apartment was redone. Alecia recommended a home interior designer she had used. Her name was Diane. She quickly grasped Cara Bow's desire to bring more light into the place and to keep it simple.

"Simple, simple, light, light," had become Cara Bow's mantra. She liked Diane's suggestion for mid-century modern. "Cost is not an issue."

Diane had no problem with that dictum and the final result was more than pleasing to Cara Bow. Track lighting, chalks and greys with indigo accents erased all of the heaviness from the past. Meanwhile, her time at Alecia's was spent enjoying the city and its attractions. The museums—Alecia got her a membership to the Museum of Contemporary Art for which Cara Bow immediately gave a generous donation.

Alecia and Tony had week-end catered affairs for Tony's political friends and some of Alecia's more generous donors. They seldom made use of their kitchen

"I was never much of a cook," said Alecia, but Tony likes to grill when the weather is nice. I know you make great plum jelly."

Cara Bow had laughed, "Not any more, Alecia. That was my past. All that is behind me. Far behind, not only in miles."

"What about Polly?"

"Yes, dear Polly. She wants to live with Kelwyn. My divorce attorney said I'd probably have to pay child support and I've happily agreed." She admitted to Alecia that she had never wanted children.

"Tony and I are still arguing about the kid thing. Now suddenly he wants a family but I'm not ready yet. I'm still helping my mother with Dad. He's gone about as far as he can go with his ongoing speech therapy sessions. He's hard to understand and can only get around with his wheelchair."

Maybe that explained the funny look she had seen Tony give to Alecia at that first meeting in the Banya's backyard, thought Cara Bow. "My parents moved to an assisted living center in Green Bay. They seem happy there. I call my mother every day. She doesn't answer if it's her bridge day."

"That's so funny Cara. Maybe my mom will want to do that one day. I know she's exhausted with Dad's care. Bridge, huh? I've never learned. We like to play board games."

"Nor have I, Alecia. I'm not much of a game player, either."

"Well we're having some interesting people in next weekend. Someone you'll want to meet."

"You're not trying another match-making thing, are you? The last one was a disaster."

"I'm sorry, Cara. I'd known Kelwyn for years. We grew up together. Now I think I really didn't know him at all." She quickly changed the subject. "Remember Dr. Timmer from Madison? You used to talk about him a lot. I think you had sort of a crush on him. I've invited him for Saturday night."

"He'll never remember me, Alecia. It's been more than a few years." She felt a little tingle as his name was mentioned. "Is he still at Madison?"

"No, he has his own business now. He's running a paternity testing DNA lab in Chicago. He's his own boss. I think he was tired of the tenure stuff in Madison. And he's turned out to be one of my best donors, too."

Doctor Timmer did remember her. "Well, well, Cara, what are you doing in Chicago?" he asked her over after dinner brandies.

Cara Bow poured out the whole story to his more than sympathetic ear and took comfort in his arm around her shoulder as they sat on the sofa in the Banya living room. The other guests had drifted out to the firepit in the backyard.

"My ex-wife and I parted ways two years ago. That's why I left Madison. Anyway, that's history now. It's so good to see you, Cara. You look great. I always thought you were a beautiful girl. I call you Cara. Why don't you call me Dan?"

"Dan it is," said Cara Bow. "I hope I get to see more of you." The words had slipped out. *Was she actually interested in another man? Had she so soon fallen back into the centuries old thinking of a woman's place was with a man? Subservient to a man? It hadn't worked with Kelwyn. His point of view had never been hers. Was part of the problem her inability to accommodate Kelwyn's impossible to change male mindset?* Dan interrupted her thoughts with a quick kiss on the cheek.

"I have your number, Cara. Alecia gave it to me. I'll certainly be calling." He gave her a snuggle and another longer kiss. Cara Bow make no objection.

The next several months passed in a whirl. Cara Bow's application for a spot in forensic chemistry was accepted at every college she had applied to. The hours would fit in perfectly with her part time job at the county crime lab, but she decided to hold off for a while. She was enjoying herself too much in her new surroundings. The Keck apartment had been erased of all signs of the former occupants except for one clown puppet left hanging in the back of one closet that reminded her of old Corky. She laughed when she found it. The puppet was deposited in the building incinerator. Cara Bow and Dan had several dates. He was older but not by much. Things were going well but no commitment was made.

"My divorce will be final in December," she told him. "I'm looking forward to the new year with you, Dan."

"And I with you, Cara."

They still had not had sex. Cara Bow had decided not to be on his casual sex list. It was a departure from her usual jumping into bed with whatever was offered. She and Ginger talked frequently on the phone. Ginger even came to Chicago for a visit one weekend that summer. They went to an outdoor theater production of Shakespeare's *As You Like It* done in modern dress. When they toured the Lurie Garden at Millennium Park she saw Dan in another area. He was gesticulating wildly at them from the cone flower plantings. Not wanting him to meet the beautiful Ginger, Cara Bow pretended not to see him.

Around Thanksgiving— hunting season in Cooperton, Ginger called her early one morning.

We're having a blizzard here, Caribou. It's terrible. Ice and snow! There's been no school for three days. Plows can't keep up. We're in the deep freeze. It's below zero and the electricity has been out for the last twelve hours. Floyd can't get into his office. He's disgusted and even talked about moving south—at last. Oh, I hope he means it. I'm always bringing it up after we have sex. You know how I miss Mississippi. We've never had a storm this early in the season. I've been so scared and so is Louise."

Ginger really did sound frightened. "The storm moved in from South Dakota, Ginger. We've had a little of it here, too. Don't worry, Honey. The weathercaster said it was moving east. Keep warm by your fireplace. It's going to be okay. Maybe bring up moving south before sex," she added.

Cara Bow wondered how Kelwyn and Polly were doing. She called his cell number but there was no answer. The plows in Cooperton finally got the main roads cleared and then began on the side roads. The last road they plowed was the narrow lane to Kelwyn's hunting camp. They found Kelwyn on the floor near the table. He had been shot in the stomach. A rifle was near the body. There was no response to the EMT's ministrations. Blood around his body was frozen. There were several jars labeled plum jelly on one shelf and one jar opened on the table. The jars were all cracked due to the cold temperatures and some of the jelly was mixed in with the blood.

The body of Polly Judy was found about twenty feet from the camp lying stiffened on the snow where it looked as though she had been making snow angels. There was no autopsy as the cause of death was evident to the coroner. Darla Albert testified that Kelwyn had promised to teach Polly to shoot. It was an accident, ruled the coroner. Polly must have tried to go for help and she froze to death. She was not wearing a jacket.

Pastor Cornwall agreed to conduct the service though Kelwyn and Polly had not been regular attendants. Cara Bow returned to Cooperton for the double funeral in the Presbyterian church. Two bronze coffins were on the chancel. One extra-large size box for Kelwyn and the other child size. The coffins were closed. Though the Alberts were Catholic, many of them filled the pews. Ginger came, of course, and Floyd. Ginger sat next to Cara Bow and whispered in her appealing drawl that Floyd had at last agreed to move to Mississippi. He was tired of the monthly small claim court appearances to get payment from the Albert clan. Cara Bow promised to visit her during the winter months. She said she hoped Ginger had a piano so they could resume their duets. She never told Ginger what Polly had done to her saxophone.

Cara Bow directed the remains to be interred in Fond-Du-Lac near the plot of Kelwyn's father, Doctor Keck, as soon as the ground thawed the following spring. She thought it fitting to keep the family together in whatever universe they now inhabited. She smiled at the idea.

Her attorney informed her that since the divorce wasn't final and there were no other relatives, all of Kelwyn's estate would go to her. He said there was a retired couple from Chicago who wanted to live in the country and had made a good offer on the house if necessary repairs were made. They had lived in Cooperton for a few years as children. A Mr. and Mrs. Thornton Albert.

"Of course, I'll see to it," she said. *Full circle*, she thought.

Cara Bow hired a trash service from nearby Rhinelander and told them to bring a dumpster and clear everything from the house. "Throw it all away. Keep nothing," she said in a resolute voice. "Keep nothing."

A cleaning service followed and then inside and outside painters. She had the siding painted a bright sunshine yellow. She hired a landscaping company to remove the quack grass from the front lawn and replace it with sod. The two stone lions were removed but the sign was kept—*Just Be Kind*.

"Let the swallows stay," she said. "Also, the wasp nests. They were here first. And be sure to leave the two plum trees." She told the landscapers to encircle the trees with cat memorial stepping stones. Mewmew would not be disturbed.

End

Acknowledgments

I must thank my first readers and great spellers, Katherine Jeans and Judy Martin and also Carol Smith, who was the artist for the book jacket painting for Plum Jelly. Special thanks to Jo Pilecki, the Sand Castle Writers loving guide for her encouraging words and lastly my son, Noel Frigo, for his uncomplaining help with my computer glitches. I'm also grateful to everyone who purchased my first novel, A Loved Place/ Paradise Lost. It's been a wonderful 2018.

Lightning Source UK Ltd.
Milton Keynes UK
UKHW040430240219
337804UK00002B/29/P